MASTERING A SINNER

Books by Kate Pearce

The House of Pleasure Series

SIMPLY SEXUAL

SIMPLY SINFUL

SIMPLY SHAMELESS

SIMPLY WICKED

SIMPLY INSATIABLE

SIMPLY FORBIDDEN

SIMPLY CARNAL

SIMPLY VORACIOUS

SIMPLY SCANDALOUS

SIMPLY PLEASURE (e-novella)

The Sinners Club Series

THE SINNERS CLUB

TEMPTING A SINNER

MASTERING A SINNER

THE FIRST SINNERS (e-novella)

Single Titles

RAW DESIRE

Anthologies

SOME LIKE IT ROUGH

LORDS OF PASSION

Published by Kensington Publishing Corporation

MASTERING A SINNER

KATE PEARCE

APHRODISIA
KENSINGTON PUBLISHING CORP.
www.kensingtonbooks.com

APHRODISIA BOOKS are published by

Kensington Publishing Corp.
119 West 40th Street
New York, NY 10018

All Kensington titles, imprints, and distributed lines are available at special quantity discounts for bulk purchases for sales promotion, premiums, fund-raising, educational, or institutional use.

Special book excerpts or customized printings can also be created to fit specific needs. For details, write or phone the office of the Kensington Special Sales Manager: Kensington Publishing Corp., 119 West 40th Street, New York, NY 10018. Attn. Special Sales Department. Phone: 1-800-221-2647.

eISBN-13: 978-0-7582-9022-9
eISBN-10: 0-7582-9022-5
First Kensington Electronic Edition: January 2015

ISBN-13: 978-0-7582-9021-2
ISBN-10: 0-7582-9021-7
First Kensington Trade Paperback Printing: January 2015

10 9 8 7 6 5 4 3 2 1

Printed in the United States of America

1

London, 1828

Alistair Maclean glanced at the clock on the mantelpiece and realized it had stopped. With an exasperated sigh he drew out his battered pocket watch and studied the scratched glass face. Stepping over the accumulated odds and ends on the floor, he picked up the clock, rewound it, and set the correct time. It was almost three in the morning. He was due at his desk at the Sinners Club at eight sharp.

Where the devil was Harry? He went over to the window, pulled aside the tattered lace curtain, and studied the empty cobbled street. His brother's lodgings were in a street that bordered the seamier side of East London and he never felt at ease there. If he hadn't been nursing an old injury, he'd be pacing the tattered hearth rug worrying about what scrape his younger brother had gotten himself into now. And why *was* he still worrying? At twenty-five, Harry wasn't a child, even though he sometimes behaved like one.

Alistair built up the fire again using the few remaining lumps of coal in the scuttle and sat back down in one of the wing chairs. A faint sound echoed down the street and grew louder, a chorus of yells and shouts that evolved into hunting cries and catcalls that eventually burst through the door of the house. One of the revelers almost fell into Alistair's lap. He recognized most of the men—bored younger sons of the aristocracy, accompanied by the upcoming sprigs of new wealth that clung on like a particularly thorny rose.

He rose slowly and stood amidst the shouting and sway of inebriated flesh, which reminded him all too forcibly of being stuck in a pen full of Scottish cattle on market day.

"Good evening, gentlemen. Or should I say good morning?" He registered the blaze of his brother's red hair amongst the mêlée and bowed. "May I speak to you alone, Harry?"

With a groan, his brother staggered away from his companions. "Devil take it, Alistair, who let you in here?"

One of the other men belched loudly. "Want us to toss him out for you, Harry?"

Alistair turned to the leering drunken fool who'd just spoken. "I beg your pardon?" He'd faced Napoleon's armies in Spain. A few wild aristocrats didn't frighten him at all.

The man's piggish eyes narrowed. "Damn you, sir, I—"

"Don't start, Foster. When he looks like this, my brother means business, and as he pays my bills, I suppose I'd better listen to him." Harry grinned at his companions and started to herd them toward the door. "I'll see you all tomorrow."

"Night, Harry."

For once the men were willing to behave themselves and leave quietly. Alistair slowly let out his breath. He hadn't expected it to be so easy to disengage his brother from his drinking cronies. In truth it was becoming harder and harder to have any kind of conversation with Harry at all.

As soon as the door shut, Harry's easy smile disappeared and he swung around to glare at Alistair.

"What's wrong with you? Skulking in here, acting like my bloody father, and sending my friends away."

"They're hardly your friends, and in certain respects I do stand in place of your father."

Harry flung himself down into the nearest chair and unbuttoned his waistcoat. "You certainly do your best to control me just like he did."

Alistair took the seat opposite. "I came to tell you about a change in my circumstances."

"Let me guess, you've decided to petition Parliament to restore our ancient family title, and see if they're willing to offer us a large annuity to go with it."

"Hardly."

"I was jesting. I know you wouldn't do anything to draw attention to our family."

"Why would I bother when you do a perfectly good job of that yourself?" Alistair snapped.

"Oh, for God's sake, leave me alone." Harry shoved a hand through his unruly red hair. "You nag like a fishwife."

Alistair reminded himself that he was too old to rise so easily to his brother's taunts. "I've taken a new position. I thought you should know about it."

"Why?"

"It's at the Sinners Club."

Harry went still. "So what?"

"I'll be working as the private secretary of Benedict Lord Keyes and Mr. Adam Fisher."

"As I said, so bloody what?"

"You were . . . friends with Adam Fisher once."

"Not anymore." Harry scowled and ripped off his cravat. "You should do well there. Adam's almost as prosy an old bore as you are."

Alistair set his jaw. "I just wanted you to know that if you come looking for me, or take part in any of the activities on the second floor, that you might encounter me or one of my employers."

"And *I* said that Adam Fisher means nothing to me and I'm extremely unlikely to come chasing after you at your place of business. I'm not that indiscreet."

Alistair studied his brother. "Are you quite sure about that? Your current bout of drunkenness and irresponsible behavior began just after you parted company with Mr. Fisher."

Harry shrugged. "He wanted me to settle down and behave myself, wanted me to—" He stopped speaking and flashed his most charming smile. "It's none of your business, anyway, is it? Don't worry. I won't spoil your precious new job by turning up and starting a fight with Adam. I know how much you like the salary it brings you." He paused. "Adam doesn't want to see me again, anyway."

"I'm quite happy to visit you here if you need me, Harry." Alistair rose to his feet. "And your scorn for my having an occupation is hardly merited seeing as it is my income that puts a roof over your head, and supports our mother and sisters."

"And damn you for having to remind me of that every time I see you!"

Alistair met his brother's furious blue gaze. "Why does it offend you to be reminded of your current lifestyle, brother? From all accounts you don't just live off me, but off your aristocratic friends. Does it truly make you happy to be a parasite?"

"Go to the devil. What I do is no concern of yours."

Beneath Harry's hard-edged scorn lurked that touch of pain and self-derision that stopped Alistair from washing his hands of his brother and walking away. He took a steadying breath and unclenched his fists.

"Believe it or not, I didn't come here to fight with you. I simply wanted you to be aware of my new position before someone else told you about it, and that became my fault too." He bowed and turned to the door, kicking Harry's discarded boots out of his way.

"You're the one who should be worried."

"And why is that?"

"Because when Adam discovers you are my brother, he'll kick you out on your arse in an instant."

Alistair opened the door and looked back over at Harry, who remained sprawled in the chair, his eyes already half-closed. "Actually, you are completely wrong on all accounts. Who do you think recommended me to Lord Keyes for the position in the first place?"

He had the momentary joy of seeing Harry's face frozen in shock before he closed the door and let himself out into the street. His brother wasn't the only person who'd been surprised at the recommendation. After a great deal of thought, Alistair had ended up asking both his new employers if they knew his brother. Both of them had confirmed they did and that it didn't affect their decision to employ him in the slightest.

A cold wind hurried down the center of the street and Alistair picked up his pace, his slightly uneven gait making his right leg drag slightly. He doubted Adam Fisher had meant what he'd said. There had been too much pain and sadness in the man's eyes to believe he hadn't been affected by Harry's desertion and subsequent relationship with a man old enough to be his father . . . but then perhaps that was what Harry thought he needed—a father.

Sometimes he hated his brother's ability to breeze through life like a summer storm with his good looks and charm leaving devastation in his wake. He seemed incapable of deciding who to love, and left broken hearts everywhere. Alistair had wanted to tell Adam he'd had a lucky escape and that he should be thankful Harry's roving eye had moved on to someone else. Except this time, it felt different. Harry seemed more out of control than ever, as if he was trying to prove he was the wildest, most sexually provocative being in the whole of London.

And he needed to be careful. By law a man who was accused

of sodomy could still be flogged and put in the stocks, or even worse imprisoned, tried, and executed. He might find Harry exasperating, but he wouldn't wish that fate on someone he loved. It was a shame that every time they talked, Harry tried to shock him, and *he* ended up acting like the prosy old bore his brother insisted he'd become. They'd been close once, back in Scotland when their father was alive. They'd roamed the countryside together pretending to be border lords who vanquished the English in every battle. . . .

Alistair turned onto the main thoroughfare and saw an empty hackney cab standing at the corner. Waving a hand at the driver, he gave in to the temptation to get back to the Sinners as fast as possible and at least attempt to get some sleep before his day started. As he reached the cab, a woman came around the opposite corner and almost knocked him over. He instinctively grabbed for her elbows to steady them both.

"Oh my goodness! Thank you, sir."

Her voice was low and she sounded far too cultivated to be out alone at this time of night in this sort of neighborhood. She wore a bonnet with a veil and such a deep brim that he could barely make out the outline of her pale face.

"Ma'am." He bowed. "I must apologize. I almost knocked you down."

"I'm so sorry. It was my fault. I didn't see you there, sir." She kept her hand on his arm. "I was too busy trying to attract the hackney driver's attention before he left me stranded here."

With a mental sigh, Alistair stepped back. "It seems as if we were on the same errand, but please, be my guest."

"Thank you."

She accepted his help and went up into the body of the vehicle and then turned back to him. "Perhaps we could share the ride, sir? In which direction are you headed?"

"To Mayfair, ma'am."

"I am going to Barrington Square, myself."

"Then our destinations are quite close."

She held out her gloved hand. "Please, join me."

Ordinarily, Alistair wouldn't have complied with her polite request, but his hip was paining him, and he really couldn't see the harm in accepting her offer.

"That's very kind of you, ma'am."

He managed to lever himself up into the small interior and settled on the seat opposite her. He'd damaged his hip thirteen years earlier fighting the French. Most of the time it behaved itself, but occasionally when it was damp and cold, or he was stupid enough to fall off his horse, it caused him some pain.

The cab driver clicked to his horse and they set off, the only sound the *clip clop* of hooves on the cobblestones. Alistair leaned back against the seat and briefly closed his eyes. Dealing with Harry always sapped his energy, and he already had a busy day ahead of him. Both of his employers were present at the Sinners, which meant twice as much work for him. It was also rumored that Lady Benedict Keyes had accompanied her husband to London this time. She might have social arrangements he would need to see to as well. . . .

He liked his new job, but the unconventional nature of his employer's occupations wasn't quite what he was used to. Stately judges and government officials in Whitehall never behaved quite so *spontaneously.* He constantly struggled both to impose order on the chaos of their irregular working lives and on the inner mechanisms of the club itself. The place wasn't quite as he'd envisioned it. The Sinners was not simply a gentlemen's club. It allowed female members, which was shocking enough, and *other* activities within its walls, more reminiscent of the Delornay pleasure house than a private club.

But while he might be expected to *arrange* some of those salacious activities on the second floor, he would never take part in them. It wouldn't be fitting. He had a reputation to maintain. Even as he framed the thought, he imagined Harry laughing at him.

He caught a yawn discreetly behind his gloved hand and stared out into the night as the ramshackle streets became wider and more prosperous. He desperately needed to down a large glass of whisky and go to sleep. At least his small apartment in the Sinners came rent-free and had a door he could lock. He raised his voice so that the hackney driver could hear him.

"Please stop in Barrington Square, and let the lady out first."

"Right you are, sir."

He turned his attention to his silent companion, who had her head down and was searching for something in her reticule. A hint of lavender soap teased his senses as she snapped the bag shut.

"We're almost there, ma'am."

"I realize that, Mr. Maclean." She looked up. He blinked as the newly installed gas lamp on the corner of Barrington Square illuminated the barrel of the small dueling pistol she held in her hand. "Please don't move."

Alistair slowly raised his hands and considered his options. "I don't have any money to give you."

"This isn't a robbery."

"Then why are you holding a pistol on me?"

"To get your attention. I have a message for you from a client of mine."

"And what might that be?"

"My client wishes you to know that if you do not control your brother, my client will."

"That's a rather ridiculous statement. My brother is an adult. I am not responsible for his actions."

"My client doesn't believe that's true. If you don't rein him in, the consequences will be dire for your brother, and possibly ruinous for your career."

Alistair smiled as anger pushed aside his surprise and shock. "Indeed. Perhaps you might care to tell your client that unless he is willing to stop hiding behind a woman and speak to me *di-*

rectly, I will take no heed of his words." He leaned forward and she jerked the pistol up until it was an inch from his face. "And you, ma'am, are a fool to allow yourself to be part of such a cowardly attempt at intimidation."

She laughed. "I've been paid well to deliver this message. That's all I care about." The carriage stopped and she drew back from him. "Good night, Mr. Maclean."

He waited until she got out of the carriage and then asked the driver to move on until they'd cleared the corner of the square again. Stepping out of the cab, he paid the fee and turned back to the large houses. There were few lights on in any of them and all was quiet. In less than an hour the maids would be up lighting fires and boiling cans of hot water for the household. He retraced his steps to where the woman had alighted and considered the steps up to the two front doors of the large stone-terraced mansions.

As far as he remembered, one of the houses was vacant. The other he recognized immediately. He'd wager his monthly stipend that the woman had entered a world he knew all too well. Not many of the patrons of the house of pleasure realized that the mansion they visited extended into the building behind it. Which happened to be the very one he was standing in front of on Barrington Square.

Not only did he know how to get into the house, but he also, courtesy of Jack Lennox, another Sinner, had a key. Sleep forgotten, he strode forward, went down the basement steps, and unlocked the door. The scent of lavender lured him on as he passed through the deserted scullery, out into the passageway that connected the two houses underground, and into the main kitchens of the pleasure house.

A footman stopped to wish him a pleasant evening and Alistair paused.

"Did you see a woman pass through here about a minute ago? She was dressed in black and wearing a bonnet."

"No, sir. I haven't seen anyone in the last half hour, but then I've just come up from the cellars, so I might have missed them."

"Thank you."

"Mr. Delornay is in the kitchen if you want to ask him, sir. I'll also inquire of the other staff."

"Thank you." Alistair forced a smile and went through into the homely kitchen, where several members of staff sat eating and drinking around the large pine table.

"Mr. Maclean." An elegantly dressed blond man stood up and inclined his head. "Were you looking for me?"

"Good morning, Mr. Delornay." Alistair bowed. "I was looking for a woman who just came in through the Barrington Square entrance."

Christian Delornay frowned. "Through the Barrington house? That shouldn't be possible." He came around the table to Alistair's side. "Do you know who it was?"

"It was not someone I recognized." He hesitated, but Christian Delornay, the owner of the pleasure house, was the soul of discretion. "Actually, she held a gun to my head and threatened my family."

"Obviously an enterprising female. Come and speak to Elizabeth. She knows everyone who comes here and works here."

Alistair followed Christian out of the kitchen and into the offices on the ground floor. He was quite familiar with the layout of the more practical areas of the house, having learned that if he wanted to fulfill his duties to provide entertainment at the Sinners, the Delornay family could offer him everything he needed.

As they walked, Christian spoke to every member of the staff they encountered asking after the woman in black, but to no avail. He knocked on a door at the end of the corridor and went in.

"Elizabeth, we have a mystery on our hands."

His wife looked up from her perusal of the account books. She was one of the most beautiful and serene women Alistair had ever met. "Good morning, Mr. Maclean. And whatever do you mean, Christian?"

The smile Christian gave his wife was almost too intimate for Alistair to bear. It reminded him of how he'd felt about Gelis when he'd persuaded her to marry him.

"A mysterious woman gained entrance into the premises through Barrington Square. Mr. Maclean followed her inside, but there's no sign of her now."

"What did she look like?"

"I don't really know," Alistair said. "She wore black, and her bonnet shielded her face from me. Whoever she is could simply take off her pelisse and hat and I'd never recognize her again."

"What did she want?"

Alistair hesitated for a second and then reconsidered. Anything he said to Christian and Elizabeth Delornay would remain between them and they already knew the worst about his brother.

"She'd been paid to give me a message concerning Harry. That I need to bring him under control." He met Christian's amused gaze. "As if I could."

"Oh dear," Elizabeth said. "I must confess to being worried about your brother. Christian and I were speaking of him only the other day."

"He seems intent on finding his way to the devil's very door," Alistair agreed. "And I don't know how to stop him."

Christian sat on the edge of the desk and took his wife's hand in his. "Perhaps you could ask Adam Fisher to speak to him."

"I wish I could. He was the only man whom Harry ever *did* listen to. But he wants nothing to do with my brother anymore, and as he is my employer, I can hardly start meddling."

"Agreed. Perhaps it is time to let your brother face up to his responsibilities."

"But he'll fail and . . ." Alistair tried to swallow. "I'm afraid he'll end up dead and I'll never forgive myself."

Silence followed his confession and was interrupted by a knock on the door.

"Come in," Christian called.

A footman entered and bowed. "Mr. Delornay, the door-keeper reports that about five minutes ago, a woman dressed in black came through from the back of the house and went straight out the front door without acknowledging him at all."

"Why on earth would she do that?" Alastair asked. "Why come in here and leave straightaway?"

"Well, perhaps she did it to show she had the ability to get into the pleasure house, which I don't appreciate at all, *and* she found out something about you."

"And what might that be?"

"That you had the ability to get in here, too." Christian raised an eyebrow. "Now, why do you think she wanted to know that?"

2

"Good morning, Alistair."

"Good morning, my lord." Alistair placed a stack of letters on the corner of Lord Keyes's desk. "I have gone through the first post, and these are the matters that require your attention. I also need to remind you that you have an appointment with your solicitor at ten regarding the purchase of your new town house."

"Ah, yes, thank you." Lord Keyes grimaced at the pile of mail. "Malinda is here, so I suspect she will want to speak to the solicitor as well. Perhaps you might go and remind her? She's in the breakfast room with Faith."

"Yes, my lord."

Alistair took himself out of the room and down the corridor to the sunny room at the back of the house that served as the gathering place for the various members of the Sinners who had rooms within the large mansion. Lord Keyes and his wife occupied one suite, but were planning on moving out to accommodate their ever-increasing family. Adam Fisher had the second set of rooms, and the original founders of the club, Faith and

Ian Carmichael, the current Earl and Countess of Westbrook, sometimes stayed in the third.

He wasn't surprised to find most of them around the breakfast table, chatting amicably to each other. Seeing them in such a domestic setting, no one would guess that the Westbrooks had led one of the most complex spy rings of the Napoleonic wars. The countess looked up as he came in through the door and patted the seat next to her.

"Alistair, how is your hip? You have stopped using the cane, I see. Come and sit down and have some breakfast. You look tired."

"That's very kind of you, my lady." He bowed. "But please excuse me if I have to decline your kind invitation. I have a message for Lady Benedict."

"Don't call me that." The auburn-haired wife of Lord Keyes looked up and scowled at him. She had a piece of buttered toast in her hand and six more slices on her plate. "I don't consider myself to be Benedict's possession. Call me Malinda."

Alistair nodded. "I apologize, my lady. Lord Keyes asked me to remind you that your solicitor will be arriving at ten this morning to discuss the purchase of your new house."

"At ten?" Malinda turned to the countess. "I thought we were going shopping then?"

Faith looked up from reading her correspondence. "We can still shop, Malinda. You need to decide whether you have to be at the meeting or not. We can always go out later."

Alistair gently cleared his throat. "You have an appointment with the furniture manufacturer at two, my lady."

"And I think there might be something else to do after that." She looked inquiringly at Alistair. "Is there?"

"You can hardly expect Alistair to know all this, Malinda." Adam Fisher's quiet voice drew Alistair's attention to his other employer.

"I do my best, sir."

"I am sure you do, but I'm beginning to believe we are overburdening you and need to get you an assistant."

"Or Faith and I could find ourselves a secretary," Malinda said.

"What an excellent idea!" Faith glanced at Alistair. "You don't look too enthusiastic about the notion."

"I can cope with the work, my lady. There is no need to worry." The thought of another person being allowed to meddle with his rather complex job was highly alarming.

Adam stood up and came around to Alistair's side. "Perhaps we should leave the ladies to their discussions. I have some news to share with you and Benedict."

"Yes, sir."

They walked back together to his office, which sat in between his two employers' rooms.

Mr. Fisher gave him a slight smile. "You can call me Adam, you know. We're all quite informal here."

"I . . . wouldn't feel comfortable doing that, sir."

"You'll get used to it." Mr. Fisher knocked and opened the door into the other office. "Benedict, can you spare us a moment of your time?"

"Certainly." Lord Keyes came through and sat on the edge of Alistair's desk. "What is it?"

"I had a message from Christian Delornay this morning informing me that he and Elizabeth are no closer to finding out who the mystery woman in black was." Adam looked at Alistair. "Do you know what he's talking about?"

Damn Delornay. He'd hoped to keep the whole event secret.

"Yes, sir, I do. Last night I followed a woman into the back entrance of the pleasure house on Barrington Square. She apparently walked straight through to the front door and left immediately."

"She must be the first person in London to ever have done

that," Lord Keyes commented. "But if Christian doesn't know who it was, how did she have a key?"

"That's what Christian was wondering," Adam said. "He was hoping Alistair could tell him more about what happened *before* she entered the house. You mentioned that she tried to rob you?"

"Not quite, sir. I hailed a hackney cab late last night, and as I approached it a woman came around the corner of the street and we collided. Once I realized she was after the cab, I ceded my place."

"And took the next one."

"Unfortunately not. She offered to share the cab, and as we were traveling in the same direction, I agreed. Just as we reached Barrington Square, she took a gun out of her reticule, pointed it at my head, and threatened to shoot me if I didn't control certain members of my family."

Mr. Fisher looked down at his boots. "From what I remember of your references, Alistair, you only have one brother here with you in London."

"That's correct. The female seemed to think I had the power and authority to change Harry's behavior. I assured her that I did not, and suggested her employer stop being such a coward and deal with the matter himself."

"All while she held a gun to your head. You could've been shot."

"I wasn't prepared to give in to such a demand, and I don't like being threatened."

"None of us do." Keyes paused. "Do you believe you are in danger?"

"No, my lord."

"What about your brother?"

"Quite possibly. I will, of course, write and let him know what happened, but I can hardly protect him from the consequences of his own actions."

"No, you cannot," Adam said quietly. "If this woman approaches you again, will you let us know as soon as possible?"

"Certainly, sir." Alistair hesitated. "If you believe this matter might complicate my position here, please tell me immediately."

Keyes glanced at Adam, and then they both smiled at Alistair. "There's no need to do that. Don't you know that the members of the Sinners thrive on just this sort of mystery? We are all sadly out of practice since the war ended, and need something to keep us all amused."

"*Amused*, my lord?"

"I suspect you don't find this very amusing yourself, Alistair, because it concerns your family, but rest assured we will find out who this mysterious woman is, and, more importantly, who is behind her actions. You're part of the Sinners now, and we protect our own."

"I . . . appreciate that very much, my lord."

And he would do his damndest to make sure that Harry realized the danger he was in and laid low for a while. Perhaps he could persuade his brother to return to Scotland to visit their family. . . .

"Well, I must get on." Lord Keyes stood up and brushed down his coat. "I have a busy morning ahead."

Despite Keyes's claim that the Sinners had ceased operating after the war, Alistair knew that his employers were still unofficially employed by the government to deal with clandestine matters such as spies, political uprising, and the monitoring of foreign undesirables—hence the full workload and the need for his secretarial services.

Speaking of which, he needed to consult his diary and report back to Malinda Keyes as to exactly what she was supposed to be doing for the rest of the day. After he'd done that, he'd write to Harry and warn him of the interest he'd stirred up. If his brother agreed to go to Scotland, he'd even pay for his coach ticket, but he doubted Harry would listen to reason and go.

A day later, he hadn't heard back from his brother, and there was no further news about his mysterious lady in black. What there was, however, was the task of settling the monthly household bills, paying the staff their quarterly wages, and dealing with any queries that arose from either of those two tasks, which was as likely to happen as the sun rising.

By lunchtime, Alistair was deep into the accounts books and barely noticed when there was a knock on his door. When he finally looked up there was a woman standing in front of his desk dressed in a blue pelisse, ostrich-plumed bonnet, and a matching feathered muff.

He revised his first impression when she looked down her nose at him. Not a woman. A *lady.*

He whipped off his spectacles and rose to his feet. "Good afternoon. May I help you?"

The lady consulted a letter she held in her gloved hand. "Is this the Sinners Club?"

"It is."

"Are you Mr. Maclean?"

He bowed. "Yes, I am. How may I help you? Are you here to settle up an account?"

"No, I'm here for an interview."

Alistair studied her anew. She wasn't a young woman, and she bore herself with a quiet certainty that couldn't fail to impress. She also didn't look like the sort of person who needed to earn her keep.

"If I might be so bold, an interview for what?"

Her finely arched eyebrows rose. "I begin to understand why I might be needed here. Does no one in this place consult with each other?"

Alistair met her unamused blue gaze. "I can assure you that I keep a very firm eye on everything, ma'am." He gestured at his desk. "As you can see, I am rather busy with the end-of-the-month accounts, so if you could plainly state your business, I would be more than willing to assist you."

She considered him for a long moment. "I was invited here

by the Countess of Westbrook. Does *that* name sound familiar to you, or have I arrived at the wrong address?"

"The countess wishes to interview you, then?" Alistair turned to ring the bell. "Then I will call the butler to ascertain if her ladyship is receiving visitors. If she is available, one of the footmen can take you up to her sitting room."

"I don't need to see the countess. I've already met her. She told me to present myself at this address at two o'clock so that you could interview me too."

"You are seeking employment here?"

Her fingers began to tap against her reticule. "Obviously."

"In what capacity? With all due respect, I doubt you wish to be employed as a servant, and all our special acts on the second floor are sourced from another place."

If possible, her gaze became even more glacial. "Do I look like a domestic servant or a circus performer?"

"A governess, maybe?" Alistair hazarded a guess. "But Lady Benedict Keyes will not need such a person for at least four or five more years."

Just as she began to speak, the door opened and Faith appeared.

"Oh, Alistair, I'm so glad that you two have met." She beamed at them both. "So, what do you think?"

Alistair glanced helplessly at the countess. "I'm not sure I understand what is going on, my lady."

"But didn't Diana explain?"

"Diana" turned to the countess and curtsied. "I've tried, my lady, but Mr. Maclean seems to be remarkably lacking in intelligence and believes I must be some kind of domestic!"

"That's not quite true, my lady, I—"

"Oh, I forgot, your other suggestions were a governess or a thespian."

"Didn't you get my note, Alistair?" The countess came around to stare at his desk. "I'm sure I left it here last night."

"It's probably somewhere under the accounts book, my lady." He hesitated, one eye on the imperious figure poised on the other side of his desk. "What exactly did it say?"

"Just that Malinda has found us the perfect secretary." The countess waved a hand in the direction of the visitor. "This is Diana, Lady Theale, our new secretary for the *ladies* of the Sinners Club."

If Diana hadn't been so annoyed, the stunned expression on Mr. Maclean's face would've made her laugh out loud. That would teach him to dismiss her so easily. What an odious, officious little man.

"New secretary?" He actually stuttered.

Diana gave him her most gracious smile. "Yes, Mr. Maclean." She allowed her gaze to sweep over his cluttered desk. "And it seems as if I have arrived just in time to prevent you from being overwhelmed by your current tasks."

"I'm not overwhelmed, my lady. It's quarter day," he snapped. "The complexity of the payments requires the use of all the household accounts books—hence the current disorder."

He didn't even attempt to smile at her, and his Scottish accent grew stronger with every word.

"Then one can hope you will be more organized in the future," she said soothingly. It would not do to antagonize him too much. She needed the job to complete her mission successfully. If the answers to her questions lay anywhere—it would be at the Sinners. "I've had experience dealing with quarter days both in London, and on my late husband's country estate, so I'm sure I can be of service to you."

The countess clapped her hands. "There, Alistair. Diana will be able to help *you* too." She glanced across at Diana, who was still trying not to smile at Mr. Maclean's obvious discomfort. "Would you give us a moment, my dear? I'll get my butler to take you through to my sitting room, and we can share some tea with Malinda and discuss our requirements further."

With a gracious nod, Diana went toward the door where the butler still hovered outside and allowed herself to be escorted to the countess's sitting room. She already knew that the innocuous frontage of the Sinners Club held many secrets. Her hope was to discover a few more that might unlock the keys to her past, and offer her a far better future.

But those issues were for another day. Her first task was to assume her new duties, and lull all the occupants of the Sinners into believing she was harmless. She doubted Mr. Maclean would be much trouble, and her new employers seemed manageable and even quite likeable. Not that she would allow herself to like them *too* much. She was tired of being naïve, and determined to succeed in her objectives.

Squaring her shoulders, she walked into the sitting room, curtsied to the obviously pregnant Malinda Keyes, and made herself agreeable.

As soon as the door closed behind the interloper, the countess started speaking.

"I know you didn't think you needed help, dear, but Malinda and I talked it over and we realized that our social engagements were hindering your ability to do your work properly, and we couldn't have that."

"I assure you that I can do all the work necessary and more, my lady, there is no need—"

The countess sat down and gazed at him, her blue eyes clear and guileless. "There is *every* need, Alistair. If I might be brutally frank, Diana has fallen on hard times, and she needs the salary I intend to offer her just as much as you need yours."

"Then can she not find something more genteel, more *ladylike,* to do?"

"Are you suggesting that a woman might not be as capable as a man of being a secretary?"

He thought of his mother and eldest sister running the meager Maclean holdings and how they'd held the family together financially and physically after his father had died.

"She is undoubtedly capable, my lady, but still—" He frowned. "Theale . . . is she related to Mr. Nicodemus Theale who sometimes provides the Sinners with information?"

"Yes. It's a rather complicated situation. Diana was married to Nico's father."

"Then she is his stepmother?"

"I suppose she might be considered as such, but Nico is illegitimate and wasn't brought up by the Theales. He grew up in Hackney with his mother, who married someone else. Diana was Lord Theale's third wife. When he died, she was left nearly penniless."

After sorting through all the countess's information, Alistair grimaced. "Having been in a similar situation when my own father died, I have great sympathy for her plight. Does she not have any family to care for her?"

The countess fixed him with a rather intimidating stare. "Not all women wish to be taken *care* of, Alistair. Some of us prefer to stand on our own two feet."

"I am well aware of that, my lady. I meant no offense." He considered his choices and faced the inevitable. "If you intend to employ Lady Theale, she had better set up an appointment with me after I've finished going through these books, so that I can hand over all the relevant information pertaining to you and Lady Benedict."

The countess rose. "Oh, don't worry too much about that, Alistair. I've agreed to let Diana use our apartment until she is more settled in London. She'll be here all the time, so I expect you'll be seeing a lot of her."

"Indeed."

He pictured the elegant face of Lady Theale, her aristocratic nose and the intelligence in her fine blue eyes. He didn't think she held him in very high esteem. He might not appreciate having to share his responsibilities with another person, but he couldn't deny that working with the lady might prove to be an interesting experience.

"Now, come along, Alistair. You can join us for tea and begin to get acquainted with Diana. She really is a remarkable woman."

Having already learned that life was never as predictable as one might wish it to be, Alistair opened the door for the countess and meekly followed her to her sitting room. He could already hear Malinda Keyes's distinctive voice and the quieter replies from Lady Theale. She'd taken off her bonnet and revealed her black, glossy hair, which was braided into a crown on the top of her head with just two curls dangling over her ears. Her neck was long and her olive skin held the warmth of the sun.

She didn't bother to acknowledge him when he took his place opposite her at the fire. Her attention was fixed on Malinda, who was describing the renovations to her new house, the upcoming baby, and various other matters at a speed and complexity that made his head spin but seemed to make perfect sense to her listener.

After a little while he turned his attention to his tea and discovered that the countess was staring intently at her new employer.

"What is it, my lady?"

"Diana reminds me of someone."

"She does bear a slight resemblance to her stepson, but one must assume that is just a coincidence."

"One would hope so." The countess chuckled. "Unless she and Nico are actually siblings, and share the same mother, in which case she would have married her mother's lover and the father of her brother."

Having become used to the unconventional nature of the Sinners, Alistair took her remarks in his stride. "Stranger things have happened, my lady. I believe Jack Lennox recently married his own aunt by marriage."

"Who wasn't really his aunt at all."

Alistair shrugged. "I don't believe either of them cared what society might think of them. It must be nice to feel so far above social conventions."

"The aristocracy have always considered themselves above such things, Mr. Maclean, didn't you know that?"

He looked across as Diana Theale spoke up. "I know it all too well."

She smiled at him. "As do the poor French."

"And the Scottish, my lady."

"Alistair's family have an ancient Scottish title, which was taken away from them when his grandfather took part in the last Jacobite rebellion," Malinda said.

"That's correct, my lady."

"Which perhaps explains your animosity toward the current ruling class," Diana Theale murmured.

"I have no animosity, my lady. My grandfather was a fool who risked everything for a fool, and lost."

"And if one of the Stuarts came asking for your help, now, Mr. Maclean, would you turn him away?"

"Of course I would."

"Even if he promised you untold riches and the restoration of your title?"

"Such promises are easy to make, and treacherous to keep."

She raised her eyebrows. "You are a hard man, Mr. Maclean."

"I've had to be, my lady." He smiled back at her. "Would you care for some more tea?"

Once the ladies were settled, he politely excused himself and went back to his office. There was still a lot of work to do, and if he were to provide information for his new female counterpart, he would be working long into the night.

"Mr. Maclean."

He looked up to see the butler barring his path.

"Yes?"

"Your brother is here. I have put him in your office."

"Thank you." Alistair increased his pace. So much for Harry's avowal that he would never bother him at work. . . .

"Good afternoon, Harry, how can I—?" He went still. "What the devil are you looking for?"

His brother was casually investigating his desk drawers. "Calm down, Alistair. I'm not stealing state secrets or anything. I just wondered if you had my signet ring, the one Grandfather left me."

"I've never had it, Harry." Alistair leaned back against the door. "What do you need it for?"

"What do you think?" Harry's hard blue gaze met his. "I need to pay back a gambling debt."

Alistair's hand clenched into a fist. "How much?"

"Nothing that need concern you."

He advanced toward his brother. "How *much?*"

"I don't need a lecture, Alistair. I need money, fast." Harry held up his hand. "I know what you are going to say. I deserve your scorn and your anger. I'm also fully aware that I am a disgrace to the family, and all the rest of it, so could we avoid the moralizing and could you just give me the ring or the money?"

"I don't have any money."

"I don't believe you." Harry's charming smile flashed out. "Come on, Alistair, help me out. I don't know what I'd do without you."

"You don't understand. I don't have any money left to give you."

Harry's face went blank. "Then I'm doomed."

Alistair reached into the pocket of his coat. "I'll fund your coach ticket to Scotland. Why don't you take me up on that offer and rusticate for a while?"

"Because I'm not like you! I can't run away every time something happens!"

"Then what do you intend to do?"

His brother gave a careless shrug. "Find someone who *will* help me."

Alistair half-turned as his office door opened and Adam Fisher came in.

"Alistair, I—"

"My brother is just leaving, Mr. Fisher."

Harry came around the desk, his charming smile firmly in place. "Adam, how lovely to see you."

"Maclean."

Harry winced. "And we were once so close." His gaze swept Adam's tense features. "I miss you, you know." He sauntered even closer. "I probably made a mistake in leaving you." He reached out his hand and Adam stepped back.

"Good-bye, Maclean." Adam turned to Alistair. "Come and see me when you're free."

"Yes, sir."

Harry pouted. "Am I nothing more than a nuisance to you both, now? The two men I thought would always love and support me most?"

Adam opened the door. "I heard what you were saying to your brother, Maclean. I don't have any money to give you either."

Something flashed behind Harry's eyes, and his face grew hard. "Is that the case? Perhaps I should seek out one of the scandal sheets and share the details of our *friendship* with them? Would the public wish to know that a man entrusted with the nation's secrets loves nothing more than to get down on his knees and suck cock?" He slowly shook his head. "I'm fairly certain they would be suitably shocked and demand your resignation, and what would you do then?"

"Harry—" Alistair growled.

Adam Fisher held up his hand and looked calmly across at Harry. "You can say whatever you like about me, I can't stop you. All I know is that I will never pay you a penny to keep that information to yourself. I've no desire to be blackmailed for the rest of my life."

Harry bowed. "Then you are a brave man, Mr. Fisher." He blew his former lover a kiss. "I must be off. I have a signet ring to search for. If you find it, Alistair, please let me know. Good afternoon, gentlemen."

He went through the door whistling under his breath as if he didn't have a care in the world. Alistair turned on his heel to follow, but Adam touched his arm.

"Will you let me handle this?"

"It's not your problem, sir."

"I'll just make sure he is safely off the premises and then make certain he isn't admitted again." He pressed Alistair's arm. "Stay here."

With a groan, Alistair sank down into the chair behind his desk and lowered his head to his hands. When he eventually looked up again, his employer sat opposite him.

"There's nothing to worry about, he's gone." Adam paused. "He won't reveal my sexual inclinations to the public."

"How can you be sure of that?"

"Because if he exposes me, he'll ultimately expose himself, and I stand a much better chance of weathering the scandal than he does. Harry can't afford to let society kick him out completely. He lives off them."

"But he seems desperate, and I have nothing left to give him. . . ." Alistair sighed. "In truth, I've sworn not to give him any more money even if I have it. He simply uses it to gamble or drink and we're right back where we started."

"That's an excellent decision, but one that I should imagine is very hard to keep." Adam smiled. "I have to keep reminding myself not to fall for his charm. I gave him all the coins from my pocket as he left."

"I offered him his coach fare to Scotland."

"Then we are both fools, are we not?" Adam shook his

head. "He will not bother you here again, at any rate. I've instructed Maddon not to admit him."

"I fear I am bringing more trouble to your door than I am worth."

Adam stood and smiled down at Alistair. "The Sinners always attracts trouble and we always deal with it. You do your job very well. We have no intention of blaming you for the sins of your brother, or of your employer's foolish choice of lovers."

"That is very good of you."

"I hear we are to have a new secretary. Have you met her yet?"

"Yes, she is most agreeable."

Adam nodded. "Good. I'm sure you will work well together. Now I must get back to writing this report or Keyes will give me hell."

"Thank you, sir."

"For what?"

"For coming to my aid."

Adam paused at the door and looked over his shoulder. "To be honest, I did it more for myself than for you. I've been avoiding your brother and that didn't solve anything. Seeing him today, hearing him speak to you like that, reminded me of why I'd decided to walk away in the first place. It was most illuminating."

He nodded and went out leaving Alistair staring down at his unfinished accounts while his mind warred with his body. It was far easier to walk away from a person when you weren't related by blood and guilt. He would stay until the books were safely balanced and put away and then reward himself with a trip to the pleasure house. It was that or drink his way through a bottle of brandy, which would leave him with a terrible headache. Better to abuse his body in a different way.

With that thought to sustain him, Alistair turned back to his books with renewed enthusiasm.

3

"Back again, Mr. Maclean?"

"Yes."

"Private or business tonight?"

"Private." Alistair nodded at Donal Murray, one of the pleasure house staff who managed the notorious top floor.

"There's a good crowd here." Donal held the door open for Alistair. "Is there anyone in particular you're after?"

"Is Lady M here?"

"I believe she is, sir."

"Then I'm sure I'll find her. I'll just go and change."

Alistair hurried through to one of the small retiring rooms set aside for those who wished to play on the third floor where sex had no boundaries and anonymity was guaranteed. He took off his clothes, folded them neatly, and put them in a pile on one of the shelves. He changed into the livery of the pleasure house—old-fashioned tight black satin pantaloons, white shirt, and a blue waistcoat.

He didn't bother with a cravat or a coat. It would be hot in the rooms and those items would soon be discarded. And it made him feel gloriously free not to wear much clothing or even put on his shoes. The last item was a black mask that tied at the back and concealed half his face. Not that any of the patrons would recognize him. Dressed like this, he was merely one of the staff, and obviously of no account. Even in this, his secret life, he preferred to remain anonymous.

After a deep breath, he opened the door and made his way down to the main salon. One of the other liveried men came up to him and smiled.

"Do you wish to serve food or drinks, Mr. Scott?"

"Whatever you wish." Alistair took the tray of red wine that was passed to him and began to circle through the chattering guests. He reckoned there were about forty people in the room, which was a lot for the upper floor.

As he offered the tray of drinks to the guests, some touched his arse, or stroked his arm, or simply stared at him, measuring his assets in a way that reminded him of a horse fair. Not that he objected. The stares only made him lower his gaze and his heart beat faster.

"Scot!"

A be-ringed hand waved imperiously at him, and he headed toward a cluster of chairs.

"My lady."

The blond-haired beauty beckoned him forward impatiently. "Where have you been, my little Scottie dog? Put down that tray and come here immediately!"

She snapped her fingers, and Alistair carefully put the silver tray down on one of the tables. Without a word, he went down on his knees beside Lady M and allowed her to pat his head.

"Where is your collar?" The gentle caress turned into a sudden tug of his hair that made his breath hiss out. "You naughty boy. Did you lose it again?"

He nodded and her grip tightened. "Well, I'll have to punish you for that, won't I?" She raised her voice. "James, will you fetch me a collar?"

Alistair waited quietly on his knees until she yanked his head up by his hair again.

"Let's put this on you."

He let her fasten the simple leather collar around his neck and buckle it rather too tight. He swallowed convulsively, and her brown eyes narrowed. "Is it too tight for you, my dear? But if you insist on losing it, I have to make sure it stays put, don't I?"

He quieted his breathing, aware of her gathering her skirts and rising above him. She snapped her fingers again, and he rose too, keeping his gaze on her slippered feet.

"Come with me."

He followed her out of the noisy salon and down to one of the smaller rooms that branched off the main corridor. Usually, she liked to deal with him in public, so this change of plan made him a little nervous. He'd chosen her because of her predictability. Even in this setting he preferred to know what he was letting himself in for.

She left the door of the room open, and he followed her inside. There was an upright wooden rack at one end and a few chairs at the other. The far wall was shelved and displayed a fine collection of whips, chains, and sexual toys for those who liked to use them or endure them.

Lady M sat on one of the more comfortable chairs and pointed at her feet.

"Kneel down, draw up my skirts, and make me come with your mouth."

"Yes, my lady." He was aware of a sense of relief, as she demanded he do exactly what she always asked for.

"Keep your hands behind your back while you do it, mind."

"Yes, my lady."

He knelt and carefully folded her silk skirts away from her legs until he could see the tops of her ribbon-tied stockings and her shaved mound. Breathing in her scent, he bent his head and licked her clit until she sighed and spread her thighs even wider.

"Keep going."

He obliged her, keeping his hands locked behind him, and used just his tongue and his teeth to bring her to a sharp, gasping climax. His cock was hard now and pressed against the confines of his breeches in a way that made his body ache with need. Speaking of aching, his right hip wasn't entirely happy with having to kneel on the hardwood floor, but he refused to acknowledge the pain. It would disappear when he got what he craved.

"Stand up."

He stood awkwardly, trying to keep his hands away from her.

"Fetch me a riding crop."

He bowed and turned to the wall of supplies, selecting the implement she requested, and returned to kneel before her.

"Now, do I punish you first, or wait until you've finished pleasuring me?"

Her gaze wandered over him, but he didn't make direct eye contact. That wasn't part of the game they engaged in. He was her plaything, and he wasn't allowed to have an opinion—although he knew her well enough now to know what she'd do next.

"Stand by the rack and place your hands on the top bar."

He almost smiled as she spoke. She couldn't resist the opportunity to watch him suffer. It would only heighten her pleasure when she finally let him fuck her.

The rustle of silk announced her presence behind him, and Alistair wiped all traces of amusement from his expression and stared at the opposite wall. He had a sense that Lady M wasn't the only person who was watching him, but that wasn't unknown in the pleasure house. The door was open, signifying anyone was free to look in, and there were plenty of peepholes within the walls for those who preferred a more voyeuristic approach.

"Widen your stance."

The crack of the riding crop against his arse made him jump

and tighten his grip on the wooden support over his head. A pleasurable heat built on his skin as she wielded the whip, and then it became mixed with pain and he was no longer smiling, but enduring. He closed his eyes and started to count the strokes, aware that she was being more brutal than usual and wondering why.

Unlike her, he knew exactly who she was in real life. He always investigated his partners. It meant he had information on hand if things went awry. She was the bored, much younger wife of a promising aristocrat who was steadily working his way toward the most senior of government positions. He understood why she came to the pleasure house and her need to take her frustrations out on someone else. He probably understood her better than he understood himself.

She paused and he became aware of the harshness of his own breathing and the way his fingernails were biting into his palms. She moved closer, the scent of her perfume filling his nostrils, and undid the placket of his breeches. He groaned as she roughly freed his hard cock and wrapped her hand around the base.

"Lie on the floor on your back, Scot, and put your hands over your head."

He sank down onto the hard floor, wincing as his well-beaten arse came in contact with the wooden planks, and stretched out, arms obediently over his head. She retrieved one of the already prepared sheep-gut condoms the pleasure house provided, slid it down over his cock, and tied the ribbon tightly at the base.

"Now . . ." She straddled him. "Don't move. I just want your cock, not the rest of you." She pinched his cheek. "And don't come until I give you leave."

"Yes, my lady."

She slowly sank down over his cock, and he concentrated on behaving like her personal dildo. Just a hard cock for her to move on, with no say in the matter, no input, and no value. Just how he liked it. He might enjoy being used, but even that would be on his own terms.

The release of the previous evening made the sight of Diana, Lady Theale, sitting in his office when he walked in much less alarming than it might have been. She wore a plain, round-necked gown in a blue patterned fabric with a modest bodice and no jewelry apart from a gold cross around her neck. Her black hair was again braided on top of her head in a rather severe style that suited her all too well.

"Good morning, my lady. How may I help you?" He took his seat behind his desk and smiled at her.

"Good morning, Mr. Maclean. I was hoping that you might have time to go through the duties I am assuming for the ladies of the house."

"Of course, my lady." He patted a stack of papers on his left. "I have all the information you require right here, including copies from my diary of all the upcoming social and business engagements the countess and Lady Benedict have already committed to."

"That is most efficient of you."

"You didn't see me at my best yesterday, my lady. I must apologize for that." He risked another smile, but she didn't offer one in return. "Did the countess take you around the house?"

"No, she hoped you might have time to do so."

Alistair rose and bowed. "I am always happy to oblige the Countess of Westbrook. We can do that now before we settle down to business."

With a nod, she stood up and smoothed down her skirts. She was of average height for a woman, but she carried herself like a queen.

"Let's start in the kitchens, my lady, so that you can meet the staff."

* * *

Diana wasn't surprised by Alistair Maclean's more gracious attitude to her. She'd already deduced that, unlike his loathsome brother, he was the kind of man who made the best of things.

He'd also spent an evening at the pleasure house.

"And these are the more public rooms of the Sinners. Our members can congregate here just as in any club in London, read the papers, meet other members, and have a decent dinner."

"There are also rooms set aside for those who wish to stay?" She asked the question, even though she already knew the answer.

"Yes." Mr. Maclean picked up a badly folded newspaper and straightened it out before replacing it exactly on top of the periodical underneath. "I assume you are willing to deal with general matters arising from the female members of the club? I fear I sometimes do not understand their needs as well as I should."

"I am quite willing to do that, in fact Lady Westbrook suggested it." She followed him through to the deserted dining room, where the tables were already laid for anyone who wanted luncheon. "Is there anything else I can help you with? The countess did mention something about the second floor, and appreciating some female input into what goes on there."

"She did?" Mr. Maclean blinked his vivid leaf-green eyes at her. "Did she specify exactly what she meant?"

Diana held his gaze. "I understand that certain *entertainments* are provided on a monthly basis as suggested by some of the members of the club. Is that not correct?"

"Indeed."

He walked back out onto the landing and continued up the stairs with her a step behind him. It was almost amusing watching him struggle with what he considered suitable to share with her. Even more amusing if she considered what she knew of him.

He eventually stopped at the top of the stairs, and waited for her to join him.

"What exactly did Lady Westbrook tell you about these entertainments?"

"Just that they were of a sexual nature and were entirely private and much enjoyed by the membership."

"She was correct about all of those things." A muscle twitched in his cheek. "I am responsible for gathering the suggestions and seeing whether I can bring their 'fantasies' to life."

"And how would one do that?"

He opened the nearest door for her, and they stepped into a small cozy salon with doors that led into another room and then another.

"There is a book where suggestions for the entertainment can be left." He pointed out a large red leather tome on a pedestal. "I read them and consult with my employers before seeking assistance from another, outside party if necessary."

"Why would you need to do that?"

"Because sometimes our membership does not include fire swallowers, or snake charmers, or acrobats from Asia who can contort themselves into the most erotic shapes imaginable."

"Oh, I see." She opened the book at random and read through a couple of the suggestions. "Or pirates or marauding vikings, from the sound of it." She raised her gaze to meet his. "I've just realized that I should be insulted."

"In what way, my lady?"

"You asked me if I had come for an interview for the activities on the second floor. Did you think I was an exotic prostitute looking for work?"

His pale skin flushed, and he looked away from her. Idly, she wondered if the rest of his body reacted in the same way.

"I have already begged your pardon for that incident, my lady. Perhaps we might put it behind us."

Even though he still wasn't looking directly at her, she continued to study the lean angles of his arresting face. He wasn't a handsome man, his features chiseled out of the same mountainous rock as the harsh place where he was born. Not a man to cross easily—unless one wished to take on a tiger. She closed the book and turned away from him.

"I'll be more than happy to help you choose suitable acts for the second floor, Mr. Maclean. I have been married, and I am not easily embarrassed."

"So I see," Mr. Maclean murmured. "Shall we move on?"

She was an interesting woman. Alistair shut the door behind Lady Theale and went back to his desk. He had no doubt that she would manage the ladies of the Sinners with great aplomb. She'd asked intelligent questions, seemed unruffled by any of his answers, and was more willing to listen to his advice than he'd anticipated.

Which made his sense that something was not quite right even harder to understand. Had the countess and Lord Keyes had her investigated before she joined their organization? It would be most unusual if they had not, but that information hadn't reached him. Was it possible that because of her connection to the countess and to Nicodemus that such checks were considered unnecessary? And if that was the case, how could he find out?

The clock on the mantelpiece chimed twice. He automatically delved into his pocket to check that his own watch had the correct time and found nothing. He checked his other pocket and then his trousers, but there was no sign of his much treasured pocket watch.

With a soft curse, he hunted through his desk and then rang the bell. Maddon appeared and bowed.

"May I help you, sir?"

"I appear to have lost my pocket watch. If anyone finds one in the house, will you let me know?"

"Indeed, sir. I will also ask the staff to keep an eye out for your watch as they work."

"Thank you."

Alistair waited until Maddon left and then stood up. It was most unlike him to lose anything. He tried to remember when he had last handled his watch. After the disruption of the previous day, was it possible that he had forgotten to wind his watch at his usual time? He couldn't recall doing it, which meant he'd either lost his timepiece at the pleasure house when he'd removed his clothes, or his brother had taken it.

He'd damn well kill Harry if he'd stolen it. The watch was the only thing he'd managed to save of his father's after the bailiffs had come in. He'd carried it through all the military campaigns in Spain and considered it something of a lucky charm.

Much better to imagine he'd lost the thing at the pleasure house. Forcing down his anxiety, Alistair picked up his pen. He had seven letters to write for his employers. He'd go back there later tonight after he'd finished his work and hope to God that this was one mystery Christian Delornay and his staff would be able to solve for him with ease.

The clock chimed eleven times, reminding Alistair both of his lost watch, and that he needed to stop working. He had no concerns about the pleasure house being closed. It was open most of the day and all night and busiest when most decent folk had gone to bed.

Maddon had brought him something to eat on a tray, so he took the remains of his supper down to the kitchens on his way out. Most of the staff was also asleep, but one of the footmen was at his post and more than willing to fetch Alistair's hat and cane for him. There was no light under the door of Diana Theale's new office, which sat beside the breakfast parlor. She hadn't bothered him for the rest of the day. He assumed she was far too busy reading through the copious notes he had given her.

It was a fine night, so he decided not to bother calling a hackney and instead walked through the collection of mews houses that backed onto each new square and led him directly to his destination. He used his key to access the rear of the property and made his way into the kitchens. There was no sign of Christian Delornay, but Donal Murray sat at the table eating a bowl of soup and chatting to the French cook.

Alistair made his way over and sat opposite him.

"Mr. Murray, I have a question for you."

Murray put down his spoon. "Good Lord, Mr. Scott, you are prompt. I barely sent that message off to you not five minutes ago!"

"What message?"

"That the lady found your pocket watch. She said she'd wait for you in the room where she found it."

"That's excellent news." Alistair smiled at Murray. "I'll just go up and retrieve it, then. Thank you."

He took the servants' stairs to avoid the majority of the guests. The room he'd occupied on the previous night had been the one closest to the door leading to these particular stairs, so if his luck held he would be able to escape undetected. His steps slowed. *If* Lady M simply gave him back his watch. If she was in an unpleasant humor, she might demand more from him and he was still sore from the night before.

He shrugged that consideration aside. He was willing to do whatever it took to regain his watch. Another beating with a crop or a quick fuck was not going to stop him.

The door was shut, so he knocked briskly and went in, closing it behind him.

"Lady M, I—"

"Good evening, Mr. Maclean."

His horrified gaze fastened on Diana Theale, who sat at her ease in one of the chairs. She held something out to him.

"Were you looking for this?"

4

Mr. Maclean took a step backward and almost collided with the door. "I was not expecting to see you here."

"I can see that." Diana tilted her head to one side. "You were expecting Lady M."

"I do not understand—"

She smiled. "How could you?" She gestured at the chair opposite her. "Perhaps you might care to sit down and discuss the matter?"

"I don't wish to sit down. If you give me my watch, I'll be on my way and we can forget this ever happened."

"Do you think this is an unfortunate accident, Mr. Maclean? That I picked up your watch from the floor, recognized it immediately, and sought to return it to you with the least amount of embarrassment possible?" She paused to study his face. "If that was the case, surely I would've waited until the morning, and left the watch among the papers on your desk, leaving you none the wiser?"

His green eyes narrowed. "Then perhaps you might tell me what is really going on."

She held his gaze. "Sit down."

After a long moment, he did as she had asked and she breathed a little easier.

"Lady M found your watch and she gave it to me."

"Why would she do that?" His tone was faintly amused, as though they discussed something of little importance. She had to admire him for that. "Are you, perhaps, her secretary too?"

"No, we share other tastes." She let her gaze linger on him, and he looked away.

"Does this have anything to do with my brother?"

She sat back, his watch dangling from its chain in her fingers. "Now, why would you think that?"

"It's hardly likely that two women wish to blackmail me in the same week."

"*Blackmail* you, Mr. Maclean?" She widened her eyes. "I have absolutely no intention of doing that."

His skeptical expression didn't alter.

"Perhaps I merely wished to return your watch to you?"

"I doubt that, or why would I still be sitting here?"

"One has to agree." She paused deliberately to consider him. "You would look much better on your knees."

"I beg your pardon?"

"Did you wonder why Lady M brought you in here last night? Doesn't she usually play with you in the more public salons?"

He didn't speak, but his hands fisted by his sides.

"She says that you need more training, and from what I witnessed, I would have to agree." She waited, but he remained silent, his expression resolutely remote. "You need someone stronger, who won't let you get away with such behavior."

"Do you really expect me to stay here while you discuss my sexual proclivities?" This time he raised his head and glared at her. "I am what I am. I'm not ashamed of myself."

"Of course you are not," she said soothingly. "There is no shame in wanting to be mastered."

"Then give me back my watch."

"But you don't really want Lady M to master you, do you? You expect her to give you what you want on your terms."

"This has nothing to do with you, or the return of my watch."

She kept talking. "You *pretend* to submit, but you don't actually intend to let go of your control."

"I haven't had any complaints." He shrugged. "This is a house of pleasure. I give my mistresses what they ask of me."

"No, you do not. You give them what *you* are prepared to give." She shook her head. "That's not the nature of true submission."

"And what the devil would you know about it?"

Despite his faint smile and relaxed stance, he was quite angry now. She could only stoke the flames—and that would be a pleasure.

"If you were mine, I'd show you the difference." She licked her lips. "But you are far too conceited to ever want to learn anything from a mere woman. You pick your partners, don't you, Mr. Maclean? God forbid that one of them should pick you because that would mean you weren't able to control them."

"You know nothing. I do what I am told."

She laughed. "Good gracious, Mr. Maclean, you are such a liar. You wouldn't even sit down when I told you to."

"*You* are not my mistress."

She smiled into his eyes. "Only because you are too scared to relinquish control to me."

She flinched as he erupted from his chair and went down on his knees in front of her. "You're wrong. I assure you I can take anything you choose to do to me."

"Then strip."

He started tearing off his clothes and throwing them to the floor into an untidy heap, which spoke volumes for his disquiet. When he was completely naked, he returned to kneeling in front of her. His cock was hard and arced toward his flat stomach.

"Put your hands behind your back."

She smiled as he instantly complied, and stood up to circle him, noting the faint whip marks Lady M had left on his buttocks the previous night. When she reached the front again, she gently dropped his pocket watch onto his discarded coat.

"Good night, Mr. Maclean."

She moved toward the door, but he was up and on her in a second, one hand grasping her wrist. She tried to pull free, but he held on, his wet cock tangling in the silk of her skirts.

"Let me go," she ordered, but he didn't comply.

"What do you want from me?" he snarled. "I did exactly as you asked, and you walk *away*?"

"I did what *I* wanted, Mr. Maclean. That's the whole point, isn't it? It's supposed to be about what *I* want, and not what you think you deserve. I *tell* you what you deserve. I *tell* you what I am willing to give you."

She shook free of his suddenly slackened grasp. "If you decide you want that kind of relationship, please let me know. Otherwise I'll let you go back to playing silly games with women like Lady M who don't know how to treat you." She patted his cheek. "Good night, Mr. Maclean." And whisked herself out of the door.

Picking up her skirts, she ran along the corridor and through to the staff quarters. She didn't think Alistair Maclean was quite angry enough to pursue her naked, but one never knew, and she had certainly unsettled and enraged him.

Knocking on the door, she waited until she was admitted and went in, smiling at the figure on the bed.

"I escaped unscathed!" She sank down on the side of the bed and pressed a hand to her bosom. "Now I'll just have to wait and see if he takes the bait."

Charlotte poked her arm. "Tell me more."

"There's nothing much to tell. I took him by completely by surprise. He didn't have time to think about what I knew, or how I was able to gain access to the pleasure house, he just reacted."

"He didn't hurt you, did he?"

"Of course not. He was furious, but when I challenged him he stripped and knelt at my feet." Diana shivered as she allowed herself to remember that extraordinary moment of capitulation.

"And what did you do then?"

"Gave him back his watch and walked away. If he wants to take things further, he knows where I am."

"At the Sinners."

"Exactly."

"But won't this make it more difficult for you there? What if he demands your resignation?"

"He won't."

"How can you be so sure?"

"Because he would have to explain why he wanted me dismissed. I don't think he is going to do that."

"But Lord Keyes and Mr. Fisher are members here themselves. They are hardly going to be shocked at what Mr. Maclean chooses to participate in when he isn't working."

"Mr. Maclean goes to great lengths to conceal his presence here. I suspect he doesn't want *anyone* to know what he does."

"Which works in your favor."

"And also makes the task far more interesting." Diana sighed. "*If* he chooses to let me train him. Even if he doesn't, I'll still be able to find out what I need to know at the Sinners. I'm not comfortable being so underhanded, but I cannot think of another way to accomplish what I need."

"You could just ask."

"The Sinners doesn't work like that. If Nico can't find out the truth, there must be a reason. They must be hiding something."

"I think you are overcomplicating matters."

"Says the woman who's already allowed herself to be drawn into the tangled lives of the Maclean brothers."

Charlotte shrugged. "I simply passed on a message to your Mr. Maclean about his horrible brother, Harry, who, in my opinion, *deserves* to be held accountable for his actions."

"But now if he finds out we are connected, the older brother will assume I'm in league with Harry's blackmailer," Diana said.

"Well, we *are* in league."

"I suppose we are, even though our goals are somewhat dissimilar."

"We both want to find out the truth, don't we?"

Diana studied Charlotte, who looked rather belligerent. "Yes, we do, and you know I'll do anything in my power to help you. But I'd much rather deal with *my* Mr. Maclean than yours."

"Harry Maclean doesn't belong to anyone except himself. That's why I dislike him so excessively." Tears sprang into Charlotte's gray eyes. "He destroyed Maria and he didn't even notice."

Diana wrapped an arm around Charlotte's shoulders. "I know, my love, and we'll make him pay for that."

"Do you think your Mr. Maclean knows what his brother is really like? When I held the gun on him in the hackney cab, he seemed unwilling to accept that Harry had done anything wrong at all."

"He's a man. You had him at a disadvantage. He was extremely unlikely to confess all." She paused. "I have a sense that he knows more about his brother than you might think. His loyalty to his family also does him credit."

"I suppose so, although Harry doesn't deserve a thing."

"I know." Diana pursed her lips and remembered how Alistair Maclean had looked naked and on his knees in front of her, his cock hard and wet, his gaze lowered. . . . She shook off the pleasurable sensations the image evoked and turned to her companion.

"Can I stay with you tonight? I don't want to go back the Sinners in case Mr. Maclean is lurking in the shadows waiting to question me about my deplorable behavior."

"Of course you can stay. It will be just like old times."

Diana yawned as Charlotte blew out the candles and plunged the room into darkness. Below them the hum of noise from the pleasure house continued unabated, but it wasn't annoying. She'd grown used to it when she'd lived there. Despite her confrontation with Mr. Maclean, she felt much more secure. If he didn't want to play her game, she still had power over him. He wouldn't like that, but it might stop him attempting to eject her from the Sinners. If he did want to play . . . she sighed with anticipation.

No matter what, she wouldn't forget her true task, but if it came with the additional thrill of taming Mr. Maclean, it might make her days far more interesting than she had anticipated.

5

Alistair paced his office, one eye on the clock as he considered for the one-hundredth time exactly what he was going to do about Diana Theale. By the time he'd struggled back into his clothes the previous night and gone in search of her, she'd disappeared. No one had seen her leave, which meant she'd either left in disguise, or had escaped unseen.

He paused, his gaze on the window that looked out over the back of the Sinners toward the mews. Or she hadn't left at all and had an accomplice within the house of pleasure. If that were the case, it would also make sense of the other disappearance that had occurred within the pleasure house.

He started pacing again. The simplest thing to do would be to approach his employers and ask them if Diana Theale could be removed from her position. But he suspected if he tried that, the ladies would become involved, and then information would be revealed about his private activities that he'd much rather stayed private.

But if he did nothing . . .

With a curse, he gave in to temptation, went out of his office, and walked straight into Diana Theale's without even knocking.

"Good morning, my lady."

She glanced up at him and then held up one finger. "Good morning, Mr. Maclean. Would you excuse me for just one more moment? I need to finish this task. Perhaps you might care to come back later at a mutually agreeable time?"

"That's all right." He took the seat in front of her desk. "I'll wait."

She resumed writing, her pace unhurried and her features composed. She wore another of her serviceable, high-necked gowns that reminded him of a schoolteacher. Her black hair was neat, her fingers bare of jewelry apart from a gold band she wore on her right hand. She wasn't a beautiful woman, but she was a handsome one. He couldn't even remember if she'd been dressed differently in the pleasure house the previous night. His shock at seeing her had obliterated all such observations from his mind.

He barely restrained his impatience as she finished her list, inspected it with pursed lips, crossed out three things, and then blotted her page.

"How may I help you, Mr. Maclean?"

"I would like an explanation."

"About what?"

"About what the devil happened last night."

"At the pleasure house?"

"Naturally," he snapped the word out. "Do you usually walk out on men you have ordered to strip naked?"

"I explained why I did that, Mr. Maclean."

"You—" He took a deep breath. "Perhaps I should try another tack. Why were you watching me at the pleasure house?"

"I believe I told you that as well. Lady M and I share similar tastes. She mentioned you to me, and invited me to watch her school you. When I realized who you were, I tried to think of a way to let you know of my interest without impinging on our professional relationship."

"You are suggesting that your interest in me has nothing to do with the position I hold here at the Sinners?"

She smiled. "Well, it does add a stimulating element to our potential relationship, doesn't it?"

He ignored her smile and her attempt at levity. "And what about my brother?"

"What about him?"

"What does Harry have to do with your sudden 'interest' in me?"

"Nothing at all." She raised her eyebrows. "Why are you so obsessed with him? What has he done?"

"He—" Alistair stopped talking.

"Well?"

"Everyone who has admission to the pleasure house knows my brother."

"I have heard of him, but I can't say I've ever been interested in meeting him."

"Or making him strip?"

"Oh no, Mr. Mclean. I don't do that to every man I meet. Only those I wish to further my acquaintance with."

He ignored the surge of interest that comment aroused in him and forced himself to go back to his list of prepared questions.

"Be that as it may, one might wonder how you miraculously managed to be in the right place at the right time."

"It was rather remarkable, wasn't it?"

He met her gaze, but she didn't blink, and he was the first to look away.

"If I told our employers that you were attempting to blackmail me, they would terminate your employment immediately."

She tapped the top of her quill pen against her top lip. "I don't think they would. They are both members of the pleasure house. Nothing you do there would shock them."

"You're suggesting that if I tried to have you dismissed, you wouldn't feel obliged to share those details of our time in the pleasure house with my employers?"

She folded her hands together on the desk. "As I've already pointed out, I don't intend to blackmail you. If you don't wish to pursue a relationship with me that's perfectly fine, but please don't use *that* as an excuse to avoid it."

"I'm not trying to avoid anything, I'm merely trying to establish what is going on here."

She sighed as though he had disappointed her. "Excuse me for being frank, Mr. Mclean, but both of us need to earn a wage, and neither of us wishes to leave our present positions. Am I correct?"

At his reluctant nod, she continued. "So neither of us will risk betraying the other."

"We are at a stalemate?" Alistair asked. "I don't request your dismissal and you keep quiet about what you think you know about my activities at the pleasure house?"

She nodded. "It seems fair. Our business relationship has nothing to do with our private liaison at the pleasure house."

Alistair rose to his feet. "It's far simpler than that, my lady. We *have* no private relationship, and we never will have." He inclined his head a frosty inch. "Good morning, Lady Theale."

He'd reached the door before she spoke again.

"If you do change your mind about that, Mr. Maclean, please meet me in the same room on the top floor at midnight this Friday. I will expect you to be naked and on your knees."

He looked over his shoulder at her. "Go to the devil, Lady Theale."

She blew him a kiss and returned her attention to her work. Alistair slammed the door behind him and stormed into his office. He stood and stared at his desk for several minutes as if he didn't know what it was.

Damn her. She'd had her chance. He would never abase himself at her feet again. She bloody *unnerved* him and that was completely unacceptable.

He made his way to his chair and sat down, his head in his hands. After a few deep calming breaths, he picked up the first letter on the pile on his blotter and slit the seal with his knife. Smoothing out the paper, he read the contents about four times before they started to make sense and even then he was confused.

The letter was a politely worded request for him to repay a gambling debt of a thousand guineas to the Demon Club.

He didn't gamble, and he was fairly certain that he'd never been to any club of that name. He read the letter again and turned it over to see the seal and to whom it was addressed.

Ah. It was addressed to Mr. Maclean, which made sense. It wasn't the first time he'd been sent a bill for his brother's debt. He would forward the letter to Harry's lodgings and ignore it. He considered the expensive writing paper and the fashionable address. Perhaps he should apprise the sender of his brother's direction. But he didn't wish to be the architect of his brother's downfall, and Harry blamed him for everything anyway.

With a sigh, he drew out a fresh piece of paper, wrote his brother's name and address on it, and wrapped it around the original letter without adding anything. It was time for Harry to grow up and take care of his own debts. Placing the letter in the tray for delivery, he turned back to his pile of correspondence and continued to apply himself.

Unfortunately, Diana Theale's words rankled and kept running through his head. She thought him a coward who manipulated women to give him what he wanted. She was completely wrong, of course. He gave his lovers what they *craved*, a man on his knees who allowed them to dictate to him. He remembered stripping for her, the anger he'd felt, the intense desire to show her that he was everything and more than she would ever need. . . .

And she'd walked away from him.

Alistair lifted his gaze and stared at the door. He wanted to prove that she was wrong, but that meant putting himself in a potentially vulnerable position and he hated that. But what if he called her bluff and brought *her* to her knees and then *he* walked away? That would make his apparent submission as meaningless as her argument that he was a coward and show her that she was just as weak as he was.

But he had to be cautious. He still wasn't convinced that her interest in him was accidental. There were very few coincidences in life, and her appearance at the pleasure house *and* at the Sinners bore close examination. Of course, if she capitulated to him in bed, he might find out exactly what was going on there as well. . . .

Dammit, he had to stop thinking about her. It was too dangerous. Ignoring the sound of female laughter outside his office, he forced himself to work. Nothing good would come of his involvement with Diana Theale. He would do well to remember that.

Diana put down her pen and wiggled her fingers. She'd been writing for hours and needed to escape her desk. Even as she had the thought, she chided herself for complaining. Being a secretary was the easiest job she'd ever had. It was far better than being paid to lie on her back or placating an older husband.

She'd worked hard to recover her social status, and she would work even harder to maintain it. The generous wage she was paid by her employers would be fully earned even if she had taken the job under false pretenses and had to leave.

A knock at the door made her look up. Was it Mr. Maclean wanting a second chance to argue with her? Or even better, begging for the chance to capitulate completely? She considered what she would do if he did. Would she make him strip right there in her office? Make him come on her desk while she spanked him with her wooden ruler?

"Diana?"

Nico's head appeared around the door.

She smiled at him. "Come in."

Her stepson closed the door behind him and took the seat in front of her desk. He wore his usual sober black coat and trousers, brown waistcoat, and modestly tied cravat. His ability to disappear into a crowd and remain anonymous was part of the reason for his success in discovering the kind of information that was never meant to surface. He had an amazing ability to fit the pieces of a scandal together and detect the lies.

She'd liked him from the moment she'd met him and trusted him more than anyone apart from Charlotte. Despite her being his father's wife, they were almost the same age. They had been mistaken for siblings more than once, which had enraged her husband. But then everything had enraged him by the end.

Nico took out his notebook and placed it on his knee. "What's going on, Di? Why are you here?"

"Because I needed a job. You know that."

"But why here?"

"Why not?"

He frowned at her, reminding him rather of his father. "Your interest in the Sinners Club has always been excessive."

"Then perhaps I am finally in the right place."

"Di . . ." He sighed. "I've already told you. There is nothing here for you. This place wasn't even established until 1815. The official records, which are very few, start from there. I've *checked*."

"I know you have. I also know these people are your friends and your employers and I don't wish to destroy that relationship. You've done everything you can. The rest is up to me." She held his worried brown gaze. "All I ask is that you don't tell them anything that might lead to them drawing the wrong conclusions."

"The right ones, you mean." Nico grimaced. "That's actually why I'm here." He consulted a page of his notebook. "I had a message from Alistair Maclean this morning asking if the usual checks on your past had been completed before you were employed."

"And what did you say to that?"

He looked up. "I haven't said anything yet. Until I read his note, I didn't even know you'd taken the extraordinary step of becoming Lady Benedict and the countess's secretary." He hesitated. "I wish you'd consulted with me first. I'm very fond of the countess. She has always believed in me."

Diana fought down a wave of guilt. "I swear I'll do everything in my power to protect you from my actions, Nico, but I have to know. You do see that, don't you?"

"I suppose I do." He fidgeted with his notebook. "Finding my father was the quest that set me off on my investigative career. If it hadn't been for that, I would never have crossed paths with the gentlemen of the Sinners."

"What are you going to tell Mr. Maclean?"

"That I can't investigate my own stepmother."

She smiled at him. "Thank you."

"I owe you a lot. You forced my father to acknowledge my existence."

"Much good it did us," she muttered, and he grinned. "We were both cut out of his will after that."

"But we survived, didn't we?" He paused. "What if you can't find what you seek?"

"Then I have a perfectly respectable position as a secretary to two peeresses of the realm. I might set a new fashion." She rose from her seat and went around to him. "I know it's unlikely that I'll be able to find anything, but I have to try."

"What if I just—asked *for* you, as though the matter had suddenly come to my attention?"

"Because I don't want to involve you in this."

"But if you succeed and find your evidence, suspicion will automatically fall on me because we are connected."

"Not if I take all the credit for myself and insist you knew nothing."

He grimaced. "I don't like this, Diana."

"Neither do I."

He reached for her hand and brought it to his lips. "Just be careful. This place is not what it seems, and your employers might appear benign—even the ladies—but they aren't stupid."

She patted his shoulder. "I know. The countess is all charm and sweetness, but I detect a spine of steel and the ruthless mind of a warrior beneath that."

"Then be wary, Di. I don't want you to get hurt."

"It's too late for that." She smiled brilliantly. "But I've learned my lesson well, and I don't intend to lose this time."

Nico shook his head and walked to the door. "Good-bye, love. I'm off to report to Mr. Maclean."

"Mr. Maclean, I cannot investigate a member of my own family. It would be unethical and any evidence I presented you with would be biased in her favor."

Nicodemus Theale sat forward, one hand on his familiar notebook, the other gripping the arm of the chair.

Alistair frowned. "So, are you saying that no one investigated Lady Theale before she took this job?"

"I should imagine the Countess of Westbrook did her own investigating, sir. She certainly has the ability."

"But she didn't ask you."

"No, sir. If she had I would've refused just as I am doing now."

Alistair gave a reluctant nod. He might not like it, but he respected the man's ethics. "Do you think Lady Theale is suitable for the position?"

"Yes, sir, I do. She managed my father and his estate for the last five years of his life."

"But I understand he left her nothing."

"That's because she stood up for me. His two legitimate children disliked her and hated me. They convinced my father that he was being swindled by the pair of us—when, in fact, the opposite was true. Diana was simply trying to save what was left of the estate from the constant depravations of the pair of them."

"I suppose they considered her an interloper. She was a lot younger than your father, I understand."

"Yes, sir, she was."

Alistair reminded himself to check into the details of the Theale inheritance issue. It might prove interesting.

"Do you know where she met your father?"

"I have no idea, sir. You would have to ask Lady Theale." Nicodemus put his notebook away, signaling the interview was at an end. "Is there anything else I can help you with, Mr. Maclean?"

"There is one more thing. Have you ever heard of a place called the Demon Club?"

Nicodemus went still. "I have, sir."

"Is it a respectable gaming house?"

"It's . . ." Nicodemus shook his head. "It's a den of iniquity where a man might lose his soul and never recover it."

"That makes sense," Alistair murmured. "If one was in debt to such a place, would one be in trouble?"

"One would. With all due respect, Mr. Maclean, if you owe them money I suggest you do everything in your power to repay that debt as soon as possible. If you do not, the club will consider you fair game."

"And what exactly would that mean? Would they come after me?"

"If they had to." Nicodemus actually shuddered. "If you cannot pay, they consider you as collateral."

"In what sense?"

"They'll use you to repay the debt by whatever means they choose."

"That doesn't sound good at all."

"It isn't, sir. As I said, if you owe them a single penny, pay it back immediately."

"I'll bear that in mind, Mr. Theale." Alistair considered for a moment. "If you have any other information about the club, please let me know. It might come in handy later."

"For your sake, I hope not, sir." Nicodemus bowed. "I must be off. I have several other matters to investigate for Lord Keyes."

"Then thank you for your time."

Alistair waited until his companion had closed the door, and then sat back down. The Demon Club sounded appalling. He had to assume that Harry knew what he'd gotten himself into, but he was still uneasy. His brother didn't have a hundred pounds, let alone a thousand to pay a single creditor. Was the holder of the debt connected to the woman who had held him at gunpoint? It was definitely a possibility.

Alistair pushed the problem to the back of his mind and addressed his thoughts to the speech he was writing for Lord Keyes to deliver in the upper house. He'd trained himself never to be distracted from the task at hand, but even he was having difficulty concentrating when his thoughts skipped about from Harry's problems to the tantalizing opportunity of getting his own back on Diana Theale.

He snorted as he dipped his pen in the ink. She thought him undisciplined. She had no idea what he was like at all. He had no intention of obliging her by turning up at her command on Friday night, but he almost wished he could. . . .

A knock at the door several hours later had him looking up to see the butler advancing toward him.

"There is a Lord Blaydon Kenrick here to see you, sir." Maddon presented a tray with the man's card on it to Alistair.

He examined the card, but it held nothing other than the man's name. "Did he mention why he needed to see me?"

"No, sir. Do you wish me to inquire?"

"That's not necessary. Please send him in."

If he was not mistaken, Kenrick was the family name of the Marquess of Killkenny, an Irish peer.

The gentleman who was ushered in by Maddon was dressed in the height of fashion and about Alistair's age.

"Mr. Maclean?"

"Yes, please sit down. How may I help you?"

Lord Blaydon ignored the invitation and stood his ground, a calm smile hovering on his lips.

"You do not look much like your brother."

Alistair's smile disappeared. "We share similar coloring, but that's about it. How may I assist you?"

"Your brother owes the Demon Club a thousand pounds."

"So I understand. You had the wrong address. I passed your letter on to him." Alistair met Lord Blaydon's dark gaze. "That is the extent of my interest in this matter."

"I'm afraid that isn't quite how it works, Mr. Maclean. Your brother used your name when he incurred the debt."

"A mistake, of which you are obviously aware, so I cannot see what it has to do with me."

"Your name is on the voucher."

"And I deny all knowledge of it. Are you done, my lord? I have work to do."

"If your brother does not pay us in full by the end of the month, or appear at the Demon Club, you will be required to honor his obligation."

Alistair stood up and glared at his visitor. "I repeat. I am not obliged to pay my brother's debts."

"Then you are happy to watch him suffer?"

"I am not responsible for my brother. He is a grown man."

"Be that as it may, if he doesn't turn up, you *will* be required to fulfill his responsibility."

"And if I refuse?"

Lord Blaydon smiled. "You will not be given the opportunity to refuse, Mr. Maclean." He put on his hat. "I wish you a good evening."

Alistair let him leave and then sat down again. Damn Harry for dragging him into yet another mess. He had no choice but to go to his brother's lodgings again and lie in wait for him.

"Devil take it!" Alistair muttered as he put away his work and tidied his desk. "My brother is going to pay for this!"

He hailed a hackney cab and arrived at Harry's rooms less than half an hour later. He managed to get into the house, but his brother's door was locked so he had to find the manager of the property who lived in the basement and get him to open up the place. He also had to endure a tirade about his brother's wild ways and a threat of Harry being evicted if he didn't pay his rent on time. It was only after placating the man and offering him a substantial bribe that Alistair was given the spare key.

He wrinkled his nose at the sour smell that permeated the place. He discovered a half-eaten meal on the table, disposed of the rotting meat, and opened a window. The apartment looked as if no one had been there in days, but that didn't necessarily mean that anything bad had happened to Harry. He quite often cadged off his friends, staying a night here and another there until they became tired of him and he moved on.

But this time, things looked different. Alistair wandered into the adjoining bedroom and surveyed the chaos of open drawers and chests and an unmade bed. There was a sense that someone had left in a tearing hurry. . . .

Checking more carefully now, Alistair looked in vain for a note or any clue to his brother's whereabouts. He returned to the front room and studied the collection of screwed-up paper on the floor around the desk. Had Harry attempted to write to him, or someone else, and given up in his haste to be gone? He bent down and picked up some of the paper and unfolded it. One of the pieces was written in his hand and was addressed to his brother. He thought it was the paper he'd used to wrap his message in. The rest were all his brother's work.

Harry's agitated writing covered half the page, begging someone for more time, insisting that he would pay as soon as he was able and that he would be back . . .

Alistair read through five attempts at the letter, which were all pleas for extra time, but none of them specified what debt Harry referred to or the name of the debtor. It didn't matter. He had a shrewd suspicion that his brother had bolted after receiving his forwarded letter from the Demon Club. From what Nicodemus had told him and his own encounter with the icily polite Lord Blaydon, he could see why Harry had panicked.

But what of Harry's latest lover and protector? Alistair frowned as he tried to remember the name of the peer who had pursued Harry after his tumultuous relationship with Adam Fisher had finally ended. Would Harry have gone to this man for protection or was he, too, involved with the Demons?

Nicodemus might have the answer to that, so might Adam Fisher, but Alistair didn't want to bother him. Alistair took one last look around the lodging. He placed the rubbish in the grate and burned it before locking the door behind him and leaving for the Sinners. He'd have the place watched to see if his brother returned, but at this juncture there was nothing else he could do. It was quite like Harry to run away from his problems, but this time, Alistair wasn't prepared to save him from his fate.

He felt like someone was squeezing his heart as the heavy weight of his responsibilities sank over him. He'd always protected Harry, first from the wrath of their father, and later from everything and everybody in society. And all he'd done was make his brother believe he would always save him. How many times had Harry begged him to make something right? Promised to change, to pay him back, to—

With a weary sigh, Alistair decided to walk back to the Sinners. Adam Fisher had mentioned that he'd given up trying to save Harry because Harry never changed. He conveniently forgot everything that had been given to him and headed straight for the next crisis, leaving a swathe of wounded hearts and minds along the way.

But no more. Alistair was done with him. He was tired of being the responsible brother, the one who was always in control. His thoughts turned to the pleasure house, to a night of anonymity sexually serving whoever wanted him without protest . . .

But even that sanctuary was in jeopardy now. If he went back, he'd have to deal with Diana Theale.

It started to rain and he turned up his collar and jammed his hat more firmly down on his head. Harry needed to learn a lesson, and he had to step back and let him fail. Alistair could only hope he could convince his heart and his conscience to agree with him.

6

Diana opened another box of old correspondence and studied the date of the first letter. Whoever had curated the records of the original Sinners Club had done an excellent job. The content of each box was meticulously recorded in a document placed at the top of the box and organized by date and by subject matter. As a result, Diana knew rather too much about the kitchen accounts and how much alcohol the Sinners consumed and even where it had been obtained.

But she hadn't found anything of a more personal nature. Not even a hint about the origins of the club, or the person she was attempting to trace. Nico had warned her, but she thought she'd find something, some little trace that would've escaped a man's eye. And she knew more than she'd told Nico. Some things were too private to ever share.

She sat in the front attic of the house, a cushion on the bare floorboards beneath her bottom and a candelabrum at her side. It was quite late and none of her employers, male or female, were supposed to be home. Even Mr. Maclean had gone out, but she suspected he'd done that deliberately to avoid her reminding him that it was Friday night.

She packed the box away and rose to her feet, brushing off the dust, and surveyed the ordered ranks of boxes that filled the shelves and disappeared off into the darkness. Perhaps Nico was right and she should simply ask the countess what she knew. . . .

With a shake of her head, she picked up the candles and turned to leave. She would not allow herself to become dispirited. There was always another day and a chance to make a discovery that would change everything. Even if she couldn't bring herself to ask outright, she might be able to find out where the Sinners kept the more secret and personal correspondence.

After carefully closing the door into the attic, she paused on the landing to blow out the candles and listen for the sounds of activity below. As she stood in the darkness, she looked down over the bannisters and observed Adam Fisher's return to his apartment on the floor below, locking the door behind him.

Poor Adam. She knew he'd cared deeply about that scoundrel Harry Maclean, but he was well rid of him. If Charlotte and the Demon Club had their way, Harry would receive a punishment that might just fit the crime.

Picking up her skirts, she descended the staircase and went down two floors before crossing over another landing to the door of her borrowed apartment. She locked the door and considered her opulent surroundings. A portrait of the Earl and Countess of Westbrook painted shortly after their marriage hung over the fireplace. Diana went over to study it, her gaze drawn to the contrast between the strong English features of the bride and the exotic coloring of her Anglo-Indian groom.

Before his marriage, the earl had been known as the "Savage Rake" both for his unusual birth, and for his propensity to sweep women off their feet and into bed in a remarkably short space of time. He'd apparently become a reformed character after his unexpected marriage to the plain bluestocking older daughter of a minor peer.

Diana hadn't met him in person yet. Lady Westbrook had

told her that the earl was on a diplomatic mission for the government and was expected back within a month. She had no desire to meet him. She'd heard he was extremely hard to deceive, and one look at her would make him suspicious, she was quite sure of that.

She went through to the bedroom and considered her choices. Regardless of whether Mr. Maclean joined her or not, she was going to the pleasure house. If he was too much of a coward to submit to her, she would enjoy showing him what he was missing as he fawned at the feet of someone less worthy, like Lady M. Her friend had no idea what Mr. Maclean was like or any desire to find out. All she required was a lapdog, and despite what he wanted to believe, Mr. Maclean was more of a lone wolf.

Unbuttoning her practical day dress, she considered what to wear and settled on a black silk gown that showed off her bosom and the warm tones of her skin to advantage. Underneath the dress she would wear just one thin petticoat and her lightest set of stays. If Mr. Maclean *did* decide to participate, she wanted to be ready for him. The thought of him touching her made her purr. The thought of *preventing* him from touching her until he was a begging, shaking mess made her nipples ache and her cunt throb.

But he wouldn't demean himself before her.

She was fairly sure of that, which was a huge disappointment. With a resigned sigh, she rang the bell for her maid. The dress needed to be hooked up at the back, and her hair required a softer, more natural style than the tight braids she wore all day. While she waited for Nelly, she applied some discreet cosmetics to accentuate her eyes and her mouth. Even if Mr. Maclean didn't turn up, she intended to enjoy herself.

Half an hour later as the clock struck midnight, she tied the ribbons of her velvet cloak and accepted an escort through the streets to the door of the pleasure house. It was as busy and crowded as always. She spotted Charlotte in the main salon talking intently to an older man and didn't interrupt her. As she mounted the stairs, the crowds faded away until she was on the top floor and being ushered in through the locked landing door by Donal Murray, who gave her his usual wink. She didn't stop to ask him whether her room was occupied, but made her way down to the smaller of the two salons, where a select number of guests were circulating and choosing their partners.

One of the half-naked servers offered her a glass of red wine, which she accepted while she considered his muscular body and the tight black pantaloons that barely covered the hard bulge of his cock. His smile was an invitation to sin, but he was rather too obvious for her tastes. She preferred a partner who was so aware of her that their behavior changed.

After speaking to one or two of her acquaintances and consuming some excellent food, she strolled back along the narrow corridor to her room at the end and slowly opened the door.

Alistair Maclean knelt in the center of the bare wooden floor, his back to her, his hands by his side. Diana slowly closed the door and leaned against it, admiring the view of his strong back, the curve of his muscular buttocks, and the evidence of his career as a soldier that marred his pale Celtic skin.

To his credit, he didn't turn around, but she was amused to see him shiver and watched the goose bumps appear on his skin. She walked forward and stroked one finger over the fine erect hairs on his arm.

"Good evening, Mr. Maclean. Link your fingers, and put your hands behind your head."

He did what she asked, his shoulders flexing as he assumed the position. Diana trailed her finger down from his throat, along his collarbone, and finally down his arm, letting him feel the scratch of her fingernail. A faint red line appeared on his skin, and she was the one to shiver at the possibilities ahead.

"Kiss me."

Diana paused and took a step away from him. "Mr. Maclean, do we have to go through all this again? I tell *you* what to do."

"You want to kiss me, I can tell, so why not get on with it?"

She smiled at the rough impatience of his tone. "I have no intention of kissing that demanding mouth of yours, Mr. Maclean." She turned to the tallboy against the wall, opened the top drawer, and extracted a black silk scarf. "In truth, until I give you leave, you don't need to speak at all."

When she approached with the silk held loosely between her hands, he jerked his head away from her.

"I don't like being—"

She pressed one finger hard against his lips, silencing him.

"Either cooperate with me, Mr. Maclean, or get out." She waited to see what he would do, but he didn't move a muscle. "Then be quiet."

She gagged him with the silk, wrapping it twice around his head and securing it with a tight knot at the back. His breathing slowed and his interlocked fingers flexed as if he wanted to strangle her.

"That's better. Now, stand up but keep your hands where they are."

He rose slowly and she noticed he favored his left leg. She slid one slippered foot between his bare feet and guided him into a wider stance. His cock was already hard and curving toward his stomach.

She began to touch him. Her hands swept over his chest and hips, the hard columns of his thighs, and the curve of his tight arse. As she touched him, she observed his reactions to her, the way his breathing altered when she brushed his nipples and the inside of his thigh, the way his cock strained toward her, the crown pushing past the foreskin to reveal his true length and impressive girth.

He was beautiful.

But still far too sure of himself.

She indicated the wooden rack that stood on one side of the room. "Stand over there and put your hands up over your head."

He moved more easily now, the scar on his right hip from some old wound obviously troubling him less. She would have to remember that while she played with him. Following him over to the rack, she fastened the leather cuffs that hung from the top of the frame around his wrists and buckled them tight, before adjusting the pulley-and-chain system to raise him slightly so that his feet barely made contact with the floor.

It stretched his body out to its fullest extent and made her lick her lips. A bare canvas to create on . . . Each mark she made would be unique and help form the pattern of their relationship.

She placed her palm on his buttock and he flinched. Had he expected a slap or the curl of the whip? She knew he liked that, had watched him with Lady M. She smoothed her hand over his taut flesh, cupping his tight buttock, and then eased a finger lower to rim the pucker of his arsehole. His reaction was immediate as he attempted to remove himself from her touch. She did it again, and this time he jerked his whole body away.

Intrigued, she walked around to face him, enjoying the flash of anger in his green eyes.

"You don't like being touched like that?"

He vehemently shook his head.

She smiled. "Oh dear."

His eyes widened, and he made a concentrated effort to fight off the silk gag. Diana waited until he realized the futility of that and returned his wary gaze to her face.

She knelt at his feet and calmly attached cuffs to his ankles and chained each one to a wooden support at the side of the frame holding him immobile. Before standing up, she leaned forward and licked off the pre-cum glistening on the crown of his cock.

"Mmm." She took a moment to savor his taste before sucking her own finger into her mouth and wetting it. She smiled and walked behind him, watching as his whole body tensed against his restraints. She ran her wet finger down between his buttocks and he shuddered.

"If I wish to touch you here, Mr. Maclean, I will do so. I do not expect you to attempt to avoid anything I wish to do to you."

She waited a moment before picking up a bottle of unscented oil and drizzled some on his skin waiting as it dripped down over his arsehole and taint. She coated her finger with oil as well and trailed it down to his tightly clenched hole.

"Relax, Mr. Maclean."

He shook his head again, his mouth working to bite through the silken gag darkening and knotting the silk.

She stopped touching him. For a long moment, Alistair held his breath, but she did nothing more sinister than walk around to observe him, her blue gaze calm. She studied his face and then yanked the gag down.

"I fear I have been remiss, Mr. Maclean. We did not discuss terms before I tied you to this frame."

He swallowed down what felt like a pint of spit. "There are no terms. You want me to fuck you, and I'm more than willing to do so."

Her eyebrows rose. "You are rather overconfident, sir. I told you to be in this room so that you could attend to *my* needs, not to yours."

"Surely they are the same?"

"Hardly."

He glanced down at his cock. "You don't want this?"

"That isn't the point of this discussion, Mr. Maclean."

"Then what is?"

"We need to agree on something. If I hurt you, or push you into doing something you do not want, you must tell me."

"You won't hurt me."

"Again, you are deliberately missing the point. I do not wish you to injure yourself or suffer unnecessarily."

He glanced down at her slippered feet. "I'm not a coward. I was in the military. I can take any beating you choose to give me, the harder the better."

"I'm sure you can, Mr. Maclean, because that's what you pride yourself on, isn't it?"

He slowly raised his gaze to hers and swallowed hard. "I do what I am told. I take what I am given. I don't need to *tell* you to stop."

"Yet you didn't wish me to touch your arse."

"I—" He set his jaw. "That is unnecessary to our purpose. You are a woman. I can fuck your cunt and your arse. If you order me to do it, I'll keep going until you are screaming my name and I run out of come."

She sighed. "Which brings me back to my original point. What if I don't want you to fuck me, but wish to fuck you instead?"

"You can't. You don't have the necessary equipment."

She strolled away from him and returned with a slim leather phallus that she'd taken off one of the shelves.

"Oh, I can fuck you."

He glared at her to hide his sudden apprehension. "Why bother with that when I can satisfy you far better with my real cock? You can beat me bloody and I swear to God that I'll still be able to perform for as long as you want."

She stared at him for so long that he had to look away. "You don't wish me to make you come with my fingers and this nice leather phallus?"

He set his teeth and continued to study the floor.

"Then *tell* me you don't want me to do that to you."

Rage burned through him, and he raised his head. "I won't beg. I'm not a coward."

She turned her back on him and for an instant he forgot how

to breathe, but she didn't leave, she just went to the wall of implements and took something down. His gaze settled on the leather cock rings she held in her hand.

Without speaking, she buckled the leather straps around his balls, bringing them up tight against the root of his cock, and then added the third strap around his shaft. His breath hissed out as she tightened the strap until he could feel his rapid heartbeat throbbing through his trapped cock. He lowered his head to watch her work, torn between salacious delight at her handling him so roughly, and anxiety as to how she expected him to come at all when he was trussed up so tightly.

She moved behind him again, and he felt her finger circling the oiled bud of his arse, rimming the circle, pressing inward with each swirl of her finger. He clenched his muscles as hard as he could, but she gained a fingertip of entrance. It felt like her fist . . .

"If you don't like it, Mr. Maclean, or if I am hurting you, all you have to do is tell me to stop."

His thoughts swirled into a chaotic muddle. He didn't want her anywhere near his arse, but if he told her to stop, she'd think she'd won . . . He groaned as she eased her fingertip fully inside him. Despite the restriction, his cock was pumping out pre-cum, soaking the leather and making him ache with pleasure.

He tried to focus on what he wanted, of what to say to make her stop . . .

"Let me fuck you properly, Lady Theale. Keep me in these bindings, fuck me like this, don't let me come until you are satisfied." She pushed her finger deeper and he shook with the strangeness of it. "Beat me until I'm bloody, and then deny me your cunt. I'll beg for you then."

She started pumping her finger back and forth, and there was nothing he could do to stop her. Panic almost made his lungs seize up. He had to stop her; he had to stop this *now.*

"Are you too afraid to set me free, Lady Theale? Are you scared because what you really want is for me to overpower you and fuck you until you're the one who is screaming?"

She removed her hands from him, and he started to smile until she walked around to face him.

"Nice try, Mr. Maclean, but I don't need you to fuck me. I *need* you to act like a responsible man and *tell* me when you are uncomfortable with a sexual situation I might put you in." She cupped his chin. "I'm not interested in beating you to death because you won't accept your limits!"

"I have no limits. Fuck me properly, and I'll show you. I can tell you this—I won't come if you use me like this. I won't bloody *allow* myself to."

Her blasted smile widened. "We'll see about that."

She washed her hands, went to the door, and consulted with someone who sounded rather like Donal Murray. Eventually she turned back to him.

"I wish to offer you one more chance to be reasonable, Mr. Maclean. Accept that you need to tell me what you don't like, and also when I've gone too far."

"A little slip of a girl like you?" He managed to grin. "You'll never get me to that point."

"So be it." She drew up a chair and sat down on it. A knock on the door made Alistair tense as she told the person to come in.

"Ah, James, I have a job for you."

The young man dressed in the livery of the pleasure house bowed. "Yes, my lady?"

In front of Alistair's incredulous gaze, Lady Theale handed over the vial of oil and the slim leather phallus to the footman.

"I wish you to use this on him until he comes."

The footman studied Alistair warily. "All trussed up like this, my lady?"

"Yes, please."

"No!" Alistair bit out the word. "You will not let him bloody touch me!"

"Did you say no, Mr. Maclean?"

"Not to you. But he's not touching my arse."

"All you have to do to make him stop is ask me nicely, Mr. Maclean. It's as simple as that." She smiled into his eyes.

"Damn you," Alistair said.

She nodded at James. "Proceed."

He was fighting so hard not to come that she wanted to shove her skirts up and finger herself until she came with him. Because he would climax. She had no doubt about that. He'd almost bitten his lower lip bloody biting down on it as James dutifully pushed the oiled phallus in and out of his arse in a regular pounding motion. His cock was straining at the leather restraints and his hips were bucking as far forward as his shackles allowed.

She held his gaze and saw his fury boiling to an incandescent rage. It might seem cruel, but if she was truly to master him, he had to understand that what he wanted was of no interest to her. Some of her lovers learned faster than others. Mr. Maclean wasn't going to capitulate easily, but that was what made him such a prize. When he did succumb to her—if he did, he would be worth it.

"God . . ." he muttered.

She went over and cupped his cheek. "Do you have something you wish to say to me, Mr. Maclean? Have you had enough? Do you want James to stop? Just tell me and I'll make it so."

He tried to pull free of her fingers, his breathing labored, his skin now glistening with sweat.

"Go to hell."

She looked over his bowed head at James.

"Faster, please."

He nodded, and she noticed the excitement in his eyes and the thrust of his own cock pushing at his pantaloons. She would make sure that he was rewarded well for his part in Mr. Maclean's training.

She saw the moment when Mr. Maclean could take no more and gripped his damp auburn hair, forcing him to hold her gaze as he climaxed in long spasms that made his body arch against his restraints.

"Leave the phallus inside him, James, if you please, and come here."

"Yes, my lady."

She beckoned for the flushed young footman to stand right in front of Mr. Maclean.

"Did you enjoy that, James?"

"Yes, my lady."

"So I see." She cupped his balls and rubbed her thumb over his hard cock. "Perhaps you might do one more thing for me before you go off to find some relief for yourself."

"Anything, my lady."

"Take the cock rings off him."

"Yes, my lady." James rushed to kneel at Mr. MacLean's tethered ankles. He carefully started unbuckling the soaked leather and dropped it to the floor, hissing in sympathy. "He'll be sore after this."

"Good. He deserves to be." She waited until he'd completed the task and he stood up. "Thank you, James." She handed him a gold sovereign. "Tell Mr. Murray you're finished."

After he shut the door behind him before returning to Mr. Maclean. He tensed as she gently inspected his balls and the red lines that had bitten into his most tender flesh.

"I told you, you would come."

He didn't answer her, so she continued her inspection, aware that even as she touched him his cock was quivering into life again.

"I can still fuck you until you can't take any more." He growled the words at her, and she hid a smile. She would've been disappointed if he'd capitulated now. . . .

"Oh, Mr. Maclean," she cooed. "How can you do that when I haven't finished fucking *you*?"

His breathing hitched and his horrified gaze sprang upward to her face. She wrapped her hand around his growing cock and gently squeezed.

"We're not done. Unless you have something to say to me?"

His lips pressed together as if to stop any words escaping.

"Are you quite certain?"

There was another knock at the door and a blond-haired footman entered. Diana smiled into Mr. Maclean's leaf-green eyes. "You did say you wanted to fuck until you ran out of come, didn't you?"

Alistair closed his eyes and tried not to moan as the third footman used the phallus on his sore arse. He'd already come twice. His hips were thrusting forward as though caught in some nightmarish mating ritual that demanded a human sacrifice. *He* was that sacrifice. His cock was in agony, he wanted to scream that he couldn't take any more, but he had to endure, he *had* to.

Because *she* sat there, watching him, waiting for him to give in and beg her to stop the torment. And he would not beg. He would *not* . . .

"Stop."

"Yes, my lady."

Alistair held himself still as she came over to him and grabbed his hair, bringing his face up to hers.

"Give in to me, Mr. Maclean. Ask me to end this."

"No." He forced the word out and heard the sound of the door shutting behind the footman. She leaned around his shaking body and removed the phallus and then returned to study his face.

"Give in to me."

"No."

She gently kissed his bloodied mouth, little kisses that teased and ignited his senses. He jerked his head away and hissed at her.

"I know that you want me to get angry with you, Mr. Maclean. You want me to lose control and flog you so you can enjoy the release that gives you."

"I want you to lose control, so I can fuck you so hard you'll be the one begging."

Damn her, he wanted to throw himself at her feet and order her to hurt him. He didn't want her to be gentle; he wanted her to beat him senseless. *That* he understood. She sank down onto her knees in a froth of black silk, leaving him staring at the lush curves of her bosom.

She licked his sore, beleaguered cock, and he moaned. She did it again and drew him gently into her mouth, bathing him in her saliva until he started to grow bigger. God, he hurt. It was heaven, but it was also hell.

"Don't be kind." He forced the words out. "Don't—do this."

She continued to hold him in her mouth licking and sucking him until he was erect again, and God, that hurt even more. Reaching around his hips, she slid her palms over his buttocks and cupped them, her thumbs sliding lower to penetrate his arse.

He bucked against her, his cock extending another painful inch and she slowly sucked him in rhythm to the pulse of her fingers.

"I can't—"

Alistair closed his eyes as she used him and fought hopelessly against the mechanics of his own body, which yearned for her to take him and to make him hers.

"Ah, God . . ." He climaxed, and it was like his cock spurted blistering molten metal. Each spasm went on for too long and racked his body until he had nothing left to give her. Nothing but the useless thrust of his hips and his now empty cock.

She released him and moved away, washing her hands and then wiping her mouth with her dainty lace handkerchief. For the first time, he was glad of the restraints holding him steady or else his knees would have folded and he would've been on the floor at her feet. He'd rather crawl away to a dark corner somewhere she couldn't see him and lick his own wounds. When he finally had the strength to look up, she was watching him from her chair, her gaze serene.

"Do you have something you wish to say to me, Mr. Maclean?"

He shook his head.

"Then I will leave you to enjoy the rest of your evening." She nodded at him and turned toward the door. "I'll send Donal Murray to set you free."

"You don't trust me not to hurt you, do you?" he growled. "You're right about that. If I was free right now, I'd wring your bloody neck."

She went still and slowly swung around to face him again. "I am not afraid of you." Opening the door she shouted, "Donal!"

He appeared quickly, his appreciative gaze taking stock of Alistair's nakedness, and then turned to Lady Theale. "Yes, my lady?"

"Please release Mr. Scott. I am done with him."

She smiled at Donal and left without a backward glance, leaving Alistair wanting to shout after her and beg her to return. But he wouldn't do that. She'd humiliated him, and that was unacceptable.

Donal Murray knelt at his feet and started to work on the first buckle. "Right, let's get you free."

Even as Alistair allowed himself to be helped, he had a terrible sense that thanks to Diana Theale, he would never be completely free again.

7

"Are you all right, Alistair? Is your chair uncomfortable?"

Alistair smiled at the countess. "My hip doesn't appreciate these rainy days and makes it hard for me to sit still."

"Then sit beside me on the chaise." The countess patted the seat beside her, and Alistair moved gratefully over to the well-upholstered couch. It wasn't his hip that pained him, but his arse, and he was hardly going to admit that in present company.

"Thank you, my lady." He shuffled the pile of papers he balanced on his knee. "I wanted to ask about Lady Theale."

"She is settling in very well. I have no complaints, and I think my dear Malinda feels the same. Diana's been very helpful arranging things at the new house for her."

"I'm sure she has," Alistair said. "I actually wanted to discuss another matter. As Nicodemus said he wasn't comfortable investigating his own stepmother, I wondered who *had* checked that Lady Theale was a suitable candidate for this very sensitive role at the Sinners."

The countess sat back and studied Alistair's face. "Why are you so interested in Diana's credentials?"

"I'm not. I've just learned to be careful. Her arrival just seemed somewhat propitious. How did she come to your attention?"

"I believe Malinda knows an acquaintance of hers, and heard about the terrible circumstances Diana was left in after her husband's death. When the idea of us having our own secretary came up, Malinda thought about Diana, and wrote to Charlotte to ascertain if Diana would be interested in such a position."

"So no one investigated her past? She was taken on trust?"

"I didn't quite say *that,* dear. Malinda made certain that we knew exactly what we were dealing with."

Alistair schooled his expression into one of great interest, but unfortunately, the countess didn't elaborate.

"So you are content with her story?"

"I believe so. Why? Is there something wrong?"

"Not that I know of, my lady—not yet."

"That sounds rather ominous. Are you two not getting along?"

"We—" For a second, Alistair's mouth refused to form another word. "We are perfectly in harmony, my lady. I was concerned because I hadn't received any information about her past from our usual sources."

The countess patted his hand. "Don't worry about that, Alistair. I assure you that Malinda and I are perfectly safe."

"Then I will accept that Lady Theale is a valuable member of our household." He went to rise, but she kept hold of his hand. "Is there something else, my lady?"

"Nico said you were asking him about the Demon Club."

"That's correct."

She squeezed his fingers. "Are you in debt to them? If you are, tell me how much you owe them, and I will either give you the money or advance the sum from your wages to pay the amount off in full." She shivered. "The owners of that gambling den are the worst kind of men who prey on the unwary and ruin innocent lives."

"I have incurred no debts with them, my lady."

"Are you quite sure?"

"Yes." He smiled at her. "I swear it."

"Then I will let you go."

He kissed her hand and stood up. "Thank you, my lady. If you don't mind, I'll go through to Lady Theale's office and leave this correspondence on her desk."

"She's not there, so you won't disturb her. She went with Malinda to the new house to inspect some of the new furniture that arrived this morning."

"It is of no matter if she isn't there. I've already written her a note about what to do with these letters." He had no intention of seeking Diana Theale out for the rest of his life. His cock ached in sympathy at the thought, and he bowed and withdrew.

After a perfunctory knock on her office door, he let himself in and was immediately hit by the elusive scent of her rose perfume. His shaft stirred even more and he gently cupped himself.

"No, you fool, stay down. She doesn't deserve your attention." He carefully placed the pile of documents in the exact center of Diana Theale's desk. After a quick glance at the closed door, he took the opportunity to search her desk, but found nothing of interest. If he wanted to get a sense of who she really was, he'd probably need to search her bedchamber.

But how would he gain access to that without her knowing? He suddenly thought of the large bundle of keys Adam Fisher had given him when he'd joined the Sinners. During his first two weeks he'd tried every key in every lock until he'd identified it, and then he'd labeled each one for future reference.

Hurrying back to his office, he pulled open the bottom drawer of his desk and started sorting through the carefully organized keys until he found the one he wanted. With a triumphant smile, he walked quickly through the house and up to the first floor, where the Westbrook apartment was situated. After another quick glance around to check he was unobserved, he unlocked the door and went inside.

Her rose scent was stronger here, and he paused for a second to breathe it in and remember how it had felt when she'd kissed him so gently on his bloodied lips. . . .

Damn her.

Shaking off his inconveniently lustful thoughts, he made a thorough, but careful search of the sitting room and then went into the bedroom. He couldn't help imagine her sprawled naked on the sheets while he fucked her hard, and she begged him never to stop. Not that he'd ever get to fuck her. She'd made sure of that.

There was an unfolded note on the dressing table, and he went over to read it. The handwriting was not familiar, but distinctly feminine.

> *He has not returned to his lodgings. There appears to be a man watching the house.*
>
> *Yours,*
>
> *Charlotte*

Alistair considered the cryptic note for a long moment. If he was the suspicious type, he might assume that it referred to Harry. If it *did* refer to Harry, then Lady Theale had lied to him about her interest in his brother.

Charlotte . . .

The note had obviously been delivered by hand and bore only the words "Lady Theale" on the reverse and the remains of a red wax seal. Was it possible that this was the same woman Lady Benedict knew? Alistair studied the seal closely and wondered why it looked so familiar. He thought he could make out the letter *P*.

Abandoning his search, Alistair replaced the note exactly where he'd found it, locked the door, and went in search of Maddon the butler. He found him in the kitchen reading the morning paper and drinking tea.

"Good morning, Mr. Maclean. May I assist you with something?"

"Yes, don't get up." Alistair waved him back down into his seat. "I was wondering whether you received any messages from the pleasure house recently."

Maddon frowned. "Are you expecting something, sir?"

"Yes." It wasn't a lie; he maintained regular contact with Christian over the entertainment on the second floor.

The butler put down his cup. "The only note I've taken in from the pleasure house in the last day or so was for Lady Theale. Do you wish me to inquire as to whether the message was meant for you?"

"There's no need for that," Alistair said quickly. "To be quite frank, I'm probably expecting a reply far too promptly. I'm quite happy to go and *ask* Mr. Delornay whether he has an answer for me yet. Please don't trouble yourself." He smiled at the butler. "The exercise will do me good."

"If you are sure, sir."

"If anyone asks for me, please tell them that I'll be back before dinner."

"Yes, sir."

Alistair found his hat and coat and walked around to the pleasure house, cutting through the garden at the center of the square to appreciate the flowers and the greenery that always struggled to survive in the city. It was still a far cry from his Scottish homeland, where bracken and heather predominated on the steep hillsides and the sun rarely shined. Was that where Harry had gone? Would he find some peace there?

After greeting the footman stationed in the front hall and asking to speak to Christian, Alistair was taken through to the owner's office. Christian was working at his desk, his blond head bent to his task as he filled in a huge ledger with his small, neat handwriting.

"Mr. Maclean. How may I help you?"

Alistair took the seat Christian offered him and considered how best to approach the subject. "I've reason to believe that the woman who threatened to shoot me the other night might be connected to your establishment."

"But after luring you in here, she walked right through the building and left immediately."

"She had a key for Barrington Square. All she had to do was leave through the front entrance, throw off her disguise, and reenter through the Barrington house at her leisure."

"Why do you believe that?"

"Because of further evidence I have acquired. Do you have a woman named Charlotte on your staff?"

Christian interlaced his fingers and looked down at them. "You know I am not at liberty to discuss my employees or the members of the club with anyone. This place thrives on anonymity."

"That's not very helpful."

"Unless this 'Charlotte' is officially wanted by the government for High Treason, I am unable to confirm her existence, or lack of it. You of all people should understand this. You go by the name of Mr. Scott here. I have never shared your true identity with your brother, your employers, or anyone connected to the Sinners."

"And I appreciate it." Alistair sighed. "If you do know this woman, could you at least ask her what is going on?"

Christian raised an eyebrow and remained annoyingly silent.

"Fine," Alistair snapped. "There is one more thing you might help me with. Apparently, Harry turned up at the Sinners one night with a new lover. Do you know who that might be?"

Christian sat back. "Now, I can tell you something about *him* because he was banned from the pleasure house."

"Banned? He must have behaved very badly indeed for that to happen."

"He insulted my wife."

"Oh dear." Alistair knew how fiercely Christian protected Elizabeth and was faintly surprised that the other man was still breathing. "What's his name?"

"Sir Ronald Fairbanks."

"Wasn't he ennobled by the Crown for his services to the banking industry?"

"Yes, he's been propping up the Hanoverians' finances for years." Christian wrinkled his nose. "I am all for the advancement of the *hoi polloi,* but that man is an insufferable idiot."

"If he commented unfavorably on your wife in front of you, then obviously."

Christian still didn't smile. "He met Harry here just before I banned him. I attempted to dissuade your brother from engaging with the man, but he didn't listen."

"That doesn't surprise me at all. Do you know if they are still together?"

"I haven't heard, but it wouldn't shock me if they were. Why do you need this information?"

Alistair decided to be honest. "Because Harry has bolted. He has many friends, but few who have the money to help him out of his present financial crisis. I wondered if he'd gone to Sir Ronald. I also wondered if Sir Ronald had any connection with the Demon Club."

Christian went still. "Considering what I know of that place, it should have occurred to me that Fairbanks was a member there. He seems just the type to thrive on the misery of others. It would also explain why he attempted to ingratiate himself with my wife."

"You've been there?"

"I have. He might have heard some of the old stories about what happened to me and Elizabeth there." Christian sighed. "Dammit. I hoped that after I'd dealt with Lord Kelveston and his bitch of a wife, the place would cease to exist." He fixed Alistair with his piercing blue gaze. "What do you know of it?"

"I had a letter demanding repayment of a substantial debt Harry acquired there. I sent the information on to him. Later that same day, I had a visit from a Lord Blaydon, who very politely informed me that the debt had been placed in my name and I was considered responsible for paying it back. I equally politely informed *him* that I had no intention of paying him a single penny, at which point he smiled and threatened to carry out his purpose regardless."

Christian shook his head. "The Demon Club has always enjoyed bringing debtors to justice. The problem is that in the past they were often the ones who created the debts in the first place."

"You mean the place is dishonest?"

"It certainly used to be. I don't recommend you attempt to find out."

"I certainly don't wish to have anything to do with it, but I prefer to be informed."

"Where's Harry now?"

"As I said, I'm not sure, but Lord Blaydon intimated that if he didn't settle his debt soon, I would be obliged to do so in his stead."

Christian sat forward. "May I offer you some advice? Don't attempt to pay off your brother's debt this time. Let them find him, and let him suffer the consequences of his behavior."

"But you said the place was deadly."

"It is, but if the Demon Club can't bring your brother to his senses, I suspect nothing will. Their methods of extracting payment when money isn't readily available are . . . inventive. A dose of public humiliation might be just what Harry needs."

Alistair held himself rigidly still. "He is still my brother."

"And you have protected him for years, everyone knows

that. He's twenty-five, Alistair. Don't you think it's time for him to finally grow up?"

Alistair nodded and stood up. "Thank you for your time, Mr. Delornay. And if you can find out anything about Charlotte, I would appreciate it."

"Of course. Good-bye, Mr. Maclean."

At least he had a name to put to his brother's lover. As to the rest? He'd not achieved much, but if Charlotte was living at the pleasure house, he knew Christian would alert her to his interest. If she was willing to talk to him honestly, he might be closer to solving both Harry's issues and his own.

"What did Mr. Maclean want?"

"Information."

Diana sat down and settled her skirts around her. She'd left Malinda at the door to the Sinners and taken the hackney on to the pleasure house to speak to Charlotte. She hadn't yet reached her friend, having been met in the hallway by a footman with a pleasantly worded, but definite request for her to attend Mr. Delornay before she did anything else.

"About me?"

"No, Charlotte."

"Oh dear." Diana sighed. "He's far quicker and more intelligent than I thought he'd be."

"And I'm slightly annoyed, Lady Theale." Christian sat forward, his expression cool. "What exactly are you and Charlotte plotting together, and how does it involve the Demon Club?"

Diana stared at him for a long moment, refusing to drop her gaze. "It's complicated."

"It usually is."

"Charlotte is on a quest to bring Harry Maclean to his knees. She reckons the Demon Club are the only people who can do that for her."

"I'd agree, but what does that have to do with you and the older Mr. Maclean?"

"Nothing."

"I don't think Mr. Maclean would agree with you. He is very protective of his younger brother."

"So it seems. I . . . have other plans for Alistair Maclean and the Sinners Club."

"You intend to use his particular sexual proclivities to break him down and use him against his employers?"

"No! I don't have an issue with his employers."

"Then, what?"

"I'm trying to trace someone who was associated with the founding of the Sinners."

"By using Alistair Maclean." Christian shook his head. "I don't like it, Diana."

"Why not? You didn't seem to mind when I married Lord Theale!"

"Because he married you knowing what you were, and what he wanted from you. It was a business arrangement. This"—he waved a dismissive hand—"seems cruel and unlike you."

To her amazement, Diana found herself biting back tears. "That's unfair."

"I'm just telling you how it appears to me. Can you not just tell Mr. Maclean what it is you are after, and ask for his help?"

"Life's never that simple, Christian, you know that. If I ask Mr. Maclean for help, he'll tell his employers. He's far too honest for his own good." She gathered herself and thrust the unwanted emotions down. "I didn't know he liked to submit to a woman until I saw him here."

"And you couldn't just leave him be?"

"I *couldn't*." She held Christian's gaze. "He is such a challenge. He still is. I've never met anyone like him. He fights me every step of the way, and I want to break him, I want him to kiss my feet and *mean* it."

"How inconvenient for you."

She glared at him. "It damn well is!"

His expression sobered. "At some point, you will have to tell him the truth, or he will be forced to choose between you and his loyalty to his employers."

"I'm hoping to avoid that happening. When I find out the answers to my questions, I will be able to leave the Sinners, and then he can choose whether he wants to have a relationship with me or not."

"Now who is being delusional?" Christian sighed and sat back. "Let me recap. I don't care what Charlotte is up to with Harry Maclean. He deserves to be brought down. But I don't want anyone from the Demon Club on my premises or for us to have any association with that place."

"I'll tell Charlotte."

"You can also tell her that Mr. Alistair Maclean would very much like to speak to her."

"She won't agree to that."

"I didn't think she would. I didn't confirm that Charlotte worked here, but he is suspicious. For some reason, he also knows that you are connected to her, which is why I assumed you were both after the same thing."

"Damn."

"Your language is appalling for a lady."

"I'm no lady." Diana stood and curtsied to Christian. "You of all men know that. Your wife rescued me off the streets."

"She has a habit of doing that, but I can only applaud her efforts, especially when she brings me beautiful women like you and Charlotte."

"As if you care about what we look like when you have such an extraordinary wife."

"I am well aware of that." He shrugged. "But you make my pleasure house beautiful, don't forget that, and I am, at heart, a pragmatic French businessman. Please be careful, Diana, and tell Charlotte to be on her guard. Any dealings with the Demon Club can go horribly wrong."

"I'll tell her. Now I must speak to Charlotte and then get back to work."

"And the interesting and untamable Mr. Maclean."

Diana ignored his provocative comment and headed up the stairs to Charlotte's room. She would have to tread very carefully with Mr. Maclean if she wasn't to hurt him. Christian was right, he didn't deserve that. How was she going to survive her need to own him and yet satisfy her desire to find out the truth? She had to find a way. She *had* to.

8

Alistair knocked on the door of Lady Theale's office. Despite his unwillingness to see her, he now had a genuine reason to confront her and he'd never been a man to shirk his battles. He had to find out what her connection was to the woman named Charlotte who had threatened him in the hackney cab.

"Come in."

She wore a dark green dress with a narrow lace border around the bodice and full bell sleeves. Her black hair was arranged in a sleek bun at the back of her neck and fastened with jet pins.

"Mr. Maclean, how delightful. Please take a seat."

Sunshine streamed through the single window behind her desk, which looked out over the back of the house and the mews beyond.

"Thank you."

"How may I help you?"

"I spoke to Mr. Delornay yesterday about a woman I believe you are acquainted with from the pleasure house."

"And who might that be?"

"Charlotte."

She raised her eyebrows. "Why do you think I know this woman?"

"Because of something Lady Westbrook mentioned to me about how you were hired. Mr. Delornay quite properly refused to discuss any of his employees, so this morning I asked Lady Malinda if she was acquainted with a Charlotte who currently lived at the pleasure house. She said that she was."

"Oh."

"Is there anything you would like to tell me about this woman?"

"In what respect?"

"Her relationship to you, and more importantly, her relationship to my brother."

She folded her hands together on her desk. "I've known Charlotte for several years. We were at school together. When our school closed down, we were both cast out on the streets. Elizabeth Delornay found us and offered us a home and employment at the pleasure house."

"Forgive me, but what kind of school throws its pupils out on the streets?"

She met his gaze without flinching, "The kind where the headmistress dies and the charity pupils have nowhere else to go."

Alistair digested that unexpected piece of her history. Considering her ladylike stature and accent, it had a certain ring of truth to it.

"That's where I met Lord Theale."

"At the pleasure house?" He looked up. She was volunteering information now?

"He asked me to marry him because it was cheaper than paying the fees to see me at the pleasure house."

"A true romantic, then."

"Simply a man who knew what he wanted, and was prepared to pay for it." She shrugged. "The arrangement worked very well."

"It certainly did for you, but your friend, Charlotte, remained in the pleasure house."

"I offered her a home with me, Mr. Maclean, but she preferred to live at the pleasure house and ply her trade there."

"With my brother, presumably."

"No, I don't believe she bedded Harry. His tastes run in different directions to hers."

"He prefers men, but will fuck anything if he feels the need."

Her mouth curled in distaste. "So I've heard."

"Then what does she want with my brother?"

"You'll have to talk to her about that."

"If you will recall, my lady, the last time we met she rammed a pistol in my face, threatened me, and ran away."

"She had her reasons."

"So, she set you on me instead."

"No, she asked me to determine where your sympathies lie."

"Harry is my brother."

"I understand that now. I have told her that despite everything, you are loyal to him and that appealing to you for help would be a waste of time." She lifted her hand in a gesture of dismissal. "I also told her there was nothing else I could help her with except report back on your movements with regard to your brother."

"How very generous of you."

"I understand your skepticism, Mr. Maclean, but I am at least trying to be honest with you."

"And why is that, when you have proved yourself to be untrustworthy in the past?"

She raised her eyebrows. "On the contrary, I'm telling you the truth."

"Why?"

"Because I wish things to be clear between us."

"Oh, they are clear." He glared at her. "I don't appreciate being used, my lady."

"We both know that is patently untrue, Mr. Maclean, don't we?" She held his gaze. "You want to be used more than you care about your own safety."

"I believe we've already discussed this matter, Lady Theale. I see no point in going over it again."

She had the audacity to tilt her head to one side and smile at him. "I think I know why you don't like being fucked."

He went so still it suddenly became difficult to draw in air.

She rose and came around to perch on the front of her desk, her satin skirts brushing his knees. "It's because of your brother, isn't it?"

"Go to hell."

She reached out and cupped his rigid jaw. "You mentioned it earlier. Harry prefers men. You don't want anyone to think you are like him, so you avoid anyone touching your arse if you possibly can." He flinched as her other hand cupped his balls. "But I like fucking you, Mr. Maclean. I like filling you with a nice big phallus and watching you come, I like pushing my fingers deep in your arse and making you beg."

He couldn't move, he couldn't damn move as she held him captive, his cock hardening and growing inches away from her fingers with every harried breath he took.

"So, we need to resolve this issue, don't we?" The heel of her hand grazed his thickening shaft and she pressed down on it.

"No. I've already made it quite clear that this 'relationship' is over. You have deceived me and—"

He gasped as she squeezed his balls hard. "Please listen carefully, Mr. Maclean. As requested, I have told you about my relationship with Charlotte and Lady Malinda. I have admitted that Charlotte has plans for your brother, of which I know very little. I have realized where I erred the other night when I had you tied up and at my mercy. Isn't that enough of a concession for you to reconsider our 'relationship'?"

He held still, his cock growing. "I don't know what you want from me," he said hoarsely. "You continue to confuse me."

"I want to make an agreement with you. I'll not let men fuck you if you allow me to fuck you instead."

"There's no point; we're no longer playing this game."

"Aren't we?" She squeezed even harder and he wanted to whimper. "You are twice my size, Mr. Maclean, and a former soldier. If you wanted to get away, do you think I could really stop you?"

He had nothing to say to that.

"Go and lock the door and come back to me."

God help him, he did what she asked, checking both the doors just to make sure.

"Face the desk, put your hands on each corner, and lean forward."

He fitted his hands against the polished oak, and she pressed on the small of his back until he bent over. His trouser-covered cock was jammed against the wooden edge of the desk, and his forehead was against her papers.

"I thought about how you might look stretched out over my desk the other day." She sighed. "The reality is even better than I imagined."

He shuddered as she caressed his buttocks and then slowly undid his trousers and buttons and pushed his clothing down to his knees. She lifted his long-tailed shirt away from his arse, making him shiver at the sudden exposure of his skin to the air.

"Does this remind you of your schooldays, Mr. Maclean? You would not believe the number of gentlemen I met in the pleasure house who paid in gold simply to be treated like a naughty schoolboy again."

She touched his skin with something, and he jumped. "It's my ruler, Mr. Maclean. I'm going to use it on your arse, but you must not come. Twelve strokes, so that when you return to your office and sit down, you will be thinking about me for the rest of the day."

He braced himself as the ruler came whistling down on his bare skin with a distinctive crack. She alternated between his buttocks until he no longer felt each individual blow, just the heat rising from his skin and the pain and pleasure of his throbbing wet cock jammed against the hardness of the wood.

She wrapped a hand around his neck. "Get down on your knees, Mr. Maclean."

He struggled to right himself and then obediently dropped down to the floor. Was he really allowing her to do this to him during daylight and at his place of work? Part of him couldn't quite believe it.

She resumed her position on the desk in front of him and slowly raised her skirts until he could see the whiteness of her thighs and the tops of her stockings. He swallowed hard as she eased one foot out and placed it on the surface of the desk, opening her sex fully to his view.

"I want you to make me come with your mouth, Mr. Maclean. Keep your hands locked behind your back."

He groaned as he leaned in and licked her inner thigh. The scent of her arousal made him want to rub his face into her slick wetness until he wouldn't know anything else.

"Go on," she whispered.

He plunged his tongue deep, and she moaned as he licked and savaged his way over her swollen lips and the tight bud of her clitoris. Using his mouth and tongue, he brought her to a quick climax, which had her grabbing his hair and holding him tightly against her pulsing flesh until he was drowning in her, fighting to breathe and not even caring.

He set his teeth carefully on her clit and she came again, her fingers tightening painfully in his hair as she ground herself against him. He jabbed his tongue deep inside her and felt the contraction of her muscles, humming to himself as he experienced her pleasure.

"Let me fuck you," he murmured against her thigh. "Let me inside you."

She laughed and, placing her slippered foot in the center of his chest, pushed him backward until he almost overbalanced onto his sore arse. As he scrambled to sit up, she moved off the desk and picked up her ruler again.

"Sit on the front of the desk, Mr. Maclean, and use your hands to hold on."

He obeyed her, wincing as his arse came in contact with the firmness of the wood. His cock was still hard and tangled up in his shirt. She stepped forward and dealt briskly with his clothing, baring his rigid length to her gaze.

His breath hissed out as she brought the ruler close to his shaft and placed one end against his groin.

"Eight inches, Mr. Maclean. Very impressive."

He managed to smile at her. "Even better when it's buried inside you."

"I'm sure." She withdrew the ruler and tapped it against the palm of her hand as she considered him. "You don't really think I'd allow you to fuck me on my desk, do you?"

"Why not? You're doing it to me."

"I am not fucking you with a ruler. It would hurt you."

"You are so kind to your slave."

Her smile disappeared. "You are being sarcastic, or attempting to be. Perhaps you need to be reminded of your place."

She brought her hand back and delivered a short smack to his cock with the flat of the ruler, which made him snarl a curse at her.

"Did you speak, Mr. Maclean?"

He shook his head and she did it again, but this time he was ready for it, and didn't react quite so violently.

"I was going to let you go back to your office with your arse burning and your cock hard and unsatisfied, but I think I want more from you." She pushed him down until he was flat on his back on her desk, his legs spread wide and his cock still at attention.

"You're very close to coming, aren't you?"

He wanted to close his eyes, but he refused to give her the satisfaction and shrugged instead. She moved closer between his legs, and he shuddered as she gripped his balls in her hand and rubbed the ruler up and down his hot, rigid length until he was fighting not to buck his hips.

"Handkerchief." He managed to force out the words.

"For what, Mr. Maclean? For your seed?" She laughed. "I want to see you let go, and come all over your belly and your balls. I want to see your come dripping off your skin."

Even as she said the words, it was too late to stop himself from obeying her and climaxing in hot-jetted streams all over his stomach. She waited until he finished convulsing and ran her fingers into the pool of liquid and swirled them around.

"Mmm." She tasted him on her fingertip and his cock jerked again. Bringing her fingertips to his mouth, she coated his lips with his own seed.

"I'll give you a choice. Suck your come from my fingers until you are clean, or go back to your office just like this." She slid one wet finger into his mouth and he helplessly sucked it until she fed him more.

After a little while, she took his handkerchief out of his pocket and cleaned him up more efficiently before pulling up his underthings and buttoning his trousers over the half-erect shaft of his cock.

He stumbled to his feet. "You deliberately distracted me."

She returned to sit behind her desk, not a hair out of place, and regarded him quizzically.

"From what?"

"Asking questions about your friend Charlotte and my brother, Harry. What is her connection to the Demon Club?"

"I don't know. Once Charlotte knew that I was involved with you, she decided not to share any more details of her plan with me."

"But—"

She held up one hand. "I promise that I am not involved in Charlotte's efforts to contact your brother. I will, however, pass any information that you *give* me about your brother to Charlotte because she is my best friend. The cards are in your hand, Mr. Maclean. If you don't tell me anything, I won't have anything to tell her."

Alistair took a deep breath. "And what about when I am stretched out naked on a rack for you, Lady Theale, my body at your mercy, my cock hard and dripping with wanting you. Will you ask me your questions again?"

She didn't answer him immediately, which gave him hope.

"I would not use that power to extract information from you. That would be underhanded and contrary to everything I believe in."

"What do you believe?"

She held his gaze. "That if you choose to submit to me, to *trust* me with your person, I cannot and will not betray that trust."

There was a note of sincerity in her answer that made him want to look away from her dark gaze. Instead, he shrugged.

"That sounds rather melodramatic, my lady. It is, after all, only sex and I've already told you that I don't trust you."

Her smile widened, which infuriated him. "Oh, Mr. Maclean, you amuse me greatly."

"In what way?"

"There's no need to stiffen up."

"I'm asking a perfectly reasonable question."

"You think that you don't trust me."

"I know I don't."

"Yet you just let me strip you half-naked over my desk in the middle of the working day." She refused to drop her gaze. "You are already my slave, Mr. Maclean. You just won't admit it yet."

"This conversation is ended." He bowed. "Good afternoon, Lady Theale."

"Mr. Maclean." She inclined her head a regal inch. "When you've gotten over your surfeit of masculine pride, please remember to be naked in my room at midnight on Friday."

He made an inelegant sound and walked out, his cock and arse throbbing with every indignant stride, his mind again in turmoil. By the time he reached his office, he was sure of one thing. He'd learned rather more than he'd bargained for on a Wednesday morning. Some of it was helpful, and much of it too confusing for him to wish to deal with. But that was the problem with Diana Theale. There were moments when he was with her that everything seemed so obvious and clear that he couldn't imagine what he had to argue about.

And then she would say something provoking and upset all his certainties about himself and his world and his sexual needs. He slammed down into his chair and regretted it immediately as his arse protested. If he could live his life naked and tied up with Lady Theale, he'd be a happy man . . .

That traitorous thought had him ringing the bell for Maddon and immersing himself in his work. Then he needed to see if Nicodemus had found out the information he'd requested about Harry's lover.

Even as he thought about the matter, there was a knock on the door and one of the footmen delivered him a note in Nicodemus's distinctive spiky black handwriting. Having checked that he at least looked respectable, even if he didn't feel it, Alistair put on his coat and hat and went out to do battle.

* * *

"You are Harry's brother?"

Sir Ronald Fairbanks studied Alistair's calling card as if it might grow horns. He was a dark, heavyset man with a moustache and hard gray eyes. Alistair guessed him to be in his forties.

"Yes, Sir Ronald, I am."

"You work for a living?"

"Someone has to support the family, sir."

He'd been ushered into Sir Ronald's study after a lengthy wait in the hall, but he had expected that. He didn't have the necessary credentials to attract Sir Ronald's attention, and was probably only being seen out of curiosity.

"And what can I do for you, Mr. Maclean?"

"As you are acquainted with my brother, Harry, I wondered if you had seen him recently?"

Sir Ronald looked down at the calling card again. "I understood from your brother that the two of you were estranged. Is that not the case?"

"If by estranged, you mean that every time I am unable to do what my brother demands of me he disappears in a huff, then I suppose we are. I do, however, consider him a part of my family and under my care."

Sir Ronald sat down behind his desk. "I saw him two nights ago. He came here in something of a state."

"Did he mention what was wrong?"

"Only that he was horribly in debt and had no means to pay his creditors." Sir Ronald's smile was sharp. "Nothing I haven't heard from him before."

"I apologize in advance for the personal nature of this question, sir, but did you give him money to settle his debts?"

"I did not." Sir Ronald snorted. "He had the audacity to suggest that as I had taken him to the gambling den in question, I was somehow responsible for the debt he had incurred."

"That sounds remarkably like him. How did he react to your refusal to help him?"

"He told me to go to the devil and stormed out. I haven't seen him since."

Alistair glanced longingly at one of the chairs. His hip was paining him, but he hadn't been invited to sit down. He doubted the invitation would be extended at this point in the uncomfortable conversation.

"He hasn't been seen at his lodgings for two days either."

Sir Ronald pocketed Alistair's card. "I wonder where he went? I gave him a guinea that I had in my pocket." He chuckled. "I made him grovel on the floor for it."

Alistair looked away from his companion's gloating smile. "I have no idea where he is, sir. I must confess to being slightly concerned. If you do hear from him, would you be so kind as to contact me at my place of business?"

"I will certainly do that, Mr. Maclean. In fact, if he turns up I might well bring him along to one of your jolly end-of-the-month events on the second floor."

"I believe those are restricted to our members, sir." Alistair made no attempt to sound regretful. "After Harry repudiated Mr. Fisher, his membership of the club was revoked."

"Oh, pity that." Sir Ronald didn't extend his hand. "Good afternoon, Mr. Maclean."

"Good afternoon, sir." Alistair bowed, turned on his heel, and left the study, none the wiser as to his brother's whereabouts, but with a deep and unswerving loathing for Sir Ronald Fairbanks. If the man had introduced Harry to the dark play of the Demon Club, he was in some part to blame for what had transpired.

Alistair put on his hat and tilted the brim against the breeze, sweeping down the wide modern street where the banker had built his ostentatious new house. But Harry would probably have found his own way to the club eventually. He had a nose for trouble. . . .

There were no hackney cabs around, so Alistair decided to walk down to the busier street below. A woman dressed in a blue pelisse and bonnet waited to cross the road at the lower end of the street, reminding Alistair of his shared hackney cab ride with the gun-wielding Charlotte.

If he'd had any brains, he would've asked Lady Malinda what her friend Charlotte looked like. Even if he went to the pleasure house and stared at all the female employees, he doubted he'd know which one she was. He was also fairly certain that such behavior would have him thrown out on his ear.

A reluctant chuckle escaped him. If Harry had indeed escaped to Scotland, perhaps he was in the right place. A few weeks of their mother's bracing company and sharp wit might be just the thing to set him on a new course. Or make him run even further. Fiona Maclean was a wonderful woman, but all her softness had been bled out of her over the years of dealing with her infuriating husband. She had no time for dreamers, or revolutionaries, or rakes, which meant her loyalty was to Alistair rather than his younger brother and always had been.

He stopped on the curb to avoid a carriage and considered what to do next. A letter to his mother might confirm his brother's whereabouts eventually and was probably worth the expense and the effort. He had nowhere left in London to try, and Nicodemus had been unsuccessful in finding any further clues as well.

As he turned the final corner into the square where the Sinners Club was, his thoughts turned to Diana Theale. It was far easier to think rationally when she wasn't standing over him, ordering him out of his clothes and making him hard for her . . . If she wasn't at the Sinners to involve him in his brother's tangled affairs, why was she there? There had to be a reason. Despite everything, he still intended to find out exactly what it was.

Lady Westbrook had indicated that she and Lady Benedict had investigated their new secretary. If that was the case, where was the information? He would have to look harder, and if he was questioned, he was sure he could come up with some excuse. He might reluctantly admit that he appeared to be under Lady Theale's spell in the bedroom, but his mind was perfectly capable of analytical thinking and swift action outside of it. With that resolve firmly in mind, he spent the remainder of his walk mentally composing the necessary letter to his mother and ignoring the thought of whether he'd be on his knees to Lady Theale on Friday night.

If she was lying to him . . .

His thoughts stuttered to a stop, and he stared out of the window at the seething swell of population on the London street.

Then God help them both.

9

"I just don't understand it. I've been through all the records I can find about the origins of the Sinners and there is nothing, not a scrap of evidence, to suggest anything untoward ever happened."

Charlotte set down her glass. "Then perhaps there isn't anything left to find."

"There *must* be." Diana scowled at her friend. "The very fact that there is nothing, is suspicious in itself."

"I suppose that's true. Mayhap you need to forget about your fears and simply ask?"

"That's what Nico said too. But I can't. I need some scrap of evidence to support my claim, or they can simply ignore me."

"Have you thought about going to the newspapers?"

"And speaking to a *journalist?*"

"Why not?"

Diana shuddered. "I have no wish for my entire life to become breakfast fodder for the whole of London. I'm scandalous enough as it is, and not accepted by polite society."

"So, what do you have to lose?"

"I want to live quietly and respectably. I want"—Diana flung her arms wide—"to be boring and conventional and to sink into comfortable obscurity."

"Whilst continuing to wield a whip over a man such as Mr. Maclean." Charlotte had the audacity to laugh. "You couldn't be boring if you tried, Di."

"I suppose that's true." She looked up at her friend. "Have you given any more thought to speaking to Mr. Maclean?"

"Alistair Maclean?" Charlotte shrugged. "He has nothing to tell me."

"When I peeked into his office, I noticed he had written a letter to his mother in Scotland and left it for Maddon on his desk. Do you think it's possible that Harry has gone up there?"

"If he has, he still won't avoid the Demon Club. They'll simply wait until he thinks it's all blown over and then pounce when he returns to England."

"Then your quest for vengeance is temporarily stalled?"

Charlotte grinned. "I suppose it is. But there is a delightful sense that Harry Maclean will get what he deserves in the end."

"Are you sure about that? Mr. Delornay told me that the Demons is renowned for its shady dealings. Even Elizabeth warned me away from the place. Have you actually been there?"

"No, but my client has, and he says it will be just the thing to bring Harry to his knees."

"Do I know this client?"

Charlotte fixed her with an intimidating stare. "I thought we agreed that I wouldn't tell you anything more about this matter while you are involved with the ever-so upright and moral Mr. Alistair Maclean."

"That's right, we did. I forgot." Diana faked a remorseful sigh.

"Fibber, you just want to know everything, you always have." Charlotte glanced at the clock. "Are you expecting Mr. Maclean tonight?"

"Yes, I am. I think."

"You're still not sure of him?"

"He's not sure of himself. He resists his nature at every turn and makes things far more difficult than necessary." She considered her reluctant lover. "It's rather like taming a wild stallion."

"So enjoyable and well worth the ride."

Diana laughed, kissed her friend, and climbed off her bed. "I need to go and change."

"Have a good night, my love."

"I think I will."

She shut Charlotte's door and headed back to one of the guest rooms where she kept some of the more outrageous clothing she'd worn when she serviced clients at the pleasure house. She chose a tightly fitting deep red velvet dress with a tiny slip of a bodice that barely covered her nipples and left her petticoats and stays off. Piling her hair up on top of her head in a loose bun, she allowed two black ringlets to fall on either side of her face to brush her cheeks. A judicious use of cosmetics and she was ready to go and find out if Mr. Maclean awaited her.

If he had decided to stay away, she would be disappointed. She loved the way he struggled to obey her, his arrogant male certainty and his need to be in control at war with his nature.

Ah, good. He was there. Naked and kneeling in place, his eyes lowered to the floor, his hands coming up to link behind his head. She let out a silent breath and walked around him. His cock was already hard. Reaching out, she nudged his shaft with the toe of her velvet slipper.

"I like that you are always ready to fuck for me, Mr. Maclean. I have come to expect it of you now."

He didn't say anything, although his throat worked as she rubbed her shoe against his tender flesh. Turning to the wall that contained all the implements she needed to tame her wild stallion, she took her time selecting what she needed and then went back to him.

"Stand up."

He obeyed, again favoring his left side, his beautiful green eyes flicking over her.

"Lower your gaze. I did not give you permission to look at me."

"But you look beautiful in that gown, my lady."

His soft murmur made her want to smile. "Thank you." She buckled the leather collar around his throat and attached the long supple leash that fell to the floor. "Keep still."

She picked up the cock harness from the bed and the small phallus.

He grimaced. "Do you have to use that on me?"

"Do you wish me to gag you?"

He bit his lip, his whole body now tense.

"I make the decisions about what you will endure, Mr. Maclean—unless you would prefer me to leave your arse open to the other guests to fondle and touch and *probe*?"

He shivered as she coated the leather phallus in oil and eased it inside him. "You will wear this until you are comfortable with it and think no more of being touched there than you do of being flogged or fucked."

"You haven't done any of those things to me yet, my lady, so how would I know?"

At his deliberately provocative challenge, she grabbed hold of the leash, jerked his head toward her, and slapped his cheek. His reaction was instantaneous as he grabbed hold of her wrist and yanked her hard against him.

"Let go of me *immediately,* Mr. Maclean, or God help me, I will walk out of this room and send twenty men in to fuck you senseless."

"You wouldn't do that."

"You are hurting me."

His hand fell away, and with a curse, he dropped down to his knees.

"I'm sorry, I *never* want to hurt you, I—"

She held her wrist and stared down at him before turning to the door.

"Don't go, my lady. God—*please,* don't, I'll do anything you want to make this up to you, I swear."

"I'm not sure I believe you, Mr. Maclean." She kept her back to him and her hand on the door latch.

"Please. Flog me, use me, make me bleed for daring to touch you without permission. I deserve it."

Diana took a long, slow breath and turned around, keeping her back to the door. He immediately averted his anguished gaze to the floor.

"Please . . ."

She shook her head. "I think I've been a fool."

"No!"

He crawled toward her on all fours and bent his head to kiss her feet. "Don't leave me."

"You don't understand. The failure is mine, not yours." She drew an unsteady breath. "I thought I could master you, but maybe I'm not strong enough. Maybe you do need someone who will beat you into submission, but I'm not that person."

He didn't say anything, and she bent to touch his beautiful auburn hair. "Good-bye, Mr. Maclean. I can't play this game anymore."

He tried to catch her skirts, but she skillfully avoided him and ran down the corridor and up into the attics to one of the empty rooms set aside for visiting servants. She flung herself facedown and realized she was already weeping. She'd been a fool. It was obvious that he only wanted a superficial relationship where he controlled everything. God, he'd practically told her that to her face, but no, she had to want more, to have him submit to her entirely. To trust her with *everything*.

But why should he? He wasn't a fool. Perhaps he could tell that she wasn't being honest with him about her appearance at the Sinners. Or perhaps it was even simpler than that. At some level, he knew she couldn't control him; he'd shown her that tonight. He was too big, too strong, and too defiant . . .

A knock at the door had her wiping her eyes and sitting bolt-upright on the bed. Christian put his head around the door.

"Are you all right?"

She dashed away the few remaining tears. "Yes, I'm fine."

He remained in the doorway, observing her with his usual cool precision. "Donal asked me what to do about Mr. Scott. Apparently, he's refusing to leave your room until you return to give him your permission."

"That man is so contrary!" She punched the pillow. "Tell him to leave and not to bother coming back."

Christian raised an eyebrow. "Isn't that your job?"

"He doesn't respect me, he doesn't . . ." She glared at her former employer. "You own this place. Order him to leave."

"Yes, my lady." He pretended to bow. "I'm quite willing to act on your behalf, but I have to mention that it isn't like you to back down from a challenge."

She practically bared her teeth at him. "He defies me at every turn, he challenges me—he"—she ran out of breath and simply glared at him—"I don't know what to do. I want him so *badly* and yet . . ."

"May I make a suggestion?"

Diana looked at him. "If it is a helpful one."

He flicked a card at her. "An old acquaintance of ours is in Town with his family this month. I suggest you write to him for his suggestions as to how to resolve this matter. I don't know of a better man to advise you."

Diana read the name and address on the card and stared at Christian in awe. "You are a genius."

He bowed again. "Please remember to tell my wife that. I'll get rid of Mr. Scott for you." He searched her face. "You are welcome to stay here tonight, but you will have to return to the Sinners at some point."

"I know." Diana sighed. "But one thing I can rely on is that Mr. 'Scott' will never allow our disagreement to influence his behavior at work."

"Sir Ronald Fairbanks is an extremely wealthy man, Mr. Maclean. There is no danger of him losing his money anytime soon." Nicodemus flipped over a page in his notebook and stared at Alistair. "Unfortunately."

"You don't like the man?"

"In my opinion, he is an unscrupulous bastard with the morals of an alley cat."

Alistair forced himself to concentrate. He hadn't slept at all the previous night and downed far too much of a bottle of whisky. "Just the sort of man my brother seems to prefer."

"From what I've learned about your sibling, Mr. Maclean, he doesn't mind what sex his current lovers are, just that the person is wealthy enough to support him."

"Which Sir Ronald is." Alistair frowned. "Having met the man, I would agree with your assessment of him. He didn't seem too friendly toward my brother either. I wonder if they have fallen out?"

"It's highly likely. Your brother tends to bleed his lovers dry. Sir Ronald is not going to allow that to happen."

"Harry will have to return to London at some point."

"I agree." Nicodemus stowed his notebook in his capacious pocket. "I hear the Demon Club are eagerly awaiting him."

"Well, I hope he comes back soon then."

"Why?"

"Because I believe they are demanding a settling of his account by the end of the month."

"Oh dear, that's not good at all." Nicodemus stuck his pencil behind his ear. "Be careful, Mr. Maclean. The Demon Club has a tendency to spread their net wide if the original offender isn't available. An acquaintance of mine who defaulted on a loan had his daughter abducted and her virginity was auctioned off at the place to recover the debt." His expression sobered. "She never recovered from the experience and drowned herself in the Thames."

He nodded and left the room, leaving Alistair staring into space.

After reviewing what Nicodemus had told him, he considered what he would do if Harry didn't return and they came for *him* at the end of the month. Surely Harry knew what would happen if he refused to pay up? Alistair rubbed his temple. Of course he did. He'd damn well signaled his intention of not returning by putting Alistair's name on the voucher.

Would Harry really want his brother to suffer the indignities of the Demon Club on his behalf?

"Yes." Alistair spoke out loud into the silence of his office. "Of course he bloody well would."

Harry would consider it Alistair's just reward for refusing to bail him out again. His brother's logic was rarely sound, and always totally self-motivated.

With a groan, Alistair buried his face in his hands. He was sick of Harry. Sick of being the responsible older brother who sacrificed everything for his family and got nothing in return. And what had his benevolence got him? A threat from the Demons, a brother who despised him, and a lover who . . .

He didn't want to think about that. Somewhere deep inside him, he was ashamed of his behavior toward Lady Theale. She'd blamed herself, but he knew at his core that he had fought her off with every weapon at his disposal, determined to keep her out, to stop himself from giving in to her too easily. And he'd achieved his aim. She'd told him to go and now . . .

The clock chimed eight times, and he realized he'd missed dinner. Had Maddon even come in to remind him to eat? He glanced down at the pile of work awaiting his attention. He might as well get on with it. He had nothing else in his life . . .

* * *

"Oh yes, Lady Theale, I've been here since the beginning."

Diana sipped at her tea and assumed her most interested expression. She'd gone down to the kitchen to steal a bite of supper, and ended up enjoying a long conversation about the intricacies of a life in servitude with the butler.

"I didn't realize you had been here so long, Mr. Maddon. You hardly look old enough."

"Oh, I wasn't the butler back in those days, my lady. I started at the Pelly house as hall boy."

"The Pellys?" A bead of excitement burned brightly in Diana's chest.

"Yes, that's correct. They had a rented house in London, but their country estate was in Cornwall, right on the coast. It was a forlorn, ramshackle place, much loved by Miss Faith, but not by the rest of her family."

"Why was that?"

"Because it was falling into the sea and would've required thousands of guineas to set it to rights, which the family didn't have."

"Is it still there?"

"No, my lady. There was a terrible storm a year or so ago, and half the cliff gave way, taking most of the house with it. Miss Faith was very upset."

"She didn't have it repaired when she married the earl?"

"It wasn't hers to fix, my lady. It belonged to her father, and then, as he had no sons, it passed to her cousin, who didn't have the funds to repair it either."

"How sad." Diana took another sip of her tea. "So you came to London with the countess when she married?"

"I did, my lady, and I became second footman here, before working my way up to the position of butler."

"What a remarkable achievement, Mr. Maddon. Your family must be very proud of you."

"I'm sure they would be, my lady, but my father and brother

passed away in a mine cave-in many years ago, and my mother didn't survive long after that."

A silence fell as Diana contemplated the all-too-common tale and the small tragedies of an everyday life. Unlike most of her new class, she had more than a passing acquaintance with the constant battle simply to survive.

"Then I suppose you had no reason to keep in touch with the staff at Pelly house after you moved on, or to go back to Cornwall to visit."

"There wasn't much need, my lady. Soon after Miss Faith's wedding, the rest of the Pelly family moved to London." He lowered his voice. "I suspect they wanted to be close to the earl, who is a wealthy man in his own right."

"Oh." Diana accepted his confidence and nodded wisely. "Was the earl inclined to help them out?"

"I believe he did his best, my lady." Maddon chuckled. "I suspect the earl felt an obligation. When he originally visited the family, he came at the invitation of Miss Faith's younger sister, Miss Margaret. She was a beautiful girl, that one. We all thought he might marry her, but he took one look at Miss Faith, and we could all see the way the wind was blowing."

"How romantic," Diana murmured. "And did the beautiful Miss Margaret Pelly marry well herself?"

"Ah, well." Mr. Maddon wiped his mouth with his handkerchief. "That one was never satisfied. I don't think she ever got over Miss Faith stealing the earl right from under her nose. She certainly made sure that everyone in the family knew her feelings on the subject."

"Oh dear. Did the sisters fall out over the earl?"

"If they did, I don't think it lasted more than a day or two, my lady. They were always very close." He sighed. "Miss Margaret died a long time ago, God rest her soul. I know Miss Faith misses her every day."

"I'm sure she does," Diana murmured.

"They were very different, but close despite everything." He rose to his feet. "There is a portrait of the two of them in the countess's office. Have you not seen it?"

Diana waited as Mr. Maddon lit a candle and led her through the back hallways to Lady Westbrook's pleasant office. The main rooms of the club were busy, but up on the second floor where the real work of the establishment was undertaken, all was quiet.

"Here you are, my lady."

The picture in question was very small, no more than six inches square, and sat on the countess's desk.

"The Pelly family didn't have the financial resources to afford a large portrait. I believe Miss Faith said this was the only one of her sister that existed." He set the candle down beside the portrait and Diana leaned in close to view it.

"They are very different, indeed."

"Yes, Miss Margaret was the one who had all the looks and was determined to marry well."

Diana studied the oval face, blue eyes, and blond curls of the younger Pelly sister. She had an arrogant expression that indicated that she knew her worth and would be hard to please.

A footman appeared at the door and Diana looked up.

"Mr. Maddon, Mr. Fisher is looking for you."

She smiled at the two men. "You go ahead, Mr. Maddon. I'll be on my way to bed."

"Yes, my lady."

Maddon bowed and followed the footman out of the room, leaving Diana alone with the picture. She touched the two young faces with the tip of her finger. They were both so sure of themselves in their own ways, but Faith Pelly had succeeded in marrying the man of her dreams, and apparently her sister had not.

It was hard not to linger over the picture on the countess's desk and retreat to the peace and quiet of her bedroom. What had happened between the sisters that their lives had diverged so dramatically? If the earl had married the younger sister, the Sinners Club wouldn't exist. Would that be a blessing or a curse?

Diana carefully blew out the candle and carried it out into the hall. She didn't want the countess to know that anyone had been in her office at night. Although, if she asked, Maddon would surely tell her what had transpired. Would Diana's interest in the Pelly family rouse Lady Westbrook's suspicions? If it did, Diana might have to face a far harder interrogation than she had anticipated.

She reached her door and unlocked it. After the unfortunate end of her affair with Alistair Maclean, she'd been struggling to concentrate. But seeing the portrait of the Pelly sisters had at least given her something else to think about . . .

"Lady Theale."

She gasped and pressed her hand to her bosom as Alistair Maclean rose from his seat by the fire and bowed to her.

"How did you get in here?"

He held up a key. "I hold keys to all the rooms on the premises in case of emergencies."

"This hardly qualifies as an emergency." She held out her hand. "Give me the key." To her surprise he handed it over to her without a murmur. "Now go away."

"I wished to speak to you about something."

"I don't think there's anything I want to hear from you at this precise moment. I'm tired and I want to go to bed." She rubbed her forehead where the beginnings of a headache were stirring. "Please make an appointment and meet me in my office tomorrow."

"Diana—"

She held up one finger. "I don't believe I gave you permission to use my first name, and I've asked you to leave. If you intend to impress me with a new plea of devotion and submission, then this is not the best way to go about it."

He went slowly onto his knees and looked down. She had a terrible urge to kick him and then start crying until he gathered her into his arms and held her close. But that would never do.

"I . . . wish to try again. You were wrong about your inability to master me." He took a quick breath. "It's not that at all."

"Go on."

"It's that I'm *afraid*."

"Of me?"

"Of myself. I want to give you everything you desire, but the thought of doing that, of making myself vulnerable to you, to a *woman* is terrifying. And when you get too close to me, when I want to give in to your every whim, I fight against myself."

"I understand."

"You do?" He risked a glance up at her. "Then, will you take me back? I swear to God that I won't fight you over anything anymore. Even if you send twenty men to fondle and fuck me, I'll do what I am told."

Diana took out some of her hairpins and massaged her aching temple. "It is perfectly acceptable for you to have *limits,* Mr. Maclean. We have already discussed this."

"I know, but I should trust *you* to discover those limits, to test them, and to maybe make me accept what I thought was unacceptable." His breathing hitched. "I cannot set a limit until I have experienced it, can I? I can't dictate what I want if I am truly to be yours."

She sat down on the side of the bed and considered him. "You are saying all the right things, Mr. Maclean, but I still doubt you mean them. The moment you lose control of a situation you start to panic and question me."

"I don't want to do that anymore. I want to try again. I can't stop thinking about you, about what I've given up, about how you make me feel." He lowered his head and kissed her slippers. "*Please.*"

She kept her gaze on his auburn hair and allowed her thoughts to run free. Was he worth saving? She had a suspicion that he might be, but how to test out his new avowal of complete surrender to her wishes?

Diana let out her breath. "I need to think about this, Mr. Maclean. When I've made a decision, I will make certain that you know it."

He kissed her shoe again and rose unsteadily to his feet. "Thank you for at least considering my plea." He bowed. "Good night, my lady."

10

"Nico, will you just listen for a moment?" Diana interrupted her stepson. "I'm not asking you to go over the same ground again, I'm asking you to try something different."

"I still don't like it, Di."

"But you'll do it for me, won't you? All I need is for you to talk to Mr. Maddon and see if you can find out who else came up to London with him from the Pelly house in Cornwall."

"I'll do it, but I'm not sure what you hope to achieve by finding these people."

"They might be able to fill in some of the missing pieces for me."

"I suppose that's true." He frowned. "Do you know what happened to the Pelly cousin who inherited the estate?"

"I believe he spent all his time in London and never visited the old place. He had a land agent overseeing the farms and the copper mine until the revenues dried up. His older brother was convicted of treason for spying. His death sentence was commuted to transportation to the colonies because of the intervention of the Earl of Westbrook."

"That was very gracious of him, but as he was about to marry a member of the Pelly family, I assume he did it to avoid involving his new family in a scandal."

"How cynical you are, Di." Nico chuckled. "Have you met the earl yet?"

"No, thank goodness."

"He'll turn up at the Sinners soon. He always does. So you should be prepared."

"I'm not afraid of the Earl of Westbrook."

"Then you should be." He shook his head. "I still don't understand why you wanted to work here right under his nose—unless . . ." His dark gaze widened. "You don't think *he's* your father, do you?"

Diana merely stared back at him.

"You can't be serious!"

"Why not? You have to admit it's a possibility. He wasn't known as the 'Savage Rake' for nothing. He rutted like a stag before he met Faith Pelly."

"Do you intend to confront him with this ridiculous notion?"

"Not without proof. And the notion is not ridiculous. We know he visited the Pellys at their home in Cornwall."

"Which is why you want to speak to the surviving servants." Nico blew out a harried breath. "You might have mentioned this to me before. I assumed you thought one of the original members of the Sinners was your father."

She smiled at him. "I do. The Earl of Westbrook."

"He and Faith were the *founders*. I don't think you are right."

"Do you care to place a wager on it?"

Nico snorted. "No, I do not. If anyone can pull it off, it will be you. How do you intend to prove this? Did you expect to find a copy of your baptismal certificate tucked away in the records somewhere?"

"I expected to find *something*." Diana sighed. "If you help me discover the Pelly servants, one of them might have evidence to show that the earl wasn't entirely wrapped up in courting Faith Pelly."

"And was bedding someone else?"

She raised her eyebrows. "Why not? Men do it all the time. I learned that at the pleasure house."

"And if you find evidence to confront the earl, you will do so."

Diana nodded.

"To what end?" Nico asked. "Do you want him to publicly acknowledge you?"

"Why shouldn't he?"

"I'm not suggesting he wouldn't be willing to do so. Despite what you might think, he is an honorable man." Nico hesitated. "Have you considered the impact that your announcement will make on your employer?"

"Lady Westbrook can scarcely object. It can hardly be the first time this has happened."

"Oh, I'm fairly certain that due to his reputation the earl has dealt with his fair share of claims, but to my knowledge he has no acknowledged bastards. Only two young sons with his wife who are currently away at school."

"Then I will be the first."

"Do you want money from him?"

"That's—" Diana glared at Nico. "That's not fair."

"It's not like you to be so hard, Di. I'm only trying to understand."

She rose from her chair and came around to stand in front of him. "I have another appointment at three with Lady Malinda. I need to go and fetch my bonnet. Is there anything else we need to discuss?"

He rose too and stood, looking down at her, his treacle brown gaze troubled. "I'll do my best to find out the information you need, Di, but I do beg you to reconsider. What good will raking up the past do now?"

"Damn it, Nico, I helped reconcile you with your own father, how can you say that to me?"

"Because by the time I found him, I realized how much of my life I'd wasted searching for him."

She patted his cheek. "Oh, Nico, don't be cross with me. I can't explain it, but I need to do this. It is important."

"If you say so." Taking her hand, he kissed her palm. "Be careful, love."

"I always am."

"Well, then be extra careful."

His smile warmed her. As they turned to the door, it opened to disclose Maddon with a silver salver.

"There's a letter for you, Lady Theale. The messenger is awaiting your reply in the kitchen."

Nico winked and slipped past the butler. Diana took the proffered letter and slit open the seal with her knife. The note was short and took her no time to read.

"I'll reply to this immediately." She sat down at her desk and wrote quickly before sealing the reply and handing it back to Maddon. "Thank you."

"You are welcome, my lady. Is there anything else I can do for you?"

"You can ascertain if Mr. Maclean is here."

"I know he is, my lady. I just spoke to him."

Diana wrote another note and gave it to Maddon. "Can you give this to Mr. Maclean? I don't expect a reply."

"Of course, my lady."

She sat back and considered the evening ahead. If Mr. Maclean truly wished to show her that he was a changed man who wished to acknowledge her claim over him, tonight he would be able to prove he meant it.

There was another knock on the door, and James the footman came in with a sealed letter.

"From the pleasure house, my lady."

"Thank you." She opened the letter, reading quickly, and found it was from Charlotte asking her to meet her when she had a spare evening. "There is no reply necessary, thank you, James."

Depending upon how her evening with Mr. Maclean went, she might have time to see Charlotte later that night. She hadn't noticed any sense of urgency in her friend's request and wondered vaguely what it might concern, her mind too tied up in thoughts of Alistair Maclean being tied up to concentrate too hard.

Alistair pinned his cravat in place for the fourth time and considered his appearance in the hall mirror. Lady Theale had asked him to meet her at six and to wear his evening clothes. That was all she'd written in her note, and it had taken him a few moments of internal struggle not to march around to her office and demand to know more. But those days were behind him now. If he wanted the immensity of the pleasure she brought him, he would have to behave himself.

He checked the clock for the fifteenth time and it finally chimed six times. There was still no sign of his companion. With a silent curse, he fished out his pocket watch and compared his timepiece to the long clock that sat on the marble floor.

"Mr. Maclean?"

He looked up to see Lady Theale at the top of the staircase. She wore a primrose yellow evening gown with silken skirts and gauzy sleeves that made her skin glow.

"My lady."

"Will you come up here for a moment?"

Mystified, he went up the stairs, and she led him through

into the private rooms that were used to entertain the members on certain nights of the week. He knew for a fact that tonight was not one of them.

When she stepped in the small anteroom that led into the main salon, he followed her.

"Shut the door, Mr. Maclean."

"Yes, my lady."

She went toward one of the chest of drawers that lined the wall. "Please undo your trousers."

He stared at her for a full second before his hand fumbled with the buttons. "May I ask a question?"

She looked over her shoulder at him, her gaze calm. "Yes?"

"I thought you said we were going out to dinner."

"We are."

There were a thousand questions he wanted to ask next, but he knew she wouldn't answer him, or worse, tell him to get out for his impertinence. He couldn't risk that, even though not knowing what was going on unsettled him. But she knew that, didn't she? This was simply part of her mastering him.

His heart sped up as she approached him with a set of leather cock rings and a short phallus, but he didn't speak. She shoved his trousers down further and set about oiling the phallus and settling his half-erect cock and balls into the sturdy leather straps.

"You may dress now."

He struggled to button his trousers over the thick protuberance of his leather-clad cock and balls. His shaft was already straining against the leather, making his arousal obvious to even the most casual of observers.

"Come here."

Resisting the urge to shield himself from her gaze, he walked over to the floor-length mirror. She made him stand in front of it as she considered both him and his reflection. He shivered as she rubbed her thumb over the contours of his trapped cock and the prominent curve of his balls.

"Very nice, Mr. Maclean." She smiled at him in the mirror. "You may help me put on my cloak and then you may put on your own."

"Thank you, my lady."

He would've done it if she'd asked, but he wasn't sure how he would have felt parading through the Sinners trussed up for all to see. He followed her down the stairs and out into the street where a covered carriage awaited them.

"Lady Theale." The liveried coachman opened the door with a flourish and handed his companion inside, leaving Alistair with little to do but to climb in after her and offer his thanks.

"Sit beside me."

He changed direction and sat beside her, careful not to crease her dress.

"Spread your legs."

He obeyed, his hands fisting at his side and she rested her gloved hand over his cock and balls and then started stroking him. His cock responded immediately, and his breath hissed out as the leather tightened around his heated flesh.

"Do you wish . . . everyone at the dinner party to see me aroused like this?" he murmured.

"Naturally. I want them all to see how big you are and envy me."

His hips bucked forward as she increased the pace of her fingers.

"Do you want me to come?"

She considered his cock. "It is rather tempting to arrive with you in that state, but I don't wish you to come until I order you to do so."

He set his teeth as she eased off a little, but never enough to make him comfortable or for him to gain any sense that he was in control.

"Ah, we're here."

The same coachman opened the door and helped Lady Theale alight. Alistair followed her more slowly, his breathing short and his heart thumping as he contemplated the grand Mayfair mansion they were entering. Was she really expecting him to walk in there in this state? The thought of that many pairs of eyes on him was disorienting.

In the hallway, the butler helped her out of her cloak and then turned to Alistair.

"Sir?"

"Let him take your cloak, Mr. Maclean."

He felt naked and couldn't even bear to look down at his arousal.

"You will wait here until someone comes to collect you." She touched his cheek. "You will continue to do as you are ordered, and will not disgrace me."

"Yes, my lady."

With all the composure he could muster, he turned his back on the two footmen stationed by the door and gave his attention to a family portrait that dominated the largest wall. It looked fairly recent and showed a dark-haired man and his wife with three children grouped around them. Alistair moved closer. The girls appeared to be identical twins and had their father's black hair.

"Mr. Maclean?"

Alistair looked over his shoulder to see a dark-haired man who looked remarkably like the person in the portrait approaching.

"Yes, sir."

"Come with me."

The man's voice held all the arrogance of an aristocrat and something else that made Alistair reluctant to meet his gaze. He wasn't young, and he exuded a quiet confidence that made Alistair feel already naked.

"In here."

Alistair braced himself, but there was no one in the study but him and the man, who smiled at him.

"Did you think to find yourself at the center of an admiring crowd, Maclean? Would you have enjoyed that? Being touched and fondled by strangers?"

"No, sir."

"Well, that's a shame, because I'm going to touch you anyway, although by the end of our time together, we are not going to be strangers, I can assure you of that." His voice changed. "Lace your fingers and put your hands behind your head. Do not speak unless I ask you a direct question."

Alistair did as he was told and stared unblinkingly at the wall of books in front of him.

"Lower your gaze to the floor, Maclean."

He jumped as the man reached forward, cupped his trapped cock and balls, and squeezed hard enough to make Alistair pay attention.

"Lady Theale has told me all about you." He undid the top button of Alistair's trousers. "You don't like being fondled or fucked by men, do you?"

"I—will do whatever my lady commands, sir."

"Ah, she said that was your other problem, your refusal to state your limits or tell her when you were uncomfortable about a particular situation she wished to put you in."

"I . . . told her that I would do whatever she ordered me to do, sir."

Two more buttons and the man was pushing aside Alistair's shirt to examine the leather bindings around his cock, balls, and arse.

"Take off everything. I want to see you properly." The man sat on the front of his desk. "And take your time. I wish to enjoy it."

When he was naked, Alistair put his hands behind his head

again, hiding nothing, allowing his companion to walk around him and look his fill.

"You have a nice big cock and an elegant body, Maclean." He held up a small bottle. "Hold your position while I oil your skin."

Despite himself, Alistair's muscles quivered and flexed as his back and shoulders and chest were rubbed with the sweet-smelling oil. Rivulets ran down over his stomach and followed the curve of his muscle to his groin and between his arse cheeks.

His flesh quivered as the man worked the oil lower, into his thighs and buttocks until his cock was dripping too, but not with oil.

"Does your mistress punish you for getting wet when another person is touching you?"

"I—don't know, sir."

"Because you are wet, aren't you?"

"Yes, sir."

"Despite not liking a man's touch."

It wasn't a direct question, so Alistair didn't have to answer it. He flinched as the man cupped his buttock.

"Perhaps you need to be better controlled." His oiled fingers slid around Alistair's hip and beneath the buckle of the cock harness. "Tighter, I think."

Alistair fought a groan as the buckles were tightened around the base of his cock, which was now fully erect and likely to stay that way as there was nowhere for the blood pumping through it to go.

His companion traced a lazy finger around Alistair's cock, ending at the crown where pre-cum continued to gather. Using his fingernail, he rubbed a delicate path around the slit.

"There is a way to try and prevent this from dripping. Let me see if I still have the necessary equipment."

He moved over to the desk and rummaged in the drawer for a moment. "Ah, yes. Here we are."

He returned to Alistair and showed him what was in his hand. "It's like a coiled hat pin, except the spherical end goes in your slit and the curled wire twists around your shaft and is attached to the rest of the cock ring." He studied Alistair's cock. "Don't come, or I will have to punish you. But do watch. I don't want you to miss anything."

Alistair forced his head lower and watched in trepidation as the man expertly wound the thin silver wire around his cock and then bent the rounded head and eased it into the slit of his crown.

"It certainly stems the flow a little, doesn't it?"

"Yes, sir."

"Now for the rest of it. Kneel down."

Alistair obeyed, his gaze still on the silver fastening around his shaft and the cold touch of the silver-headed pin against the heat of his throbbing cock.

"You like it, don't you? Perhaps you should speak to Lady Theale about getting you permanently pierced down there. My wife enjoys the sensation immeasurably."

"*Permanently?*"

His companion chuckled, and he took a chair in front of Alistair. "I will forgive the question. Perhaps when you are reunited with Lady Theale you will be given the opportunity to see my piercing for yourself at close range. Do you suck cock?"

"I will do whatever my lady orders me to do, sir."

His breath hissed out as the man grabbed hold of the leather cock harness and twisted. "That's not an answer."

"I try not to suck cock, sir."

"But you would if your lady ordered you to do so."

"Yes, sir, but—"

"But what, Maclean?"

"She promised me that I wouldn't have to do it."

"No, Maclean, she *promised* that she wouldn't allow any man to fuck you. She was quite clear on this point. If I wanted you to take my cock out and suck it right now, what would you do?"

"I'd suck it, sir."

The man released his punishing grip on Alistair's straining shaft. "Good."

He stepped away, and Alistair braced himself, but all that happened was that a leather collar was buckled around his throat.

"We've almost made you presentable, Maclean, but not quite. You need a leash."

The leash the man chose was narrow and supple and fell to the ground.

"Are you ready? Your appearance is eagerly awaited in the drawing room."

11

Alistair had no choice but to obey the yank on his leash and follow his captor into the dining room. He steadied himself, but nothing could lessen the shock of being naked, collared, and stared at by three pairs of eyes, only one of which he knew. Even in the pleasure house, he had been the one to choose his lovers and allow himself to be used. Here it was a different matter. His glance slid to Diana Theale, but she wasn't smiling at him. In truth, she looked almost as apprehensive as he felt. Did she think he would let her down?

It was highly likely.

Without being asked, Alistair lowered his gaze to the carpet and stood still, his hands at his side, his cock throbbing along with his raised heartbeat.

"Oh, Diana. What a prize."

The only other woman stood up and came to gaze at Alistair. From what he could see from his limited vision, she was older than him and richly dressed in blue satin and lace. Her ungloved hand curved over his buttock, lingering on the leather harness and tracing the curve of his hip.

"He's quite beautiful, Blaize."

The unknown man came to study him too. He stood quietly as they stroked and caressed his oiled skin, sending shivers of awareness over his body.

"I take it from the phallus in his arse that he isn't available to fuck?" the man dressed in uniform asked.

"No, he isn't." Diana answered and Alistair wanted to kiss her feet. "His arse is mine."

His captor dropped the leash. "Perhaps you might wish to go to your mistress."

"If she wishes me to do so," Alistair said quietly.

"Oh, he's a Scot!" The lady clapped her hands.

Alistair waited until Diana nodded. "You may come and kneel at my feet, Mr. Maclean."

He walked across the carpet, aware that everyone was watching him, and came down on his knees in front of Diana. He bent to kiss her feet.

"My lady."

She tugged on his collar. "Stand up again for a moment."

He struggled to his feet and waited as she touched the silver wire wrapped around his cock.

"It's supposed to stop him getting wet. Do you wish me to position the head deeper and wind the coils tighter?"

"No, I quite like to see him like this." Diana smiled up at the dark-haired man. "He hates not being in control of everything, and this is deliciously messy."

"If he was mine, I'd have another slave kneeling in front of him, probably a man, licking it up."

"I should imagine you would. But you were always the most cruelly inventive man I ever met, and not all of us have a legion of slaves begging to do our will."

"If that doesn't appeal, you could beat it out of him. Make every drop spilled without your consent a lash of the whip?" Alistair shuddered as the dark-haired man stroked a hand down over his back and arse. "Even better, I could arrange for him to suffer both. One licking him, and one punishing him."

"I'd lick him," the officer said. "It would be just like old times."

"And I'd take care of the whipping."

"It's very kind of you both to offer, my lord, Captain, but I prefer him wet."

"As you wish, my lady, but you are depriving yourself of a very entertaining evening."

Diana wrapped a hand around Alistair's straining cock and brought him back down onto his knees. "I'm sure there are many other ways he can please us tonight."

"I damn well hope so. My wife rarely allows me to visit the city anymore, so I have to enjoy my illicit and filthy pleasures while I can."

"It's not that you may not *visit* London, my lord, it is more that you have to bring me with you so that I can enjoy your filthy pleasures too."

"Yes, my love. I am aware of that."

The butler appeared at the door. "Dinner is served, my lord, my lady."

"Thank you." The woman who had just spoken rose to her feet. "Shall we proceed? We're eating in the small dining room."

Diana stood and Alistair waited until she tugged on his leash and brought him to his feet as well. When they reached the candlelit dining room, she made him kneel beside her chair and fed him from her own plate. For the first time since he'd arrived at the mansion, shielded from the others' gazes, Alistair was able to relax a little. His cock ached and he wanted to come, but he was used to that. He'd wait until she let him come. He had his pride.

The lord and lady of the house were an interesting couple, and their other guest seemed very familiar with them both. He had a sense that even though Diana had vetoed the idea of him being licked and whipped for daring to get wet, his evening wasn't quite over yet.

Diana enjoyed the meal more than she had anticipated. Having Alistair McNeal, naked, collared, and oiled, kneeling at her feet accepting the food she offered him, was immensely satisfying. She knew her hosts would have further plans for her slave, but so far he had tried hard to please her.

At the end of the meal, Lady Jane rose and smiled at Diana. "Shall we leave the men to their port?"

She glanced down at Alistair, who had gone still. "Do you wish me to leave Mr. Maclean with you, my lord, or shall I take him with me?"

"Leave him here. Wesley and I can entertain him for a while."

She almost changed her mind as Alistair wrapped a hand around her ankle. But he had to learn when to submit, and if anyone could help teach him that, it would be Blaize Minshom. She spoke in an undertone that only Alistair could hear.

"Let me go, Mr. Maclean, or I'll send you home. It is my will that you accept what is done to you. *My* will, not yours. Do you understand?"

His hand disappeared, and he resumed his position, his gaze on the carpet.

"Yes, my lady."

"Good, then I will see you later in the drawing room."

Alistair remained kneeling as the voices of the two women receded down the hall and the door was shut.

"Well. What shall we do with him, Thomas? Do you have any ideas?"

The soldier chuckled. "I usually leave that to you, Minshom. You, after all, are the master."

The name struck a horrible chord in Alistair's memory. Was this Lord Blaize Minshom, a man whose reputation at the pleasure house for debauchery was legendary?

"Stand up, Maclean."

He stood because there was something in Minshom's voice that made him want to obey.

"Come here into the light where Thomas and I can see you properly. That's better." Minshom glanced over at the army officer. "I don't think you've been formally introduced. This is Major Lord Thomas Wesley, my wife and my lover. Sit on the edge of the table, Maclean, grip the edge, and spread your knees wide."

Alistair did what he was told, his breath hissing out as the phallus in his arse came into contact with the hard surface. His cock thrust outward, constrained by the leather straps.

Thomas stepped forward and pinched Alistair's nipple hard. "He's close to coming." He trailed a finger down over Alistair's tight stomach and rested it on the very tip of his cock. "Shall I make him?"

"No—I . . ." Alistair cleared his throat. "I promised Lady Theale that I wouldn't—" He gasped as Thomas pressed his thumb down hard over the pin inserted in his slit. "God—"

Minshom walked over to the door and opened it to speak to a footman stationed on the other side. "Jones? Will you go and find Lady Theale, please, and ask her to join us for a minute? Thank you."

Thomas kept his finger on Alistair's cock as if waiting for permission to proceed. It seemed to take forever for Diana to appear in the doorway.

"What is it?"

"Maclean says he isn't allowed to come without your permission."

"That is correct." Her gaze dropped to Alistair's cock and she licked her lips.

"If he is constrained like this in the harness for much longer, he might damage himself."

She smiled right into Alistair's eyes. "Then by all means use him as you will."

"My lady—" Alistair couldn't help himself. "I only want to come for you."

The glance she gave him was eloquent with disappointment and dismissal.

Minshom smiled, and it was one of the most terrifying things Alistair had ever seen. "You should not have spoken. I'm surprised she didn't punish you for that, but perhaps she thought leaving you with us was punishment enough? I hope you like sucking cock, Mr. Maclean, because I guarantee you are going to be an expert before the evening is out."

Turning to Diana, Minshom bowed. "Will you take a seat, my lady, and observe?"

"I would be delighted to do so."

She sat facing the table where Alistair was stretched out. Minshom found the leash attached to Alistair's collar, brought it down over his stomach beneath his already trussed-up balls, and back up behind his neck. He held Alistair's gaze as he slowly tightened the leash until Alistair had to push his palms down on the table as he raised his hips, frantic not to have his balls and cock put under any more strain.

"Ah . . ." He couldn't stop a hiss of pain escaping.

"Thomas, kneel in front of me and lick Maclean's cock, will you?"

It was torture; it was heaven, the cruel tug of the leather vying with the softness of Thomas's tongue on his slick, heated flesh. And he used his tongue well, slipping into every crevice, stirring every hair and nerve in Alistair's groin until he was groaning and begging for release.

"What do you want, Maclean?"

"I want . . . I *need* to come, I—"

"Even though your mistress isn't touching you?" Minshom tightened the leash once more, and Alistair almost leapt off the table.

"Yes, God, *please* . . ."

"Stop licking him, Thomas. Maclean, put your hands behind your head and keep them there." He slowly pushed Alistair back until he was flat on the table, only his legs hanging off the end.

Thomas stroked his thumb over Alistair's cock. "I'll suck him while he sucks me. I hope the table can hold us both."

Minshom chuckled. "It can—do you remember last Christmas with Jane, when we all had each other after the plum pudding?"

Thomas climbed on the table and straddled Alistair's head. "You'll suck my cock." He unbuttoned his trousers and freed his hard length. "Do it well."

Alistair glimpsed Minshom standing between his legs at the end of the table and beyond him Diana. Then his view was cut off as Thomas lowered himself down over him, the head of his cock pushing at Alistair's lips.

"Suck him, Maclean."

He closed his eyes and did as he was told, aware of Minshom stroking his leather-encased cock in time to his sucking. Thomas pushed deeper, almost making Alistair gag, but he kept sucking because God, Minshom was touching him and very soon he was going to . . .

Thomas shoved his cock in one more time and started to come down Alistair's throat. He took it all, the tight grip on his jaw keeping him just where Thomas wanted him.

"That was excellent. Shall we let him come now?"

"Not quite. Kneel up, Maclean, and turn around to face Thomas."

It was a struggle to do as he was ordered when he felt like his cock was about to explode. Eventually he managed it and immediately put his hands behind his head. He sensed Minshom moving behind him, but kept his gaze lowered to the table and on Thomas's unbuttoned trousers, where his cock was already stirring.

The gentle tap of a riding crop against his buttock made him quiver.

"You'll use your mouth to make Thomas hard again while I administer the punishment I'm sure your mistress would mete out to you for coming without her permission. Isn't that so, Lady Theale?"

"I have no objection, my lord."

Thomas smiled. "He hasn't actually come yet, Blaize."

"He will when I beat him. Won't you, Maclean? I want to see you lose control over your cock. I want to see your seed pumping out on your belly and dripping down your thighs. And then I want to let Lady Theale look at you." He administered the first measured blow and it goddamn hurt, barely missing the leather harness. "Spread your legs wider, Maclean, and lean forward ready to take Thomas's cock."

Alistair flinched as the second stroke landed and then several more in quick succession. His sense of being on edge became so narrow and sharp that it shaded into something else entirely, and he began to anticipate each blow, to want to beg for it. To show his appreciation, he sucked lavishly at Thomas's cock until it was hard again.

"Maclean?"

He went still, his mind already in the place where his pain and pleasure became one. His arse was throbbing along with his cock; and his mouth was full of Thomas's shaft.

"Stop sucking."

He moaned as Thomas removed his cock and Minshom yanked at his leash to make him turn around, forcing him to sit on the edge of the table again.

"Lean forward, Maclean, and suck my cock now."

Alistair forced himself to bend, his stomach touching his engorged shaft, making him groan. Minshom's cock felt different. It took Alistair a dazed minute to realize that his tongue was moving over a hard internal piercing that extended from the tip of Minshom's cock down to the side of his foreskin, anchored in place with two silver pins. As his world narrowed to the sensations he was experiencing, he lost himself to the pleasure of exploration.

"Enough." A hard yank on his hair had him protesting as Minshom thrust him away. "Your turn, Maclean. Lower your hands, wrap them around your shaft, and make yourself ready to come."

It took a moment before the words sank in and he managed to obey.

"Harder, Maclean." Minshom leaned forward and removed the silver pin from the center of Alistair's slit and loosened the buckle at the root of his shaft. "Come now. Look at your mistress and make her proud of you."

It only took two hard yanks to make him climax and keep climaxing as his long-imprisoned cock finally gained release. He groaned as he came, his hips jerking forward until he almost fell off the table. Only Thomas's hands on his shoulders kept him sitting where Minshom had put him.

When he finished, he looked up to find Minshom studying him.

"You're not done yet." Minshom glanced down at his still-hard cock and then at Thomas's, who had slid off the table to stand next to him. "Hands behind your back and bend forward." He smiled at his companion and then at Diana. "Let's see if Maclean can suck us both off at once."

Diana watched avidly as Alistair attempted to take both cocks in his mouth. It was an impressive sight. She was so wet her sex was throbbing and her nipples hard. Seeing Alistair straining to come and obeying the two men had excited her beyond reason. She wanted to go over to him and stroke his damp skin, tell him that she was proud of him, pleased with him, but that would have to wait until they were alone again.

She rose from her seat. “Thank you, Lord Minshom, Captain Wesley. That was most entertaining.”

Neither man turned toward her, both of them intent on what Alistair Maclean was attempting to do to their cocks, but Minshom waved a languid hand in dismissal.

She closed the door behind her and saw Jane in the hallway outside. She raised an eyebrow at her.

“Were you watching too? You look remarkably invigorated.”

“When you didn’t return to the drawing room, I took the opportunity of using the peephole into the dining room. It was quite an impressive performance.”

“Does Lord Minshom know about the peephole?”

“Of course he does. He’s the one who put it in, and taught me how to use it.”

“He is a remarkably understanding husband for a rake.”

“He has to be. I wouldn’t stand for anything else, and Thomas is my lover too. I can’t allow them to have all the fun.” Jane sat down by the fire and picked up her embroidery. “I think I hear them now.”

The door opened and Lord Minshom came in leading Alistair on his leash with Thomas Wesley behind. Diana studied Alistair carefully. He was dripping with come, his own and the other men’s, and his arse was crossed with red stripes, but there was a quietness about him that Diana had seen before in others but not before in him.

He came over and went down on his knees.

“My lady.”

His voice was hoarse. After a glance at Jane and the other two, who were watching with interest, Diana leaned forward and threaded her fingers in his hair.

“You did well.”

“I only wished to please you.”

"You succeeded. Lift up my skirts and use your mouth and fingers on me."

"Yes, my lady."

As he pulled up the layers of her petticoats and silken skirts, she unbuckled the remaining straps around his balls and arse, allowing the phallus to slide free.

He gasped against her thigh. "Thank you, my lady."

She swept her skirts to one side and gazed down at his head, watched his tongue flick out to capture her clit, and moaned. He needed no more encouragement, his mouth sucking and licking her sex as she ground herself against him, her fingers tangling in his hair keeping him just where she needed him until she claimed her pleasure.

He shoved his tongue deep as she climaxed, mimicking the action of a cock until she came again. It took her a while to relax her grip on his hair and let him move back. His face was wet with her juices and his mouth swollen from all the use.

"Now pleasure Lady Jane. Crawl over to her."

She let his leash trail onto the floor, and he set off toward Jane, who lifted her own skirts in anticipation. Minshom stood beside his wife's chair watching every moment, his cock already hard again as Alistair started licking. Jane's hand came up to find Minshom's, and he pressed her fingers around the swell of his shaft.

She turned and nuzzled him, and with an anticipatory sigh, he unbuttoned his trousers and fed his wife his cock. Without conscious thought, Diana rose from her seat and walked over to the three of them. Thomas approached too, his gaze on Minshom and Jane.

"Let me—" Thomas murmured. Before he even finished his request, Jane was reaching her other hand for his cock and wrapping her fingers around him.

Diana considered the tangle of limbs and then studied Alistair's hands, which were locked together at the back above his reddened arse. With a smile, she lifted up her skirts, draped herself over his back, and pressed her wet, swollen sex to his entwined fingers. His whole body convulsed as he unfurled his fingers and pushed them deep inside her, his thumb pressed hard on her clit as he worked both her and Jane.

Jane climaxed first, followed by Diana and Thomas. Minshom was the last and took the longest to pour himself down his wife's throat. They all collapsed onto the carpet, pushing Alistair down with them. Diana rolled him onto his back and studied his hard cock.

"Let's play a game with Mr. Maclean." She touched Alistair's arm. "Stretch your arms out to the sides and spread your legs. Jane, straddle his thigh; Lord Minshom and Captain Wesley, do the same to his arms." She slid her leg over Alistair's muscled thigh and settled her wet sex on him.

All four of them were now facing each other and encircling Alistair's cock.

"One kiss, one lick, one bite until he comes. The winner gets to choose the next game."

"Nothing else but our mouths?" Minshom looked disappointed.

"If you win, you may choose the next game." Diana smiled. "Can someone put a cushion behind Mr. Maclean's head so that he can see what we are doing?"

"If he can see, he'll let you win."

Diana considered Minshom's objection. "Then perhaps we should cover his eyes completely?"

She looked at Alistair. "Unless you wish to tell me something?"

He licked his swollen lips and whispered, "No, my lady."

Jane used her gauzy scarf to cover Alistair's eyes and offered to start the proceedings. Diana waited until the last to go. Watching the others enjoying her slave was an interesting experience. She felt torn between pride at his perfect behavior and dislike of anyone else touching him at all. His whole body was extremely sensitive now; every brush on his skin made him quiver and tremble with need. She hadn't finished with him yet—she wanted more . . .

Leaning in over him, she loved the way his whole body strained helplessly toward her, his stomach muscles contracting to try and raise his hips to make her take more of his cock. He would be sore tomorrow, but would he still be hers?

God, God . . . he . . . couldn't stand any more, he just *couldn't.* Alistair tried to stop his hips from thrusting forward as he labored not to come. One more nip or bite on his tender flesh and he'd have to come, he'd *have* to.

"He's very strong, Diana." Jane relinquished Alistair's cock after biting her way up the side.

"I know." Her voice was calm. What did he look like to her at this moment, straining for release, close to begging her to end it for him with one sharp pull of her lips over his swollen crown. She barely touched him, and he braced himself for the return of the two men.

"If it wasn't for us all holding him in place, he'd be fucking the air right now." Captain Wesley chuckled. "I love to see a man like this, on the brink of coming, don't you?" He trailed his finger over Alistair's balls, making him groan.

"No fingers, Thomas. You forfeit your turn." Alistair tensed as Minshom spoke. "You've all been far too lenient with him."

And then Alistair screamed because Minshom nipped his foreskin and he couldn't stop his seed flooding out of his cock until he thought he'd forgotten how to breathe.

His head fell back onto the carpet with a *thump,* and he felt his come cooling and settling on his skin and trickling down between his thighs.

"Did you make him bleed?" Lady Jane asked.

"Not quite." Alistair shuddered as Minshom traced his lips

with a wet finger until he opened his mouth and sucked the finger clean. "I do believe I get to choose what we play next, don't I?" He chuckled. "But first, I think after all that pleasure we've given him, Maclean should be using his mouth on all of us again first, don't you?"

"Now, Maclean, get up and come along."

Alistair staggered to his feet, aided by Thomas Wesley, and dazedly followed Minshom down the hallway and down a narrow set of stairs into what appeared to be a basement room. He waited at the door as Minshom and Thomas walked around lighting candles to reveal a wall of whips, chains, and leather implements, several chests, and a wooden rack facing a large mirror.

"Let's chain him to the rack."

Minshom grabbed Alistair's wrists, brought them over his head, and shackled them into the metal handcuffs, adjusting the chain until his arms were stretched out, but he wasn't in distress.

Diana and Lady Jane had also come into the room and were adjusting the position of the candles.

Alistair's throat dried as Minshom picked up a long-tailed driving whip and tested it out against the side of the rack. He looked up at Alistair and smiled.

"It is my choice what we play next, isn't it, Maclean?"

Alistair forced himself to nod.

"What do you think it should be?"

He hesitated and the whip cracked close to his flank, just flicking his skin, making his whole body arch.

"I asked you a question."

"Whatever my lady wishes."

"Even if she says I can fuck you?"

Alistair closed his eyes. He couldn't, he just *couldn't* . . . "I . . . would prefer that you didn't."

Silence fell over the occupants of the room, and Alistair braced himself.

"An excellent answer."

To Alistair's complete bewilderment, Minshom handed the whip to Diana.

"My choice is to take my wife and Thomas to bed and leave you with Lady Theale. Good night, Maclean. You have provided us with an exceptionally invigorating evening."

12

For the first time, Alistair allowed his body to sag a little in his restraints as the Minshoms and Thomas Wesley filed out, leaving him with Diana.

"Mr. Maclean." She held his jaw and made him look into her face. "I am so very proud of you for standing your ground."

He swallowed thickly. "Didn't want Minshom fucking me."

Her blue eyes were full of understanding. "He does have something of a reputation as a brute. But I'm glad that you stated your limit and stuck to it. With a man as powerful and compelling as Minshom, that is an extremely hard thing to do. He has a tendency to attract slaves who don't stop him from doing anything to them."

"You thought I'd be one of them, didn't you?"

"I did wonder."

"That's why you brought me here."

"Yes. That was part of it." She kissed his sore, well-fucked mouth. "And I wanted to show you off to a man who appreciates beautiful things." She kissed him again. "Tell me what you want to do now."

"Whatever you—"

She put her finger to his lips. "No, tell me the truth."

"I want to kiss your feet and thank you for saving me from that man."

"You saved yourself." She held his gaze. "He respected that and so do I." She climbed on a small stool and released his wrists. "Come and sit on the bench."

He barely made it over to the wide wooden bench. She made him straddle the wooden width and lie back, his hands behind his neck.

"Stay there."

He had no intention of going anywhere. His body was heavy and his mind seemed to have retreated to a quieter place where even breathing and speaking were an effort. She returned within moments with a basin of water, a sponge, and a drying cloth.

"My lady, you don't need to—"

"Let me."

He was too weak to disagree with her as she slowly and carefully sponged his chest and belly clean and then washed his face. He shivered as she turned her attention to his spread thighs and finally his cock and balls. Even though she was gentle, he was still sensitive to every stroke of the towel across his skin.

"Turn onto your stomach."

He obliged her, pillowing his head on his folded arms, and fell half-asleep as she cleaned his back and his arse with soapy water. Her fingers ventured between his buttocks and he didn't even stir, although his cock did. His eyes started to close . . .

"Mr. Maclean . . ."

He startled awake. "I am sorry, my lady, I—"

She kissed his arse, setting her teeth into the rounded curve of his muscle, making him shudder.

"You cannot sleep in Minshom's dungeon."

"No, my lady. If I can find my clothes, I will escort you home."

"No, Mr. Maclean, you will not. Come with me."

He was too dazed to argue, and followed her up two flights of the servants' stairs until they emerged on an opulently decorated landing.

She pointed at a set of double doors. "The Minshoms' suite is there."

To his great relief she kept walking until she was at the far end of the corridor. "This is my room." She paused and let go of his leash.

"Where do you wish to spend the night, Mr. Maclean?"

He went down on his knees. "With you, my lady. If you are willing. Or stretched out here guarding your threshold."

"Then come in."

He followed her into the room, which was richly appointed in crimson and gold. She turned her back to him.

"Unlace me, please."

He did so with fingers that shook and helped her out of all her garments until she was naked. His throat dried as she stared at her lush bosom, the curve of her hip, and the roundness of her bottom.

"Get into bed, Mr. Maclean, lie on your back, and pull the covers right down."

"In *your* bed?"

"Yes, unless you've changed your mind and wish to share with the Minshoms."

There was an edge to her voice that made him obey and climb onto the high bed. He drew back the covers and lay on his back, his arse appreciating the coolness of the linen sheets. The mattress sank down as she followed him and knelt at his side.

Without speaking, Diana smoothed her hand over his taut belly and chest, pinching his tight, reddened nipples until he flinched.

"You're tired, aren't you, Mr. Maclean? Your arse is sore, your cock is worse, and your poor mouth . . ." She kissed him and he fought a moan. "You've been used hard."

"Yes, my lady."

"Did you enjoy it?"

"Yes."

She smiled at his blunt answer and kissed him again, nipping at his already swollen lower lip. "That's honest, Mr. Maclean. What was your favorite part?"

"When Lord Minshom and Major Wesley made me take both their cocks in my mouth." He swallowed hard. "You looked so proud of me. I did it for you, but I . . . enjoyed it. Being used in front of you." He seemed to struggle to find the right words. "Being *owned* like that, being *had* when I know that if I'd begged, you could've made it stop . . ."

She stroked his now-stubbled cheek. "I would have done that for you. I was waiting for you to beg."

He let out a long, slow breath as she kissed his nose. Was he starting to understand that he needed to trust her to make the right decisions for him? Was he finally willing to give her control?

"When you were straining to accommodate both men in your mouth, I wanted to walk up to you and fondle you, slide my fingers in your arse, and fuck you myself."

He shuddered. "I would've . . . liked that."

His cock stirred against her hip.

"Do you think you would've come if I'd done that?" She wrapped her hand around the base of his stirring shaft.

"I don't know. Mayhap if you had told me to."

"Mmm . . ." She nuzzled his lower lip. "Your come jetting out just when Minshom and Thomas came too would've been a sight to see." He opened his mouth to her and she kissed him more deeply, feeding each faint pulse of interest building in his shaft.

"We're not finished yet, tonight, Mr. Maclean. I need your cock."

"Yes, my lady."

She straddled his stomach. "Your poor, overused, bitten cock."

"I'll do whatever you want, my lady."

"I know you will." She eased lower and brought his swollen crown against her clit and then lower. "Don't come until I give you permission."

She held his gaze as she gently lowered herself over his still magnificent cock and squeezed her internal muscles tightly around him. His eyes were wide, his entire attention fixed on her. She settled more deeply down on him.

"Give me your hand, Mr. Maclean."

She took his proffered hand and placed it over her breast. "You have my permission to touch me."

"God . . ." he breathed. "I want to touch you so badly."

With a growl he levered himself more upright and set his mouth over her nipple, his hand still playing with her other breast. His cock kicked up inside her, and she clamped down on him even harder until she could feel every pulse of his excitement. His hips tilted upward, but she didn't move on him. She just held him where she wanted him, captive beneath her and subject to her demands.

His hands started to roam her body, shaping her hips and the curve of her buttocks, sliding down her thighs, but she stayed still, letting him please her, but offering little in return, not that it seemed to bother him.

"Mr. Maclean."

He froze in place, his gaze finding hers again instantly.

"Put your hands flat on the bed."

There was an instant when he seemed to struggle, but he did as she ordered him to do, his fingers lingering on her hips until they finally came to rest on the bed. He stayed perfectly still, the only piece of him active, the deep throb of his cock within her.

She cupped her breasts and pinched her nipples until she shivered with the pleasure.

"I . . . can do that for you, my lady, let me—"

She only had to look at him to make him to fall silent. Tracing a path down over her stomach to her mound, she used two fingers to slide around her clit, opening herself to his gaze.

"My lady . . ."

She touched herself lightly, circling her bud with her fingers until she had to move faster, to slick up her juices and focus inward as the intensity of the pleasure communicated itself with the presence of his big cock in her cunt.

He bucked against her, his hips rising off the bed.

"No," she gasped. "Lie still."

She wanted to ride him now, to slide herself up and down his big cock while she climaxed. Keeping her finger pressed to her clit, she rocked against him, making him groan her name, and found she couldn't stop. Grinding herself into his buried hardness and the cradle of his groin until she started to shake and come and scream with the intensity of the pleasure.

Her climaxes began to blend, each explosion setting off another one as she continued to writhe down on his stiff length.

"God!" she screamed again and bent forward over him, her breasts touching his chest, her mouth fused to his as she experienced the best sexual peak of her life. Trembling, she waited out the small aftershocks, almost afraid to move because she might set off another one.

She lifted her head slightly to stare into his eyes. He was quivering like a bow, his lower lip caught in his teeth.

"Is there something you want, Mr. Maclean?" she managed to whisper.

"Let me come. *Order* me to come inside you. Please."

She slowly sat up so that she could see him properly; she

saw the fear in his eyes that she would deprive him of what he wanted so desperately.

"Come, then."

It took but one upward thrust of his hips and he was climaxing, each hot burst of seed deep and separate within her and accompanied by a heartfelt groan of a man who had reached his limit.

With a smile, Diana eased herself off him.

"Stay there."

His seed trickled down her thigh as she walked over to get some water. It was a long time since she had allowed a man to come in her, or wanted one to. But Mr. Maclean didn't need to know that. She washed herself thoroughly and then took the wet cloth back to the bed. He lay exactly as she had left him, hands fisted in the sheets, legs spread wide, and his chest heaving.

She washed his cock and balls, kissing them as she cleaned him until he was trembling and bucking against her hand. Discarding the cloth, she blew out the candles and climbed into bed.

"Go to sleep, Mr. Maclean."

He touched her hair. "May I hold you?"

She smiled into the darkness and found her way into his arms.

"Yes, I think I would like that very much."

13

"There is still no sign of Harry Maclean?" Diana asked Charlotte.

"No." Her friend sighed. "I suspect your Mr. Maclean is right, and he's run off to Scotland or made for France."

"But what will happen if he doesn't return?"

"I told you. We can wait. Revenge is a dish best served cold." Charlotte winked at her.

"You are a bloodthirsty wench."

"For Harry Maclean? Yes, I suppose I am. He destroys people, Di, he uses them and then discards them."

"I know, love. Perhaps with him gone, you can finally decide what you wish to do with the rest of your life."

"I'm quite happy here."

"In the pleasure house?"

"Why not? We don't all aspire to marry and become an aristocrat, Diana."

"I did what was necessary to survive. Why are you criticizing me now?"

"I'm not. I'm—" Charlotte got off the bed and went over to her chest of drawers. "I have something to show you."

She came back to the bed with a large leather-bound book and set it on the covers beside Diana.

"What is it?"

"It's one of the record books from St. Hilda's School for Girls."

"Good gracious! Where did you find this?"

"I didn't. Nico did."

"But why didn't he give it to me?"

Charlotte gave her a sidelong glance. "You'll have to discuss that with him yourself." She opened the book and a wave of damp and mildew emerged. "I assume that when the school closed down so suddenly, everything was sold to pay the debts."

"But who would buy an old book already full of writing?"

"You'll have to ask him about that."

Diana fixed Charlotte with her most intimidating stare, but her friend remained unperturbed. "This book concerns the year you and I arrived at the school."

"Of course. Nico is nothing but efficient."

Charlotte continued to turn the pages with the tips of her fingers, grimacing at the smell. "We both arrived when we were quite young. There is a question mark beside each of our dates of birth. It seems they had to guess our ages. I for one don't remember anything about my life before that, do you?"

"Not really," Diana admitted. "The odd flash of a woman's face, or a hint of her scent, but not much. Does it mention who sent us to the school?"

Charlotte sat back. "It says who originally paid our fees."

"But I thought we were charity cases."

"Apparently not."

"But that makes no sense. If we had family members willing to pay for us to attend, why weren't they contacted when the school failed?"

Charlotte tapped the page. "Read your entry."

Diana found her spectacles and squinted down at the crabbed script. After a moment she slowly raised her head. "No wonder

Nico didn't want me to see this. It says my fees were paid by the Earl of Westbrook's estate."

"So you finally have your proof."

"It would seem so." Diana shook her head. "I can't quite believe it. I don't understand why Nico didn't tell me."

"He must have had his reasons."

"To prevent me from destroying the very lucrative amount of business he enjoys with the Sinners? Perhaps I don't know him as well as I thought."

Charlotte reached for her hand. "Promise me you will talk to him before you do anything too outlandish."

"Oh, I'll talk to him." Diana got up and shook out her skirts. "I wonder whether he's at his office right now?"

"I know for a fact he is not."

"Then where *is* he?"

"When he dropped the book off to me, he said he would be out of town for a few days. He probably knew that I'd tell you what he'd found."

"Oh, I'm sure of it." Diana smacked one palm against the other. "Damn him!" She paced the carpet. "I don't need to wait for him to return. I could go to the countess and tell her what I've found out."

"But that would be cruel."

"I know!" Diana practically shouted. "I like the woman, but if her husband is my father, don't you think she deserves to know what a rake she married?"

"*Everyone* knew he was a rake. He even had a nickname, the Savage Rake. Faith married him anyway. If you have a shred of regard for the woman, you will await the earl's return, and ask him directly for an explanation."

"The Earl of Westbrook is due back in London this weekend."

"Yes, which means you might as well wait until Nico comes back and tells you what he knows before you go barging in there and make a fool of yourself."

"I will not be the fool." Diana sighed. "But I do not want to shame my employer. Dammit, I *admire* the woman. It isn't her fault either."

"Then *wait*. For goodness' sake, Di, you've waited twenty-odd years already to find out who your father is. What difference will a couple more days make?"

"A letter for you, sir."

"Thank you, Maddon." Alistair used his paper knife to slide between the thick envelope and the black gargoyle seal and eased out what appeared to be an invitation.

His name was written in slanting script in the center.

"The Demon Club requests the pleasure of your company on the last Saturday of the month for the repayment of your debt by whatever means possible."

Alistair finished reading aloud and studied the words again before flipping the card over. There was an address on the rear, a time, and another line of text. "There is no need to reply to this invitation. You will be present." He grunted. "Well, that's rather direct."

With a sigh, he put the card down in the center of his desk and stared at it. He had a sense that Harry wasn't going to return in time to deal with the Demons. All he could do was write them a note declining the invitation and reiterating why. He had a horrible feeling that his wishes would make very little difference. Would they come for him in his apartment and kidnap him? Or would they use more subtle methods to entice him to their side?

Whatever they did, he had to try to reason with them. Reaching for a sheet of paper, he wrote a short note, reminding them that it was his brother who had incurred the debt, not him.

A discreet knock on the door revealed Maddon, who took Alistair's letter and then paused. "There is a matter I wished to discuss with you, Mr. Maclean. It concerns some unusual activity within the household."

"Go ahead."

"James reports that someone has been upstairs in the attics accessing the Sinners Club records."

"And when he says 'someone,' I assume he doesn't mean one of the founding members or Lord Keyes and Mr. Fisher."

"No, sir."

"Well, I haven't been up there, so who else could it be?"

Maddon hesitated. "He thought he saw Lady Theale."

"Did he?" Alistair frowned. "And have you asked her if this is true?"

"I decided to speak to you first, sir. Lady Theale has been asking me a lot of questions about the origins of the club. I thought that bore mentioning as well, sir."

"What kinds of things has she been asking about?"

"How the club was formed, where the Pelly family came from, and about the Earl of Westbrook."

"How interesting." Alistair considered this new twist. "I will talk to Lady Malinda and the countess and ascertain if Lady Theale has been given some task that we don't know about to search the archives."

"That would seem an excellent way to proceed, Mr. Maclean."

"I appreciate you bringing this matter to my attention, Maddon."

"You are welcome, sir. I greatly respect Lady Theale, but I would not wish harm on the countess. I've known her since she was a young girl."

After Maddon left, Alistair stared at his steepled fingers. Diana had insisted that her job at the Sinners had nothing to do with her involvement with him or with his brother, Harry. If she was telling the truth, it didn't mean she wasn't after something else entirely, but what?

Information of some kind, obviously, but was it a private matter or one that threatened the security of the nation? A person who desperately needed money might be prepared to sacrifice anything to survive, and he sensed Diana was a survivor.

She'd managed to claw her way out of the pleasure house by marrying a member of the minor gentry. And now she had *him* by the balls—literally.

Having him in her power, why hadn't she asked him to help her with whatever matter she was investigating? Did she already understand that his loyalty to the owners of the Sinners was completely separate from how he felt about her? Perhaps not. Most people imagined that a man who wanted to be dominated in the bedroom wanted to be dominated in his real life. But Diana at least should know him better than that.

Was she simply waiting for him to submit completely so that she could make him do whatever she asked? And devil take it, when she ordered him to do something, he truly wanted to obey her with all his heart. . . . He'd even offered her his soul.

"Mr. Maclean?"

He jumped as Lady Theale knocked briefly on his door and sailed into his office, a letter in her hand, her spectacles perched on the end of her nose.

"Yes, my lady?"

She paused to look down at him, her expression alert. Sometimes it was hard to reconcile the way she dealt with him in bed with her efficiency at the Sinners.

"Are you all right?"

"I'm quite well, my lady. How may I help you?"

She turned to his door and locked it. "This was just delivered for you." She placed a letter on his desk and a large, flat velvet case that looked as if it might contain jewelry. "There was also a note for me. Shall I read it to you?"

"If you wish."

She pushed her spectacles further up her nose. "Dear Lady Theale, thank you for a most enjoyable evening. Your slave was everything he should be and more. If you ever need him taken care of, Lady Jane, Thomas and myself would be more than willing to offer him a place in our bed. Minshom."

Alistair swallowed hard and eyed the jewelry box. "What is it?"

"I don't know. Why don't you open it and see?"

He cautiously undid the gold latch and revealed the sleek black satin lining. Sitting on the surface was a narrow silver collar and a set of cock rings. Long, thin chains hung from either side of the collar, which he assumed attached to the rings. Alistair rubbed his finger over the brightness of the metal.

"What does his letter say, Mr. Maclean?"

Alistair opened the enclosed note and read it aloud. "This is for you, Maclean. It is discreet enough to wear under your normal clothes, yet allows your mistress to know that you are entirely hers. If I owned you, I must confess that I would keep you oiled, and naked and collared like this at all times purely for my pleasure. Minshom."

Diana sat on the edge of his desk and gently lifted the collar from its satin cushion. "It has my name engraved on it. That was rather presumptuous of him."

Alistair stared at the silver circlet, his mind in chaos. To be *owned.* To wear her collar for him permanently . . . How could he do that when she might be about to betray the very people they worked for?

"Mr. Maclean?" She replaced the collar in the box.

He slowly closed the lid. "It is very kind of Lord Minshom to think of me."

She was silent for a long while until he finally looked up at her. "You aren't willing to wear it yet though, are you?"

He shook his head.

"Then put it away." She slid gracefully off his desk and onto the floor. "Unless you wish to visit Lord Minshom and thank him in person?"

"No, my lady." He couldn't repress a shiver. "I do not want to do that."

"Yet you are still not willing to bow your knee completely to me."

"I have given you more than I've given—"

She held up her hand interrupting him, her polite smile firmly in place. He had a terrible sense that he had hurt her, but no idea what to do about it.

"I have another question. Do you know exactly when the Earl of Westbrook is arriving?"

"Why do you need to know that?"

She blinked at him and he winced. Her abrupt change of subject had made him answer her more sharply than he should have. And now he would have no opportunity to find out if she was upset about him not wanting to wear her collar.

"The countess asked me to check."

He sat back in his chair. "I sincerely doubt that. The countess is always aware of her husband's plans."

"What are you suggesting?"

"That perhaps you wish the information purely for yourself?"

She went still. "Have you been speaking to Nico?"

"I haven't seen him all week. Is there something you wish to tell me, Lady Theale?"

"No, Mr. Maclean, there is not."

"Because your business is with the earl."

"Exactly." She curtsied. "Good morning, Mr. Maclean."

"Lady Theale." He spoke to her back as she was already heading for the door. "Why are you so interested in the Earl of Westbrook?"

She unlocked the door with an audible *click*. "That is my business."

"If it affects anything within these premises it is my business too."

She turned to face him. "This has nothing to do with you."

"Only my employer."

"You are employed by Mr. Fisher and Lord Keyes."

"To *run* the Sinners in its entirety, which includes all matters involving the Westbrooks."

She sighed. "Mr. Maclean, you are simply being difficult because you feel vulnerable. You believe I intend to compromise your position in some way. I understand your concern, and I repeat that this matter has nothing *whatsoever* to do with you, your horrible brother, or our relationship. Am I making myself clear?"

"Then tell me what's wrong."

She swallowed hard and looked away from him. "I cannot."

He snorted. "So much for trust. It seems that you expect everything from me, and aren't willing to risk anything in return."

She cast him a final scathing look and left, slamming the door behind her.

Alistair glared at the wooden panels of the door. She was impossible and she was putting him in an impossible situation. Why couldn't she trust him? Didn't she know that when he gave his loyalty he gave it for life?

He stood up, took the green case, shoved it in his top drawer, and locked it. To hell with it. He needed to speak to Lady Westbrook.

"Alistair, my dear, how may I help you?"

He took the seat opposite the smiling countess and waited patiently while she poured him a cup of tea, talked about the weather, and generally attempted to set him at ease.

"I have a request, my lady."

"And what is that?" Her sharp blue gaze fastened on him, and he reminded himself that Faith Pelly was no fool, but an integral part of the continuing success of the Sinners.

"If you have information at hand about Lady Theale, may I see it?"

"Why would you want to do that, dear?" She patted his hand. "I know that you have become 'close,' but I'm fairly certain Diana would prefer you to ask her any questions you might have rather than seek information from me and her stepson."

"I have asked her. She doesn't trust me enough to answer." He put down his cup. "If you do have any information, I would appreciate seeing it."

"Nothing I know of her makes me believe she is a threat to you, Alistair."

He set his jaw. "I'm not concerned about myself. I am quite capable of dealing with Lady Theale. I suspect her reasons for taking this job at the Sinners are more complex than we realized."

"And I'm sure they are not." She held his gaze. "If I had any information about Diana that I believed could harm you or the Sinners, I would share it with you."

"Then you do know something?"

"What I know is safe in my hands." She glanced away from him. "Is there anything else?"

"Lady Theale was asking whether the earl was returning this weekend."

"Did she indeed?"

"She said you asked her to find out."

"Oh." The countess nodded vigorously. "That's correct, I did ask her to ask you. I'd forgotten."

Alistair stared at her in frustration. "Forgive me for my impertinence, Lady Westbrook, but are you protecting Lady Theale from me?"

"Why ever would I do that?"

"I'm not sure, but—"

"Alistair, dear, there is nothing to worry about. I swear it." The countess sounded very firm. "If circumstances change, or Diana decides to confide in you herself, then I am quite willing to discuss the matter again. As it is, I have nothing more to say."

He inclined his head an unwilling inch. "Then I will take my leave of you." He hesitated. "But if you need my help, please let me know."

"I will do that." She searched his face. "Have you heard from your brother?"

"No, I have not."

"Oh dear. Then what are you intending to do about the Demon club?"

Alistair stiffened. "How do you know about that?"

She shrugged. "I see all the morning post before it is distributed, and I noticed you had a letter from them. Their seal is very distinctive. Were they asking after Harry?"

"Yes, they expect to see him at one of their gatherings at the end of the month. I wrote them a note to tell them he wasn't in London, and that they would have to wait."

"They won't appreciate that."

"So I've heard."

"You will be careful, won't you, Alistair?"

"Of course I will." He rose from his seat and bowed. "Good morning, my lady."

"Don't forget to speak to Adam and Diana about the entertainment scheduled for the second floor, will you?"

"It's all in hand, my lady." He bowed again and escaped through the door none the wiser than before he'd entered and in truth, rather more confused. Whatever she said, Lady Westbrook was protecting Diana. But from what? Alistair had no idea.

14

"Mr. Maclean. Mr. *Maclean.*"

Alistair looked up from the list he was consulting to find Diana in front of him. She wore one of her plainest gowns and had braided her hair tightly to her head, giving her the look of a schoolmarm. They were on the second floor surrounded by the chaos of organizing a night of salacious pleasures for the members of the club.

"How may I help you?"

"Where have you been?"

"In the cellar with Maddon deciding which wine to serve this evening." He looked around the salon. "Is everything all right?"

"I can't find the guest list."

"Maddon should have it." He didn't move out of her path. "Are you attending the party this evening?"

"Of course I am." Her gaze raked over him. "I assume that as Mr. Fisher and Lord Keyes are busy, we are both required to host the gathering."

"I'm not sure you will wish to be surrounded by all these men."

She smiled at him. "Oh, I think I'll enjoy it immensely. It's not often a woman is invited to an all-male Roman orgy. In fact, Mr. Maclean, I was going to ask you the same question. Knowing your particular habits, I assumed you wouldn't wish to be there at all."

"I'm there in an official capacity, not as a participant."

"Of course not."

He lowered his voice and his gaze. "Unless you wish it, my lady?"

She tapped him lightly on the cheek with her pen. "We have already established that you do not wish to participate in all-male orgies. I would much rather you attended to keep an eye on me."

"I would do that anyway, my lady." He brought her hand to his lips and kissed her ink-stained fingers.

"Despite being annoyed with me?"

"Despite that."

"Then you don't deny that you *are* vexed?"

He made himself meet her gaze. "I've told you why."

Her mouth twisted. "Because you don't trust me in bed or out of it."

"In bed I've offered you complete power over me. You should not assume that my surrender means I am as easy to control in my everyday life."

Her eyes flashed a warning. "You believe I would use your nature against you?"

"Why not? You wouldn't be the first person to equate sexual submission with cowardice or weakness." He tightened his grip on her fingers. "Tell me why you came to work at the Sinners."

She looked away from him.

"*Tell* me."

"It is a personal matter concerning my family."

He let out his breath. "And?"

"And I am hardly going to discuss it here in the main salon of the Sinners with forty guests expected within the hour!"

"But you will tell me?"

She sighed. "After the conclusion of the orgy, I will . . . discuss the matter with you."

"Thank you."

Her slow smile made him stare at her luscious mouth, imagining it opening to take his cock . . .

". . . If you will do something for me in return?"

He realized she was still speaking and staring up at him expectantly.

"What?"

"Dress appropriately for the event?"

"In a *toga?*"

"Oh no, I have something far more interesting for you to wear than that." She crooked a finger at him. "Come with me."

Diana gathered up the items she required from the main dressing room and turned to face Alistair, who had followed her into the small antechamber just off the hall that the servants used to access the rooms.

"Strip."

His hands went to his cravat and then stilled. "Everything?"

"Yes, please."

He carefully removed his clothes and placed them in a neat pile on a chair. Diana shook out the folds of the red-and-green-checkered woolen cloth and showed it to him.

His green eyes narrowed. "That's the Maclean tartan."

"I know." She held it out to him. "It's quite legal for you to wear it now. I gather you pleat it rather like a skirt at the hips and throw the end over your shoulder to cover your chest."

"Aye, I know how to fashion a kilt." His Scottish accent had noticeably thickened. "What does it have to do with a Roman orgy?"

"You're a barbarian prisoner." She showed him the manacles for his wrists and his ankles. "All you have to do is allow me to lead you around like a prize in a Roman Triumph."

"Ah."

She helped him gather the folds of the tartan around his hips and secure the weight of the fabric with a heavy leather belt.

"I like this, Mr. Maclean. You look remarkably wild. We will disguise your hair if you wish, or you may wear a mask."

"A mask will be fine."

She smoothed a hand over his chest and then stroked the leather belt. "There is one more thing, Mr. Maclean."

"What is that, my lady?" he murmured.

"I want you hard under that kilt. Every time I touch your cock, I want it wet and ready to fuck. Do you understand me?"

"Yes, my lady. I'm hard now."

She reached underneath the woolen fabric and gripped his shaft. "So I see."

"If anyone else notices my aroused state, will you let them touch me too?"

She stroked her thumb over his crown, drawing out the wetness. "I haven't decided that yet. Your primary function is to please me."

"Yes, my lady."

There was a knock on the door.

"Lady Theale? The actors and musicians from the pleasure house have arrived. Shall I bring them up to the main salon?"

"Yes, please, Mr. Maddon. I'll be there in a moment."

She opened the tin of polish she'd borrowed from the kitchen and randomly smeared some of the blacking over his torso and then drew lines along his cheekbones.

"Now you look quite ferocious." She cupped his jaw and kissed his mouth. "You mustn't forget your manacles."

He half-smiled as she fitted the flimsy tin props on his wrists and then his ankles. "These are hardly capable of restraining me."

"Perhaps we shall seek out better restraints afterward. I love to see you shackled and stretched out on a rack waiting for me to decide how to play with you."

His breathing hitched.

Diana kissed him again, biting softly at his lower lip. "Go into the dressing room next door, find a mask, and meet me in the salon."

He bowed and followed her out, his bare feet making no sound on the wooden floor.

In the main salon, a group of musicians was already setting up and tuning their instruments on the slightly raised stage at one end of the room. At the other end, Maddon supervised the laying out of a Roman-style supper complete with stuffed figs, vine leaves, and elaborately decorated meats. There were also copious flagons of wine, which the all-male servers would circulate throughout the room.

Long couches arranged in groups around low tables would provide places for the club members to dine and enjoy mingling with other guests. Diana spoke to all the servers, making sure they knew that they were welcome to accept sexual offers from the guests if they chose, but would not be penalized if they didn't indulge. As all the servers were from the pleasure house and were well used to such evenings, Diana had little fear the event wouldn't progress smoothly.

She noticed there were two other men dressed as barbarians, both with long black hair who also belonged to the pleasure house and who were also willing to be fucked by the guests. With his auburn hair, Alistair Maclean would fit in well.

After making sure that everyone was in place, Diana retired to dress with the help of her maid in a diaphanous Roman tunic, which barely covered her breasts and was secured at her shoulder with a heavy brass pin. She kept her hair in one simple braid down her back and added a gold necklace and matching bracelets. Seeing as it was an all-male orgy, she certainly wasn't too worried about her virtue, but it would be helpful to have a glowering Alistair Maclean chained to her side.

As the hostess, she also donned a golden mask. She found Alistair in the main salon, arms folded over his chest, leaning back against the wall. His keen gaze observed the staff, noting every detail. She touched his muscled arm.

"It's time to allow the guests in." She moved closer to whisper. "Some of the women want to watch as well, so I told them to use the peepholes."

"Why would women want to watch men copulate?"

She chuckled. "Why wouldn't they? The idea that women don't enjoy such things is very old-fashioned, Mr. Maclean. If one man is worth having and watching, why not two?"

He was saved from replying as the double doors opened and the male guests started to crowd into the space. With a nod from her, the musicians struck up a quiet melody and the servers began to move among the guests offering sweetmeats, wine, and other more salacious services.

Diana watched for a while to see that everything was progressing properly and then turned to Alistair with a relieved sigh. "I think it is going well."

"Of course it is. We planned it perfectly."

"Well, you did."

"And you provided the necessary resources from the pleasure house."

"We work well together." She reached down a hand and toyed with the hem of his kilt before sliding one proprietal hand up his muscled thigh.

"Mmm . . . hard and hot." He remained perfectly still as she explored his cock and balls, her fingers tugging at the coarse auburn hair of his groin. "I can't wait to strip you later and see how wet you are."

"Yes . . . please, my lady."

She pinched his shaft and he shuddered. "We need to circulate, barbarian slave. Come with me."

She tugged on his chain, and he obediently fell in behind her, his manacles rattling as he walked, his head bowed and his gaze averted. As one of the servers passed her, she picked up a goblet of red wine and drank from it.

"Are you thirsty, barbarian?"

"Only for you, my lady."

She offered him the goblet and let him drink, rubbing her thumb over his mouth to clear off the drops of wine.

"You are too kind to your slave, my lady," a loud voice boomed over her shoulder.

"Do you think so, senator?"

"Feeding him wine? He should be on his knees feeding you."

"He will be, do not doubt it." With a smile, Diana moved on, bringing Alistair with her. Whenever she stopped to talk or simply observe, she put her hand on him, owning his tight bicep and even tighter stomach, exploring the gaps where his belt and the bunched fabric revealed glimpses of his muscled buttocks and the groove running from his hip to his groin.

Smiling, she bit his earlobe. "When I have you alone, I'm going to lick a path all the way down from your chest to your cock and then to your hips."

"I would like that."

"I know."

The music increased in volume and some of the men found partners to share their couches or retreated to the more discreet closed rooms along the corridor. Diana continued to smile graciously and direct the staff, as did Mr. Maclean. At one point when they were by the buffet, she made him kneel beside her while she fed him from her fingertips.

"Lord Minshom and his wife hold the occasional weekend gathering at their country house. I could bring you with me and keep you like this for three days. Do you think you would enjoy that, Mr. Maclean?"

He leaned in, took the food from between her fingers, and licked them clean. "Aye, my lady."

"Although I also wish I could keep you chained to my desk here and have your mouth on me whenever I wanted."

"That would make it difficult for me to complete my own work, my lady."

She chuckled. "That's true. I don't think Mr. Fisher would approve."

He almost smiled and she ruffled his hair. "Are you still hard for me, Mr. Maclean?"

"Yes, my lady."

"Stand up and face me."

He rose to his feet and stared down at the ground.

"Lift up your plaid and show me."

He slowly raised the tartan to reveal the hard thrust of his cock. Diana stroked a finger down the red pulsing length.

"Does the wool chafe?"

His nod was brusque.

"Do you like it?"

"Aye."

A discreet cough behind Alistair made Diana look up to find Maddon staring at her. "My lady, may I have a word?"

"Certainly. I'll be there in a moment."

She stood and pulled down the plaid. "Come with me, Mr. Maclean."

She took him down to one of the rooms, which had been decorated to look like a punishment cell for slaves. There were two other men in there, one being beaten with a whip, and the other kneeling in chains as he sucked the cock of a man dressed as a Roman soldier.

"Stand against the wall, and put your hands over your head."

When he complied, she shackled his wrists tightly to the iron spike. "You can wait for me here. I'll tell the guard that no one may fuck you, but me." She bit his nipple hard. "But they may look, and they may touch and you must not come."

Alistair watched Diana walk away to find Maddon and considered what might be wrong. Surely, she should've taken him with her? They were supposed to be co-hosting the event. He moved his feet into a wider stance, making his cock press harder against the rough fibers of the woolen cloth. Looking down, there was no mistaking the thrust of his shaft even through the tartan, and he had no ability to rearrange the cloth.

The doorway to the "dungeon" was left open so that guests could enter and participate at will. He caught a glimpse of a blonde accompanied by an all-too familiar figure and stiffened. What in God's name was Sir Ronald Fairbanks doing in the Sinners? He pulled at his restraints, but Diana had tied him up properly, and he couldn't get free. Before he could even process that thought, or act further on it, a young man in a toga blocked his view.

"And what have we here? Another barbarian Scot?"

Alistair went still as the man ran a leisurely hand down over his chest and settled his fingers on the sturdy leather belt around Alistair's hips.

"One who is hard in the presence of all these men?" He grabbed Alistair's cock through the tartan, making him wince. "Surely that is a punishable offense?"

Alistair met the man's gaze and deliberately broadened his accent. "Aye, if you free me from ma bounds, I'd be verra grateful indeed, sir."

"How grateful?"

"Enough to suck ye dry, sir, and take any punishment you wish to mete out to me while I'm down there on my knees."

"An interesting offer. And what happens if you escape?"

"After my attentions to ye, sir, I can assure ye, you'll be more than willing to let me go."

The man laughed. "I find you amusing, barbarian."

With another quick glance at the guard who was too busy watching the man sucking cock, Alistair slowly licked his lips and stared down at his companion's rapidly growing erection.

"Ye look big, sir, but I swear, I'll take every bit of ye down my throat."

The man reached up and freed Alistair's wrists from the wall. With a prayer of thanks, Alistair sank down to his knees, kissed the man's tunic, and then raised it to take his cock. Even though he needed to be fast, he didn't disappoint his companion, sucking him off fast and deep until the man grabbed his hair and held on as he climaxed deep down Alistair's throat.

"Damnation, that was—"

Alistair wiped a hand over his mouth and winked. "Good enough to allow me a moment to attempt to flee, sir? I'm fairly sure I'll be caught and punished, but give me this chance."

The man sank down onto the nearest bench and waved a hand at Alistair. "Go, you deserve it."

Alistair ran past the guard and scanned the corridor. Where had Sir Ronald gone? Did his appearance have anything to do with Harry? He went through into the main gathering place, but could see no sign of Sir Ronald or his blond companion. Slowing his pace to avoid alarming anyone, he moved through the guests and out onto the landing. There was no sign of Diana either. Was she still dealing with Maddon, or had she in fact already been alerted to Fairbanks's presence?

After a second of indecision, Alistair went down the stairs and turned into the hallway that contained the more private offices of the Sinners Club staff, including his own. There was a faint light under one of the doorways, and the latch was unlocked. Using the tip of his finger, he pushed the door panel open to reveal someone standing by the desk, red hair glinting in the candlelight.

"Harry."

Alistair shut the door and leaned against it.

His brother looked up, a pistol in his hand pointing straight at Alistair. "Is that you, Alistair? What in God's name are you wearing?"

"More importantly, what are you doing here?"

"I was just writing you a note."

"Did you come with Sir Ronald?"

Harry looked up. "No, devil take it, is he here?" He shoved his pistol in the pocket of his greatcoat. "I'll have to leave."

"You're not going anywhere until you've answered a few questions."

Harry's grin flashed out. "My dear, dear brother, always so self-righteous and pompous. Do you think I don't know why you're dressed like that? How you abase yourself for that woman?"

"I do not—"

Harry held up his hand. "I don't have time to listen to your hypocritical excuses. I have to go."

"I'm not moving from this door until you talk to me."

"Oh, *please* don't move, brother."

A figure stepped out from the shadows to Alistair's left, and the next thing he knew was a crashing pain in his skull and then he was falling.

"Good evening, Sir Ronald."

Diana finally ran her prey to ground in the main salon.

His gaze raked over her. "Where's Harry Maclean?"

She noted he didn't bother to show her any of the respect a lady of her class should receive, but that meant she didn't have to treat him as a gentleman either.

"I have no idea. Did he come here with you?"

"No, dammit, he did not, otherwise why would I be seeking him?" He looked around the crowded space. "I saw someone with red hair earlier."

"That would probably be Mr. *Alistair* Maclean. He works here."

"And is Harry's brother, which means they are probably in league with each other."

"I doubt that very much. Do you wish to speak to Mr. Alistair Maclean?"

"I *wish* to find Harry. He owes me money, but I suppose his brother would do. He might know something despite telling me the opposite, or why else would Harry come running back here?"

"I have no idea, Sir Ronald. If you would care to accompany me down to my office, I'll institute a search for Harry and ask Mr. Maclean to attend to you."

Sir Ronald turned on his heel and headed down the stairs, his expression aggrieved. Diana managed to get past him on the stairs and led him into her office, lighting more candles and checking the fire was still warm.

"I'll only be a moment."

Diana left the door ajar and turned to Maddon, who had accompanied her down the stairs. "Search for Harry. I'll go and get the other Mr. Maclean."

She went back up using the servants' stairs, which brought her out right opposite where she wanted to be. The punishment room was crowded, and she had to find a way through the men gathered around a slave being auctioned off. The wall facing her was empty. After a moment of stunned dismay, she grabbed hold of the servant guarding the door.

"Where is Mr. Maclean?"

"He—" The man took one look at her expression and his grin faded. "He escaped, my lady. Someone helped him get away when my back was turned. I'm sorry, my lady. I thought it was all a bit of fun."

"It's not important. Thank you." She picked her skirts and made her way through all the other rooms on the second floor, but there was no sign of Alistair or his liberator. She stopped at the double doors that led out onto the landing where two footmen were stationed.

"Have you seen Mr. Maclean?"

"Yes, my lady. He went down to the lower level about ten minutes ago."

She thanked the footman and carried on down the stairs and into the quieter, less ornate office quarters. She inhaled the scent of an extinguished candle and quickened her pace. One of the doors was open and a figure knelt in the darkness. Diana crept closer until she could get a good look and then froze.

"What are you doing here?"

Charlotte looked up. "Mr. Maclean's been knocked out and he's bleeding. Do you want to fetch some help?"

Alistair stirred as the voice above him strengthened. A pleasant face framed with short fair hair shimmered over him.

"Who are you?"

"The person who found you. Lady Theale has gone for help. You'll be fine now."

"Where's—?" He just managed to stop asking the question.

"Harry? Who knows? He's long gone."

Alistair licked his lips, but before he could say another word, the figure rose and walked away from him. Even as he closed his eyes against the pain in his skull, he became aware of other noises and approaching voices, the soft tones of Lady Theale, and the obnoxious bray of Sir Ronald.

"Bring more light!"

He kept his eyes tightly shut against the increasing glare and groaned as someone knelt beside him and touched his head.

"He was obviously hit from behind."

Sir Ronald snorted. "Or he's pretending to avoid being questioned about his association with his thieving brother."

"Sir Ronald, unless Mr. Maclean is a contortionist, he could scarcely have done this to himself."

Alistair tried to remember the name of the local apothecary who attended the Sinners and failed. Whatever the man's name, he was doing an excellent job of ignoring Sir Ronald's accusations.

"Gently now, Mr. Maclean. We're going to carry you up to bed so that I can have a proper look at you."

As he was carefully lifted from the floor, Alistair couldn't help but gasp in pain while the room spun in circles around him. He had to close his eyes against the dancing lights and concerned faces and focus on not crying out again. The feel of his pillow beneath him and the flatness of his mattress was more than welcome.

"Thank you for your concern, Sir Ronald. We'll let you know how Mr. Maclean is tomorrow."

That was Diana's voice. There was an implacable note beneath the sweet reasonableness that seemed to work as Sir Ronald's mutterings disappeared down the stairs, leaving them in relative peace and quiet.

"Now then, Mr. Maclean. Let's get you undressed and into bed, and then I'm going to wash the wound and give you something to ease the pain."

The next few minutes were unpleasant as the apothecary probed the wound, resulting in Alistair having to be propped up to puke in a bowl.

When his injury was clean and deemed satisfactory, he was given a dose of laudanum. Diana put another pillow under his head and encouraged him to lie on his left side.

"Thank you, Andrew."

"You're welcome, Lady Theale. Send for me if his condition worsens."

And then Alistair was left in blessed silence with only Diana stroking the damp hair back from his brow. He tried to form a question.

"How did Sir Ronald get in here?"

"I don't know. He claims he was on the guest list."

"The one we couldn't find and thought Maddon had?"

"That's the one." She sighed. "He *said* he was looking for Harry."

"Which makes sense because I found him."

"Harry was here?" Her hand stilled on his hair. "Did he knock you out?"

"No, he was with someone. Obviously, I didn't realize that until I was hit from behind. I assume they both went out the window of my office."

"But we didn't find you in your office."

Alistair tried to blink back the wave of drowsiness. "What?"

"You weren't in your office. You were in Mr. Fisher's."

15

"That . . . can't be right, I . . ." Alistair tried to sit up, and Diana pushed him gently back down.

"You are not to get agitated, Mr. Maclean. Mr. Fisher is already on his way back to the Sinners. I will go and speak to him as soon as you are asleep."

"But—"

His voice grew weaker as the laudanum clouded his senses and his eyes finally closed.

Diana gestured to the footman waiting by the door.

"James, come and sit with Mr. Maclean. Ring the bell if he becomes agitated or wakes up again."

"Yes, my lady."

"Has Mr. Fisher returned?"

"I believe he has, my lady."

"Then I will go down to him." Diana reluctantly released Alistair's hand and left James to watch over him. Seeing him stretched out on the floor, his face bloody, had given her a considerable shock. She was still shaking.

After knocking on Adam Fisher's office door, she went in

and found him surveying his desk, his gaze keen, his countenance unruffled.

"Ah, Lady Theale. What the devil has been going on here tonight?"

She told him what she knew and then added what Alistair had mentioned about seeing his brother, Harry. Some of the ease leached from Mr. Fisher's face.

"Harry was in here?"

"Apparently."

"Damn." He began to open and shut the drawers of his desk. "When we were . . . friends, he often came in here to wait while I finished work." He sighed. "I soon learned that he had a terrible habit of stealing things that didn't belong to him. When I confronted him with my suspicions, he either laughed or lied right to my face."

"What do you think he was after?"

"I'm not sure, but—*damnation!*"

"What's wrong?"

Mr. Fisher straightened a small key in his hand. "He *stole* this. I *know* he did and I hadn't gotten around to changing the lock."

"To what?"

He gestured for her to come around the desk to see the open drawer.

"My strongbox and all the important papers I don't want to leave lying around." With a strangled groan, he sank down onto his chair and clutched his hair. "Benedict is going to murder me."

"Can you tell what is missing?"

He cast a disparaging glance down at the now jumbled contents of the box. "Money and God knows what else." He sighed. "Is Benedict here?"

"I don't think he is."

"Then someone must go and fetch him. He needs to know

about this immediately. And I need to sort through this box and work out what is missing."

Diana bit her lip. "I'll send a message to Lord Keyes right away."

"Thank you."

She started for the door.

"Diana, do you think Alistair had anything to do with this?"

Turning back to Mr. Fisher, she shook her head. "No, I don't. Mr. Maclean has told me more than once that his loyalty to you and the Sinners is absolute. Whatever happened tonight was all Harry's own doing."

"I think you're right, but it doesn't hurt to be careful. Where is Alistair now?"

"Upstairs in bed recovering from a severe blow to the back of his head."

"Harry *hit* him?"

"Harry's accomplice, I believe."

"That sounds more like it. Harry isn't keen on physical violence, although he's always happy to encourage others to fight for him." He groaned into his hands. "I've been such a gullible fool, and now my stupidity might have cost this nation more than I can imagine."

"I'm sure it won't be as bad as all that, Mr. Fisher." Diana wanted to go and comfort her employer, but something about the rigid set of his shoulders sent her hurrying out to find Maddon and send for Lord Keyes.

When she'd accomplished her tasks, she went back to the second floor to check on the Roman orgy and found that everything had gone extremely well. The staff was already in the process of clearing up the remains of the feast and helping the odd drunken guest leave for home or borrow one of the bedrooms in the guest quarters.

After thanking everyone, paying out wages to the staff from the pleasure house, and making sure everything was put back in place, she went down and knocked on Mr. Fisher's door again. When she entered, Lord Keyes was standing over his partner, his expression uncharacteristically furious.

Diana hesitated. "Shall I wait outside, Mr. Fisher? I—"

"Oh no, come in. You deserve to hear Benedict telling me what a weak fool I am. How I've allowed Harry Maclean to lead me around by my cock for years!"

She remained by the door. "I think I should let you discuss this matter between yourselves."

Lord Keyes held up his hand. "Don't bother. I've said my piece now. Please come in, Lady Theale. I wish to hear exactly what happened."

Diana went through the events of the evening again and Lord Keyes nodded, but didn't comment until she reached the part when she found Alistair bleeding in the doorway of Mr. Fisher's office.

"Did he seem surprised to find his brother here?"

"I haven't asked him. But I would assume he wasn't very pleased about it."

"Why do you say that?"

"Because it was obvious that Alistair was sick and tired of dealing with his brother's antics."

"He's said that many times before, Lady Theale, and he's always changed his mind and protected him in the end."

Diana drew an unsteady breath. "With all due respect, Lord Keyes, it sounds as if you are trying to place the blame for this incident on Alistair Maclean. Why is that?"

"Because he's trying to protect my feelings," Adam interrupted her. "But she's right, Benedict. Let's place the blame where it should be, squarely on my shoulders. From my conversations with Alistair, I know that he's already given his brother everything he had. There *is* no more and I'll wager Harry knows that."

"Which is why he came back to you," Lord Keyes said and

stood up. "All right. We'll assume Alistair can be trusted and include him in all our future deliberations about how to track down his offensive brother. I'll also alert our network to the possibility of leaked information and see if anyone hears anything. Apart from that, until you can pinpoint exactly what's missing, Adam, there's little else we can do."

Diana nodded. "Alistair might have some more information, but I doubt he will be lucid until tomorrow. The apothecary gave him laudanum."

Lord Keyes shot her a keen glance. "Not the best thing to give someone who has a head injury. I've seen far too many men filled with opiates who never wake up again."

Diana brought her hand to her throat. "Then what should I do?"

He smiled at her without any humor. "Make *sure* he wakes up. Talk to him, nag him, but make certain he's able to talk to you through the night. He'll hate you for it, but you might save his life."

"Then if I may be excused, I'll go up to him right now."

"Of course, Lady Theale." Lord Keyes bowed to her. "Thank you for everything you have done for us tonight. The Sinners is a better place for having you here."

"Thank you, my lord." She curtsied and tried to smile. She'd never felt so appreciated or welcome anywhere in her life before, and it was all a sham. "I'll speak to you both in the morning."

Picking up her skirts, she ran up the two flights of stairs to Alistair's stark bedchamber and startled James as she hurried into the room.

"I'll sit with him now."

"Are you sure, my lady?" James cast a rather dubious eye over her. "Do you not want to change first?"

She realized she was still wearing her Roman costume and that her right breast was perilously close to being completely on display.

"Perhaps you might ask my maid to fetch my dressing gown and bring it to me here."

"I'll do that, my lady. We wouldn't want you catching a chill."

His embarrassed concern for her was yet another reason to feel guilty about her decision to confront her supposed father, but she wasn't prepared to let it go yet. Rubbing her eyes, and aware that the cosmetics she had used to enhance her features were probably smeared all over her face, she availed herself of the jug of water and washcloth by Alistair's bed.

With a sigh, she sat down and studied Alistair's austere features. Even in his sleep he didn't look soft; his face was all hard angles and lines that denoted his strength of character. How anyone could doubt his courage just because of his preferences in bed escaped her. She liked watching him fight his nature, to learn to yield to her when he thought he could give no more, to learn to trust her to know when to stop . . .

"My lady."

She looked up to see her maid approaching with her dressing gown and was soon more decently covered and alone with Mr. Maclean. After a deep breath she turned to him and shook his shoulder hard.

"Mr. Maclean, wake up. Wake up right now."

Alistair struggled to resist the voice that called to him. But it was impossible. Eventually he opened one eye and mumbled something obscene. For some reason Diana was shaking him.

"Stop it," he groused. "Let me sleep."

"No, you need to wake up and tell me your name."

"You *know* my name."

"Yes, but do you?"

He glared at her for a long moment, but she wouldn't look away or get off his chest.

"Alistair Ian Fraser Maclean, Laird of Duart Castle, master of nothing."

"You're a lord?"

"Was. Family lost everything in the 1745 rebellion. Father branded a traitor."

"How terrible."

"Served him right, the old fool."

"And the rest of your family?"

"Safely on the Isle of Mull, living in a cottage in the ruins of the castle." He frowned. "Apart from Harry, of course. He lives here."

"Your mother is still alive?"

"Aye, and two of my sisters." He blinked hard and tried to focus on her face. "Why are you asking me all these questions?"

"Because Lord Keyes said that head injuries can be fatal."

"Of course they can if your brains spill out. I've seen it happen."

She shuddered. "We don't need to speak of that."

"I just have a wee headache."

She smiled at him. "And now you can go back to sleep. I must warn you that I'm going to wake you up again in an hour or so."

"As you wish, my lady." But he was already slipping away, her smile the last thing he saw.

He woke by himself at dawn and turned his head on his pillow to see Diana stretched out on the covers beside him. He traced her nose and the angle of her cheekbones with the tip of his finger. His memories of the night were confusing and jumbled and his skull ached as if he'd drunk a bottle of brandy.

He frowned. Had he been drinking?

"You're awake. Thank goodness." She smiled at him and then yawned.

"For the fifth time."

"I had to make sure that you didn't succumb to the laudanum and never wake up again."

"Why?"

She came up on one elbow and looked down at him, her gaze sleepy. "What do you mean?"

"Why did you care for me rather than one of the servants or the apothecary?"

"Because you're mine." She reached for his hand and held it tightly.

"Your property?"

"You don't wear my collar, but I still feel some responsibility for you."

He thought about the implications of that and wasn't as alarmed by her words as perhaps he should have been.

"I seem to remember Harry was here."

"So you said. I don't believe anyone else saw him." She hesitated. "Lord Keyes and Mr. Fisher want to talk to you about what happened."

Alistair briefly closed his eyes. "Of course they do." He managed to let go of her hand and sit up without clutching at his head and howling. "Would you be so kind as to ring the bell and have some hot water brought up? I need to shave and make myself presentable."

She slid off the bed and rang the bell. "I expect you are quite famished. I'll see you at breakfast."

With a nod, she headed for the door.

"Thank you, my lady," Alistair said.

"For what?"

"For waking me up."

She smothered another yawn. "It was my pleasure."

He had a sense that she meant it, that her definition of caring for him was far more encompassing than he could ever have imagined. For the first time in his life, he felt *safe* with someone. Shaking off that thought, he managed to sit on the side of the bed and put his feet on the floor without puking. If Lord Keyes and Mr. Fisher wanted to see him, he'd better make sure he looked presentable even if they were going to demand his resignation.

Would he ever escape the taint of his brother's misdeeds? He tried to be a good, honest man, but there were many people who would never trust him simply because his last name was Maclean. What was the point of living an upright life when Harry constantly dragged him down? He'd felt welcome at the Sinners, *valued* . . .

"Morning, sir. How are you feeling?" James came in with a basin of hot water and some clean towels. "You're still looking green around the gills."

"I have a bit of a headache."

"I'm not surprised, sir. You were bleeding like a pig last night."

Alistair repressed a shudder and found his way to his dressing table and his shaving gear. His expression was haggard. He couldn't see the wound under the thick wad of bandage Andrew had applied to it. With fingers that shook, he untied the bandages and checked for fresh bleeding. Luckily there was none.

James hovered behind him, a concerned expression on his face.

"Would you like me to shave you, sir?"

Alistair studied the razor and then his trembling hand. "Yes, I think that would be an excellent idea."

By the time he faced Lord Keyes and Mr. Fisher, his nerves had settled, but his headache remained. He was surprised when another knock on the door heralded the arrival of Diana and the Countess of Westbrook. But he supposed if he was about to be kicked out on his arse, it was fitting that the entire private staff should witness his humiliation.

He would've preferred to stand for the *coup de grace,* but his current frail state required a chair.

Lord Keyes took center stage by sitting on the front of his desk while the others grouped themselves around him.

"I understand that you saw your brother last night."

"Yes, my lord."

"Did you invite him here?"

"On the contrary, I made it very clear to him that he was not to visit me at the Sinners."

"Then why do you think he turned up?"

Alistair shrugged. "He was probably hoping to steal money from me to pay his current debts."

"You didn't offer him money?"

"No, my lord. I have none left to give, and I made that very clear to him." He straightened his spine. "I can only apologize unreservedly for my brother's appalling behavior and for inflicting him on you all. I also wish to tender my resignation."

"Why the devil would you want to do that?" Lord Keyes asked.

"Because I should never have taken the job in the first place." He scanned all their faces. "I knew my brother's reputation. I should've realized that despite my best efforts to remain apart from him, most people believe that blood wins out and that I would be willing to do anything for my family."

"But we're not most people, Maclean." Lord Keyes glanced across at Adam Fisher, who nodded. "We don't accept your resignation."

"I don't understand." Alistair frowned. "You obviously believe that I aided my brother and encouraged him to come here. And, in truth, you might be right. I have helped him far too readily in the past, but I have resolved not to do so anymore."

"You're not the only one." Adam Fisher sighed. "I could say exactly the same thing, and I don't have the excuse of a blood relationship. I've just been a fool. Harry didn't come to steal from you last night, Alistair, he came to steal from me."

"We found you in Mr. Fisher's office. Do you remember that?" Diana asked.

"It was dark and I wasn't sure exactly whose office I was in. I suppose I assumed it was mine because that's where I expected Harry to be."

"Harry stole a key from my desk a few months ago. I'd all but forgotten about it." Adam grimaced. "It proved to be a very costly mistake."

Coldness settled over Alistair's gut. "What did he steal?"

"Gold and some rather incriminating documents about some of the political leanings of the younger aristocracy." Adam's mouth twisted. "There were several items he could have chosen, but he seemed to know what he wanted."

"He's still my brother, sir. I am to blame for all of this."

Adam's smile was sweet. "No, you are not, Mr. Maclean. We can't choose our family and there are bad apples in all of them. I *chose* to consort with your brother. I am the fool here."

"You should not blame yourself. He is very hard to resist when he wants something."

Lord Keyes cleared his throat. "The question is, what will Harry do with these documents? Will he sell them to the highest bidder, or were they stolen for a particular buyer?"

"I would assume he knows who wants them," Alistair said. "Do you have copies of the documents, Mr. Fisher?"

"Yes, I do. They are in the bank vault."

"Then perhaps we should retrieve the copies and work out exactly who would want that information destroyed."

"Agreed." Lord Keyes stood up. "And in the meantime, if you can think of any place where your brother might hide out, please let me know."

"I will, my lord. I swear I will do everything in my power to repay your trust in me."

"I'm delighted to hear it." Keyes hesitated. "However, I must warn you that Harry will face serious charges if he is caught. I am not prepared to protect him from the consequences of his actions."

"I understand that, sir."

"Do you?" Keyes sighed. "In my own experience, learning of the betrayal by a family member is a lot more complicated than you might imagine. It is hard to cast off the shackles of loyalty."

"You managed to save your father, my lord."

"Only because he is already dying. I'm still not sure how I would've felt if I'd had to go to the king, denounce him, and watch him be tried by his peers."

"All I can say, my lord, is that I will do my best and that I will not betray my country or the Sinners."

"And that"—Lord Keyes smiled—"is as much as I can expect from any honest man." He clapped Alistair on the shoulder. "Now I must get back to my wife or she will be moving furniture or something else likely to be injurious to her current condition."

"Thank you, my lord."

Alistair sat down again and allowed the babble of conversation to carry on around him. They'd trusted him enough to let him keep his job. He was finding it difficult to comprehend his good fortune.

"Mr. Maclean, are you feeling quite well?"

He roused himself to answer the countess. "I have a slight headache, my lady."

"Then you should take yourself back to bed, and not worry about another thing for the rest of the day."

"I believe Mr. Fisher might have need of me."

"Not yet, Alistair. Go back to bed. If I need you, I know where you are," Adam said.

"Are you sure, sir?"

"Yes. I need to get the duplicate documents from the bank

and read through them. When I've done that, I'll have a better idea of what we need to do next."

"If you are quite certain, Mr. Fisher." With some care, Alistair rose to his feet. "I'll return to bed."

"Let me help you, Mr. Maclean." Diana tucked his hand into the crook of her arm. "I'll make sure he's comfortable and that someone sits with him, Mr. Fisher."

"Thank you."

Alistair tottered out of the room and barely managed the stairs with her help as his head pounded as loudly as a cannon bombardment. She put him to bed, helping him out of most of his clothes and giving him some of the medicine the apothecary had left by his bedside. By then, he could barely see and was more than grateful to lie down and have her bathe his forehead with warm water scented with her perfume.

"I didn't expect that."

"What?" she murmured.

"That they would allow me to keep my job. I thought . . . I *assumed* that I would be thrown out without a character. Harry's always done this to me. He uses people. I've tried so hard to make up for his behavior, to excuse the inexcusable, and in return all I've done is ally myself with him and lose my friends."

"But not this time. Lord Keyes and Mr. Fisher are not as easily swayed as most men."

"So it seems. I still can't believe my good fortune."

"You deserve it, Mr. Maclean. You are one of the most honest and hardworking men I've ever met."

He sighed and kissed her fingers. "And what of you? If our employers are exceptional men, why can't you tell them why you are here and what you want from them?"

"I cannot."

"Why not?"

"Because my issue is not with them, but with the Earl of

Westbrook." She drew an unsteady breath. "I took this job because I wanted to look for evidence against him."

"Evidence of what?"

"That he is my father."

Alistair opened his eyes and stared up at her. "Your *father*? You do share similar coloring, although his skin is much darker than yours."

"His mother was from India."

"So I understand. Did he ever acknowledge you as his child?"

"No."

"Then what brought you to believe that he *is* your father?"

She shrugged. "Family stories, and items that were left with me when I was boarded at the charity school."

"But you felt you needed more evidence and came here to find it."

"Yes. After my husband died I had the opportunity to look about me once more, and I decided to see if I could prove the rumors were true."

"Does Nicodemus know about this?"

"He does, but he won't help me anymore. He is loyal to the Sinners and to his employers." She smiled at him. "He is rather like you, actually."

"Which is why you've been searching the Sinners records on the top floor."

She eased back from him. "You know about that?"

"Maddon was concerned." He sought her hand again. "My lady, even if the earl is your father, what can he do for you now?"

"He can acknowledge me. He can apologize for abandoning my mother in Cornwall without a second thought."

"I've met the earl on many occasions, Diana. I can't imagine him behaving like that."

She pulled her hand free. "This was a long time ago. People

change. I understand that the countess has been a stabilizing influence on his wildness."

"So when he returns in a few days, you intend to confront him with little or no evidence and demand that he recognizes you as his offspring." He let out his breath. "You don't stand a chance."

"I have new evidence."

"That is conclusive proof of his guilt?"

"I believe so."

"But what of the countess?"

"What of her?"

"She will be hurt by this."

"She knew her husband was a rake before she married him. She must have assumed that he'd sown his wild oats."

"But knowing that, and seeing the living proof of it is bound to be upsetting for her."

"So I am supposed to remain silent so that the Countess of Westbrook isn't hurt?"

He sighed. "No, that isn't fair on you either, is it? I can't think of a way to make it better for both of you. Would you like me to speak to her before you speak to the earl?"

She framed his face in her hands. "No. I don't wish you to be involved in this at all."

"But—"

"You are already embroiled in one scandal with your brother. Do you seriously think you can stand to be involved in another? I am perfectly capable of dealing with this situation by myself. In fact, if you interfere in any way, I shall consider it a breach of promise."

"I haven't promised anything."

"But you will." She held his gaze.

"Perhaps we might compromise. You show me the new evidence against the earl, and I'll decide whether I think you have a just claim."

"It has nothing to do with you deciding anything."

"I understand that. What I meant was if I agree that you should proceed, I will keep quiet about it."

"And let me deal with the earl in my own way?"

"Yes."

She cocked her head to one side to study him, a lock of black hair falling over her face. "Why?"

"Because you have a right to know who your father is, and as much as I value the Sinners, I think that trumps all."

"Thank you." She leaned over him and kissed his nose and then his mouth. "I appreciate this more than I can say."

He closed his eyes against the emotion welling in her beautiful gaze. He didn't want her gratitude. He didn't deserve it.

She kissed him once more and then slid off the bed and left him to sleep. She might not think she owned him outside the bedroom, but he was beginning to think she was wrong. Trusting her to sort out the complicated matter of her parentage without damaging the Sinners was a big concession on his part. But it also meant he was absolved from having to fight for her . . .

He was tired of fighting.

Perhaps he was more of a coward than he realized after all.

16

There was something niggling in the back of Alistair's mind . . . something to do with the night of the robbery, but he couldn't quite work out what it was. He'd slept most of the day away and awakened feeling much better. He was currently in Adam Fisher's study as his employer went through the list of items he believed Harry had stolen from his desk.

"What I don't understand, Alistair, is why he picked that particular list of names and pieces of correspondence. None of the men mentioned are major figures of government, prominent courtiers, or aristocrats. It's more a list of minor nobility and younger sons who have flirted with the idea of political rebellion or expressed more radical opinions that their families usually espouse. The kind of fools who also chose to express such opinions in writing."

"Could such a list lead to convictions by the authorities?"

Adam glanced down at the copy he'd retrieved from the bank. "Not really. It's more a list we keep for ourselves than to share with anyone else. In certain circumstances, such information *might* prove useful as an incentive for a family to act or vote in a certain manner."

"Governmental blackmail, you mean?"

Adam shrugged. "I suppose you might call it that. It is very rarely needed and only when a situation is truly dire." He hesitated. "I did wonder if perhaps your brother was involved with the Jacobite cause. There are a few Scottish names on the list."

A familiar pang of old anger shot through Alistair's heart. "I doubt it. The only thing Harry is loyal to is himself."

"I tend to agree with you."

"He's more likely to blackmail those poor sods. Perhaps that's all this is. An attempt to safeguard his own future." Alistair looked up. "He could extort small sums of money from these minor peers for years, couldn't he, and live quite comfortably?"

"That's true. But how would he have known the list was here?"

"You did say he had a habit of looking through your drawers and taking what appealed to him," Alistair said gently. "He might have read the list previously and only recently decided to take it."

Adam sat down. "I'd be inclined to agree with you, but I only compiled this particular list a month ago, and your brother has never seen it."

"Unless he is working with someone within the Sinners, or has a way in to the house we don't know about," Alistair said.

"Or we go back to our original theory that he stole the list for someone else who did know their name was on it."

"Someone on that list? How many of those men are members of the Sinners?"

"None," Adam said flatly. "They are not the kind of men who generally choose to serve their king and country and thus have no right of entry here."

"Then should we contact them all and warn them that Harry might be calling, or do we investigate them as potential candidates for having acquired the list?"

"Neither. For the next few days, we simply have them watched."

"We have the men to do this?"

"We'll find them. There are less than a dozen names on the list. If nothing happens in the next week, we'll reconsider our options." Adam nodded. "Thank you, Alistair. You've been most helpful."

"If you wish, I'll summarize what we have just discussed and send copies to the countess and Lord Keyes."

"That would be much appreciated."

Alistair rose and went toward the door, pausing as he noticed a slight red patch on the carpet. Was that where he'd fallen after being hit? He suddenly remembered the blond man looking down at him, the soft, cultured voice . . .

"Mr. Fisher?"

"Yes?"

"Do you know who found me here on the night of the robbery?"

"I assumed it was Lady Theale. She was looking for you at the time."

Another image of the blond man resurfaced and Alistair went still.

"Are you all right, Alistair?"

"Yes, sir." He bowed and left the office. Instead of returning to his own, he made his way down to the kitchens to find Maddon.

"Maddon, do we have a blond member of staff here at the Sinners?"

"Male or female, sir?"

"Either."

"No, we do not, sir."

"The night of the entertainment, did you notice any blond guests?"

Maddon scratched his head. "That would be hard to say, sir, without looking at the guest list."

"Did we ever find that?"

"It was discovered in the entrance hall, sir, concealed under a vase of flowers. We're not sure if that was done deliberately, or if it was just overlooked."

"Do you still have it?"

Maddon rose to his feet. "I do, sir. It's in my rooms. Please follow me."

Alistair accompanied Maddon to the butler's suite at the rear of the basement. He waited impatiently as the butler unhurriedly put on his spectacles and sorted through a book filled with loose sheets.

"I keep all the guest lists, sir. Lady Westbrook asked me to."

"I'm glad she did."

"Ah, here it is. See?" He pointed at the sheet. "Dated and everything, Usually I tick off the names of the guests as they arrive, so there are no surprises. This time I had to start a separate list and write them all out again after we found the original."

"Do you have that too?"

Maddon produced another list. "Here you are, sir."

"Thank you." Alistair scanned both lists but saw no mention of Sir Ronald Fairbanks on either of them. "Now, can you remember whether any of the members on this list were blond?"

Maddon took his time reading the names. "Lord Perry is quite fair and the Honorable Angus McDawd, but that's all."

"And how old are those gentleman?"

"Lord Perry is in his late forties, and Angus McDawd is around your age, sir."

Alistair gathered up the lists. "You have been most helpful. May I borrow these?"

"Of course, sir."

"I'll be over at the pleasure house if anyone needs me."

"Are you sure you're well enough to go out, Mr. Maclean? You still look a bit pale."

"I'll be fine. I could do with some fresh air."

Alistair put on his hat and coat and walked briskly around to the pleasure house. It felt good to be outside even in the mist, which reminded him of home. He asked to see Christian and was taken through to the offices.

"You again, Mr. Maclean?" Christian stood up and waved Alistair to a seat. "I heard you were in the wars this week, and that your brother has returned."

"Who told you that?"

"I have my sources. What can I do for you?"

"The staff who attended the Roman orgy at the Sinners, were any of them blond?"

"I'm not sure. Is it important?"

"It might be. And this is a government matter, not merely a personal one, so I would appreciate your help."

"Then I'll check my records." Christian moved two books off a stack and pulled another one out. "Let me see . . ."

He looked up. "Three were fair. They were all in costume as slaves. Do you wish to see them? If you are patient you can observe all of them during the shift change."

"I would appreciate that." Alistair frowned. "Although I'm fairly certain that the person I saw wasn't dressed in costume . . ."

"Perhaps it was a member of your club?"

"I don't think so. It wasn't someone I recognized." But that wasn't quite true either, was it? Something about the blond man's voice had seemed familiar.

"Are you sure about that?"

"Yes, I have an excellent memory for faces. I suppose one of your staff could've changed out of costume and come across me when they were leaving," Alistair mused.

"Where exactly were you?"

"Lying on the floor of an office bleeding."

Christian winced. "I doubt anyone from here would've been wandering around your offices, Mr. Maclean, clothed or unclothed. If they were, I will not be employing them anymore."

The clock on the mantelpiece struck four times and Christian stood. "Come down to the kitchens with me."

Alistair went down into the familiar kitchen of the pleasure house and took up a discreet position under the stairs where he could observe the staff leaving for the day and those arriving to receive their orders for the night. It wasn't difficult for him to spot the men Christian had mentioned. All three of them looked vaguely familiar, but none of them were the face of the man who had leaned over him as he lay on the floor.

With a sigh he glanced around the kitchen to tell Christian that he didn't need to speak to anyone. The back door swung open and another blond entered through the scullery. Something about the angle of the head alerted Alistair. He pushed off from the wall and followed the blond up the servants' staircase at a discreet distance. After three flights of stairs, he was starting to puff and his headache had returned.

He paused on a narrow landing to catch his breath, glancing to his left and then his right at the angled passageway under the roof of the house. He guessed he was in the staff quarters. There was a strip of old carpet down the center of the wooden floor, but the paintwork was fresh and the ceiling free of leaks.

With another look to the left, he took a wary step forward and flinched as the door beside him opened and a pistol was rammed against the back of his head.

"Mr. Maclean."

"Not again."

He was surprised when his captor chuckled. "You should be grateful that I didn't hit you with the barrel of my pistol right on that nasty cut you have over your ear."

"You still could, which is why I am standing very still."

"You might as well come in. I doubt you'll leave until you know the truth."

He let out his breath as the pistol was lowered and he turned toward the blond standing in the doorway.

"I'm Charlie. Come in."

Alistair accepted the invitation and went to sit on the bed in the small, cramped room. His companion took the chair by the fire and placed the pistol on the table.

"That's not the first time you've held a pistol to my head."

"You're very observant, Mr. Maclean."

"I am when my life is at stake. Why do you choose to dress as a man?"

"You don't think I'm a man?"

Alistair allowed his gaze to drop from Charlie's amused face to her narrow, elegant frame and endless legs.

"You are far too beautiful to be male."

Charlie shrugged off his compliment. "Some of our customers like it. Most of them are gentlemen who are too afraid to give in to their true feelings for their own valets and convince themselves that having a woman *dressed* as their valet will do just as well."

"I doubt it's as simple as that."

She regarded him with her clear gray eyes. "You might be right. Now, what do you want from me?"

"If you truly were the person who found me at the Sinners, why didn't you follow through on your earlier threats and finish me off? I've scarcely tried to help you find my brother or succeeded in warning him off."

"Because that wasn't what I'd been paid to do last night."

"I thought you were paid to warn me and then disappear?"

"That was last time." She raised her eyebrows. "This was a *separate* commission."

"Then what were you doing in the Sinners?"

"Looking for your brother, of course. Unfortunately, I just missed him." She fixed him with an innocent stare. "In truth, you should be more grateful to me. If I hadn't arrived, your brother might have decided to kill you himself."

"Harry didn't touch me."

"He had an accomplice? Someone from the Sinners, perhaps?"

"I don't think so. We check our staff very carefully indeed. How did you know that Harry might turn up at the Sinners?"

"Because you are there." She sighed. "He always comes back to you, doesn't he?"

Alistair had nothing he wanted to say to that.

"And Adam Fisher, of course," Charlie added. "Harry hasn't quite forgiven him for refusing to give him any more money."

"You seem to know my brother very well."

"I've learned a lot about him over the years." Charlie's smile died. "Nothing I've learned has endeared him to me in the slightest."

"You are not alone. My brother is an expert at letting people down."

"You sound bitter, Mr. Maclean."

"Wouldn't you be?" He met her skeptical gaze head-on. "My brother is a thief and a liar who is loyal to no one. What do you want him for, and what is your connection to Sir Ronald Fairbanks?"

"Sir Ronald?"

"Harry's latest lover. I saw you with him at the Sinners."

"I was hardly *with* him. I heard he knew where Harry was, so I kept a close eye on him throughout the event."

"Is he your client?"

"In what sense? He tried to fuck me a few times when he was a member here, but obviously not since he's been banned."

"You haven't answered my question."

She leaned forward, her eyes narrowed. "Mr. Maclean, I will do anything to find Harry. I will use *anyone*. He destroyed someone I loved. My suggestion is that we don't fight each other, but concentrate on finding your brother."

"So that you can do what? Hand him over to your 'client' or kill him yourself?"

"Are you defending him now? Hasn't he done enough to make you hate him as well? I understand that he was the one who betrayed your father to the authorities for treasonable Jacobite leanings."

"That . . . was not proven."

"I can prove it, Mr. Maclean." She looked up at him.

"I'd rather my brother was officially charged and tried by a court than by you or any of his other associates."

"So you do intend to bring him to justice?"

"If I must."

She nodded. "I actually believe you. If you have any information you would like to share with me, please don't hesitate to seek me out. And even though you haven't asked it of me, I will endeavor to do the same."

Alistair slowly stood up. "I will not allow you to kill my brother, ma'am."

"Then it is in your best interests to keep an eye on me, and make sure that I don't."

He bowed. "Indeed."

"Good day, Mr. Maclean."

"Ma'am."

He closed the door behind him and took a deep breath. The ceiling suddenly felt too close and he hurried down the stairs, his right hip aching, taking over the complaining as his headache abated.

What did Charlie want and whom was she allied to? Or was she simply so focused on finding Harry that she'd jump in bed with the devil if he promised to help her? He wasn't sure. The only thing he did know was that if his brother did meet Charlie he might be in serious danger. There had been something in her eyes that he recognized—a familiarity with death and the knowledge of how to kill without mercy.

Alistair shuddered and went through into the kitchens where Christian sat at the kitchen table.

"I take it you didn't find your man?"

"I found him." Alistair put on his hat and gloves. "Thank you for your help."

"You are welcome." Christian raised his cup of ale in a salute.

By the time Alistair got back to the Sinners, his headache was raging and he was longing for the peace and quiet of his bed. Maddon and an anxious Lady Westbrook met him in the back hallway.

"My dear Alistair, wherever have you been?"

"Over to the pleasure house. I did tell Mr. Maddon." Alistair suddenly felt like a schoolboy again. "Is there something I can help you with, my lady?"

She tucked her hand in the crook of his arm and walked with him up the stairs. "I was just worried about you venturing forth with your head in such a state."

"It feels much better today, my lady. We Scots are a tough race."

"That is true." She patted his arm. "Diana was looking for you earlier."

"Is she still in her office? I'll go and see what she wants."

"No, she went out to see Malinda. She did tell me that she'd left some documents on your desk."

"Then I'll go into my office and make sure that everything is all right."

"Then you must promise me that you will take yourself off to bed. I'll have Maddon bring you up some supper on a tray later."

"Thank you, my lady."

He managed to detach himself from her before he went into his office and shut the door. His desk was buried in a new layer of documents, books, and letters. With a groan he settled in his chair and began sorting out the mess. He might not stay awake long enough to complete every task, but he would at least attempt to prioritize the information and avoid missing anything urgent. He drew the first packet of letters toward himself and cut the seal.

"Mr. Maclean isn't in his bedroom, Mr. Maddon," Diana said.

"Are you sure, my lady? Lady Westbrook advised him to go to bed hours ago."

"Maybe he slept for a while and got up again." Diana looked back at the corridor, which held the Sinners Club offices. "I'll go and see if he's still at his desk."

She took the candle Maddon offered her and made her way to Alistair's room. There was no light under the door, but she went in anyway. A dark form was slumped over the desk. With a soft sound, she hurried over and placed the candlestick on the crowded surface.

"Mr. Maclean? Are you all right?" She crouched down next to him and gently shook his arm.

He opened his green eyes and peered at her intently. "My lady."

"You were supposed to be asleep in your bed."

"I had too much to do."

She smoothed her hand over his rumpled auburn locks. "You are far too efficient and far too careless of your health."

"I had a lot to do." He yawned and sat up, wincing as he stretched out his shoulders. "What time is it?"

"Almost ten." Diana hesitated. "Did you see the book I left for you?"

"No, I don't think I did. Where exactly did you put it?"

She stood and studied the now neat piles on his desk. "It was right here." She picked the candle up and directed the light more fully on the space. "A large brown leather book."

He waved a vague hand at one corner of the desk. "I stacked all the books here."

She leaned over and sorted through the pile, which he'd arranged in order of size, until she reached the second from last book and hauled it free.

"Here you are."

"I'll take it up to bed with me and read it there."

"I've marked the page of interest."

"Thank you."

She lingered at his side touching things on the desk, which he immediately returned to their original places. "The earl is due back soon."

"I am aware of that. Don't worry. I'm well enough to read the evidence tonight and give you my opinion tomorrow."

"There's no hurry. The proof is fairly damming." She gave him a calm smile. "I don't wish you to tire yourself out for my benefit."

He smiled back at her through the flicker of the candlelight. "That's not what you normally say."

Gathering her skirts, she turned to the door. "I have no intention of taking you to bed until you feel much more the thing."

"I appreciate that."

He followed her to the door and she turned to look at him. Reaching up, she traced a finger over his lush lower lip.

"I don't intend to wait forever, though, so please take care of yourself and don't work too hard."

He hesitated. "Will you . . . find someone else while you wait?"

"And have to start all over again? I'm not sure I have the energy to deal with another exhausting male. Mr. Maclean, before you go I must say this." She cupped his jaw. "If the Earl of Westbrook throws me out on the street, I expect you to let me fall alone."

He opened his mouth, but she stopped him speaking with the hard press of her fingers. "I do *not* expect you to support me in this matter. I want you to retain your job and your loyalty to the Sinners."

He pulled her hand away. "But what if I don't want to do that?"

"I'm not giving you a choice. You can't afford to lose this job. I can. I'm not supporting my family and a wastrel of a brother. And when I leave, Mr. Maclean, I do not intend to see you again."

He raised a sardonic eyebrow. "You seem to have it all planned out."

"Of course I do. I'm very efficient. Isn't that why I was hired to work here in the first place?"

"You were hired because the countess and Lady Malinda felt sorry for your situation."

"And we both know that I took advantage of that pity for my own ends."

"Yes, we damn well do."

God that hurt. She raised her chin. "I have plenty of friends who will make sure that I survive."

"And will you return to whoring?" His green eyes were as hard as flint.

She shrugged. "If I choose to do so."

"Or find another rich fool to marry you?"

"I will do what I want to do, Mr. Maclean, *and* what I *need* to do to survive."

"Rather than accept any type of support or protection from me."

"I doubt you can afford me on your salary." She forced herself to smile up at him. "I certainly haven't asked for any support from you."

"Because you don't consider me capable of offering any, do you?"

She met his suddenly furious gaze. "I know what you are, and I know what you need in your life."

"You know what I need in *bed*, but that doesn't make you an expert of everything about me, my lady."

"Then you'd rather I said, 'Alistair, when the earl throws me out, come with me. We can live on the streets together.' "

"It wouldn't come to that."

"But what if it did?" She searched his face. "You'd hate it. I have no intention of being poor again, and I swear to God I will never drag you down with me."

"I would find another job. I could take care of you."

"Not in London. If you left with me, the Earl of Westbrook and your employers could make finding employment impossible. Mayhap even employment in the whole of Britain."

"Now you are exaggerating."

"Maybe I am, but I can't allow you to beggar yourself and your family because of me."

"Because you don't need any help and even if you did, you wouldn't ask for it."

She wrapped her arms around herself. "This is a ridiculous conversation."

"You started it."

"I just wanted to warn you that if things didn't go well, you were under no obligation to spring to my defense," she said tiredly.

"Why not?"

"Haven't we just discussed that?"

"Why would you assume I wouldn't defend you?" He moved a step away and stared down at her.

"Because no one ever has in the past." She raised her head. "And that's perfectly fine because it taught me a lot about how to survive."

"But also made it impossible for you to trust anyone or let anyone help you."

"You are the one with the issues of trust, Mr. Maclean."

He smiled at her. "I don't think I'm the only one. Good night, Lady Theale."

He walked away, leaving her staring after him, her mouth open like a fool. How dare he misinterpret her kindly advice for him not to lose his job over her and manipulate it into something different? How dare he suggest she was unable to trust anyone? She trusted Charlotte, and Nico and . . . lots of other people. Did he have any idea how it felt to be dumped on the pavement and told to go away? How *terrifying* that was?

The fact that she and Charlotte had survived their first night on the streets was a miracle in itself. They'd been discovered by the manager of the pleasure house huddling in a doorway and brought back to Elizabeth Delornay. She'd taken them in and offered them decent work until they'd both decided to seek employment in the more lucrative part of the pleasure house itself.

She refused to be ashamed of her self-sufficiency.

She *refused.*

And if she had to strike out on her own again, she'd do it and damn the Earl of Westbrook and the Sinners. Damn Alistair Maclean too.

17

Alistair set the book down on his bed and tore savagely at his cravat. Diana Theale was *infuriating*. Her calm insistence that she could take care of herself, that she didn't need him, that she had friends . . . made him want to curse, haul her into his arms, and never let her go. And she wasn't even doing it to entrap him, he knew that. She genuinely believed she didn't need anyone to survive.

Especially him.

He left the rest of his clothes in a pile on the floor and put on his nightshirt. Despite everything, the pain in his skull had dimmed to a more manageable throbbing hum, which was almost bearable. He'd be fine in a day or so. Just in time to see the return of the Earl of Westbrook and Diana's attempt to force the man to acknowledge that he was her father.

With that unpleasant thought, he turned to the book she'd given him, lit more candles, and placed his spectacles on the end of his nose. After falling asleep for four hours at his desk, he was hardly tired. Anger and frustration made uneasy bedfellows.

He wasn't even sure why he was angry. She didn't owe him

anything. Her task in his life was to offer him the best sexual release he had ever experienced and that she performed superbly. He should be damned grateful that she wanted nothing more. After assuming responsibility for his family at fourteen, he normally shied away from taking on any other burdens, especially emotional ones. Dealing with two younger sisters and his mother hadn't been easy. He loved them all dearly, but he was always conscious of failing to protect his father from the authorities and afraid he would fail them too.

With a sigh, Alistair climbed into bed, propped the musty old book on his knees, and turned his attention to the problem in hand. . . .

Five minutes later, he threw back the covers, found his tattered silk banyan, and put in on. With the book under his arm, he made his way through the quiet corridors until he reached Diana's door.

"Lady Theale?"

She opened the door an inch and stared down her nose at him. "Yes?"

"May I come in?"

"If you must." She walked away from him and began to unpin her hair. "I hope you have come to apologize."

"No, actually, I haven't."

She sat down at her dressing table and continued to remove the pins, her movements unhurried. He put the book down and walked over to her.

"May I?" He gestured at her hairbrush.

"If you wish."

He picked up the brush and began to comb it through her luscious black locks. A hint of her perfume warmed the air, and he was instantly hard. She removed her earrings and unclasped her pearls from around her slender throat. He thought of the collar with his name on it, and wished he was wearing it right now.

She glanced at him in the mirror. "You're supposed to be

sleeping in your own bed, Mr. Maclean, not thinking lustful thoughts about occupying mine."

"How do you know they are lustful?"

She reached back and stroked the worn silk of his robe where his cock had raised the fabric like a tent pole. "You're hard."

"You have that effect on me."

"Even when you're angry?"

"Especially when I'm angry, and tied up and begging you to . . ." He resumed brushing her hair. "If I owe you an apology, I am quite happy to offer you one. I do understand about surviving."

"I doubt that, Mr. Maclean. You come from an aristocratic background and probably had the best of everything."

"Hardly. My father was accused of treason against the Hanoverian crown and dragged out of our home by English soldiers, who hung him and then burned the place down. I was reduced to running into the flames to save anything I could before the whole place came down on top of me. Some of the soldiers stood around laughing and placing bets on whether I'd survive."

He put the brush down on the dressing table. "When they finally dispersed, I had to find shelter for my mother and two sisters. It wasn't easy. None of our neighbors would help us at first for fear of reprisals. We spent several weeks living in a cave while I and some of the Maclean men made a small cottage on the edge of the castle grounds habitable."

"I . . . didn't realize that."

"Why would you?" His smile held no humor in it. "Trying to survive a Scottish winter with almost nothing to eat and three females to feed was extremely trying."

"Where was your brother, Harry?"

"He was in England."

She turned around to study him. "At school?"

"No. He was under the protection of the family he'd betrayed our father to."

Her hand came to rest on her heart. "Harry informed against his own *father?*"

"He didn't like him. He told me later that he wanted to hurt him."

"But by acting against your father, he almost destroyed the rest of you."

"That wasn't important to him. He didn't want to be cold and hungry and live like a pauper in Scotland. The money he received paid for his education and kept him safe and secure for several years."

"I don't understand how you can bear to look at him, let alone defend him."

He moved away from the dressing table to stare out of the window and then closed the curtains. "My father was a loud-mouthed fool who proclaimed his hatred of the English crown whenever offered the opportunity. If it hadn't have been Harry betraying him, it would've been somebody else."

"But still—"

Alistair shrugged. "It's all in the past. My mother and sisters are well housed and happy now."

She rose from her seat and presented him with her back, so he undid the buttons of her dress and then untied her corset. Her nightgown was hanging on the chair closest to the fire, so he handed it to her and waited as she put it on.

"If you didn't come here to apologize, what did you want?"

"To ask you about this." He picked up the book. "Are you quite certain you marked the correct page? I couldn't find any references to you at all."

"What do you mean? I indicated the place quite clearly." Her expression changed and she grabbed the heavy tome from his hands and put it on the bed. She found the red ribbon and opened the book wide.

"There's nothing there. That's not right."

"As I said."

She started flipping the pages back and forth and then turned to him. "I don't understand."

"I suspect from the fresh paper cut between the pages you marked that someone removed the evidence."

"But who would do that? Who knew what to look for?" Diana shook her head and sank down onto the side of the bed.

"At what time did you put the book on my desk?"

"It was just after one this afternoon."

"And while I was out, my office was open. Anyone could've been in there and found the damned book." He sighed. "It does make me think that someone employed here is working against the Sinners rather than for us." He sat down next to Diana and patted her hand. "It's all right."

"No, it isn't. That was the first piece of evidence I've ever found with the Earl of Westbrook's name on it."

"What exactly did it say?"

"That he paid my school fees." She looked up at him. "I thought I was a charity pupil. I was certainly treated like one."

He frowned. "But, even so, how did you end up in the pleasure house?"

"Our school was closed down when I was fourteen. The debt collectors came in at the same time as the parents arrived to pick up their children and started putting everything that they could get into their carts. By the end of the day, everyone had been collected except me and Charlotte." She sighed. "We begged for help, but no one listened. Eventually one of the bailiffs drove us out onto the street and threatened to beat us if we didn't clear off."

"The earl didn't come for you, I take it?"

"Obviously not. We were lucky that Ambrose from the pleasure house found us that night. He took us to Elizabeth, and she paid for us to board with a family of Methodists Ambrose knew.

When we were older, we both decided we'd like to work in the pleasure house."

"And now that evidence has disappeared." Alistair frowned. "I still don't understand why the earl didn't know what happened to the school, or what had befallen you. He's the head of a vast network of spies and informers. Surely he would have been able to locate you?"

"I've wondered about that too." She hesitated. "Perhaps he did know where I was and chose to abandon me there. Perhaps he has no idea that I exist at all."

Alistair had no answer for that, but he squeezed her hand hard. "I'm sorry I wasn't at my desk when you put the book there."

"You couldn't have known."

"But who did? Who knew what that book contained, Diana?"

"You, me, Charlotte, and . . ." She raised her troubled gaze to his. "Nico. He's the person who found the book in the first place. But why would he give Charlotte the evidence and then take it back? Did he really not want her to share it with me?"

She jumped up and started to pace the room. "And Nico isn't here, anyway, is he? How can it be him?"

"We don't know if he's here. We just haven't seen him. Maddon will know if he's been in the house. I can go and ask him right now."

"It's too late and we'll achieve nothing at this hour anyway." She swung around to face him. "You do believe what I'm saying, don't you?"

"You would scarcely give me a book with nothing in it, would you? The fact that someone felt the need to tamper with the evidence means it probably has value."

"Thank you."

He raised an eyebrow. "For what?"

"For believing me." She took a shaky breath. "I didn't expect it."

"Then I'm glad I surprised you." He slid off the side of the bed and pulled back the covers. "You should sleep."

She came toward him, the lush curves of her body outlined through the glow of the fire. "Will you stay?"

"I can't be of much use to you."

"Your head is still troubling you?"

He touched the wound behind his ear. "I'm recovering nicely. Scotsmen have very hard heads."

She stroked a finger down his arm. "I'll probably have nightmares about being thrown out on the street if I'm alone."

"Then I'll keep you company, as long as you wake me up if I have nightmares of my own."

She took his hand and kissed his palm. "Take off your banyan, Mr. Maclean."

"Yes, my lady." He untied the sash and let the garment fall to the floor. His cock refused to admit defeat and was stubbornly erect. "After you."

She climbed into the bed, and he blew out the candles and joined her. She pushed him onto his back and curled against his side, one hand low on his flat stomach.

"I like you hard for me, Mr. Maclean."

"So you said, my lady. You wanted me to be ready whenever you wanted to fuck me."

"Mmm . . ." Her fingers drifted lower, and he sucked in a breath. "That could be most inconvenient for you."

"I'd manage if that was your will."

"And if it was my will that you couldn't come? Would you accept that too?"

Her fingers loosely encircled the root of his shaft.

"I'd do my best." He swallowed hard. "Although coming inside you is . . ." His breath hissed out as she tightened her grip, her nails digging into his tender flesh. "Coming *for* you is far more gratifying."

"For me or for you?"

"I would hope for both of us." He licked his lips. "When I'm hard for you and I feel as if my balls are so tight, so ready to come that I can't hold on one more second, you make me wait. Sometimes I'm screaming inside and my cock is so stiff that I . . . I think one touch from you will make me climax. I yearn for that touch and yet I fear it at the same time because I want to please you and stay hard."

"You do please me. I love seeing you fight against your own needs to satisfy mine. I love seeing you hard when you can't have release." She relaxed her grip. "It gives me great pleasure to know that you are wet and ready for me. It makes me wet too."

He shuddered as she slid one leg over his thigh and he felt the sultry heat of her sex against his skin.

"Do you wish me to give you pleasure, my lady?"

"Not if it's going to make your head ache." Her laugh was low and made his cock even stiffer. "I think I'll take what I need from you, Mr. Maclean. But you aren't to move at all—especially your head." She raised herself off him and he bit back a protest. "In fact, maybe I should tie you down so that you can't move at all."

He kept still as she got out of bed and went to the chest of drawers in the corner of the room. Using the embers of the fire, she lit a candle and placed it at the side of the bed.

"Now I can see what I'm doing." She showed him the coils of silken rope in her hands. "Lie still."

She tied one of the ropes to the bed frame and drew it across his upper arms and chest, securing it on the far side of the bed. She slid an extra pillow behind his head and another underneath his arse and then tied another rope across his hips in the same manner. Touching his knees, she drew them wide apart until his thighs touched the sheets and then drew his feet up until they almost met in the center.

"Are you comfortable, Mr. Maclean?"

"Yes, my lady."

She tied his ankles together first and then brought the ends of the rope higher, sliding it under his knees and binding each wrist to each thigh. His fingers splayed against his spread thighs as if he was holding himself open wide for her gaze. He tried to ease the stress on his back but only added additional pressure on his ankles and upper thighs.

She stood to one side and considered him, her expression thoughtful, at least two more coils of rope still in her hand. He tried to breathe slowly, but he could feel the rope tightening against his chest. She leaned in and adjusted the top rope so that it ran right over his nipples making them throb along with his raised heartbeat.

"You look beautiful, Mr. Maclean, legs spread for me, cock hard. I could do anything I want and you wouldn't be able to stop me."

"I . . . wouldn't stop you anyway."

"How is your headache?"

He smiled at her. "I'd completely forgotten I had one."

"That's good." She looped a thinner silk rope around the one that bound his hips to the bed and brought it down between his legs crossing it under his cock and balls and then under his arse and bringing it back around to the front. "Be still."

He groaned for the first time when she brought the ends of the rope up and tied them around the back of his neck. His cock and balls were pushed upward now and out. Wetness gleamed on the tip of his crown as the subtle pull of the rope took hold.

"Can you see yourself, Mr. Maclean? On display for me or anyone else I choose to allow to see you this way?"

"Yes," he whispered.

"Do you like it?"

"Yes."

She tugged gently on the finer rope making his cock kick up.

"I like it too. One day, when we have more time, I'll tie you up like this and leave you all day, so that I can come back and see that you remain hard for me at all times."

A gush of pre-cum flooded down over his shaft, and she gathered some of it on her fingers and licked it into her mouth, which made him yearn helplessly toward her.

"I wonder if the staff would touch you too? Finger your nipples, play with your cock, avail themselves of your mouth?" She traced his lips with her damp fingers. "Because you wouldn't be able to stop them, would you?"

He shook his head as he imagined being played with, sucking cock, and being unable to do anything about it. He tried to move his hips, but there was no give in the ropes at all. Nowhere to go, nowhere to hide. He was completely at her mercy.

Diana stroked Alistair's hair out of his eyes, her fingers careful. "I would expect you to give everything you were asked for apart from your come." She licked her lips at the picture he made. His hard muscled body pinned to the bed, his hands helpless against his own thighs. His cock . . . God, his cock on display for her, his pre-cum soaking into the silken rope and darkening the color from blue to navy.

It would be an exhilarating sight to come home to every night. She couldn't ever imagine not thinking that, or dreaming up new ways to make him vulnerable to her, to make him see that she was the only woman who would ever master him. But there was still a long way to go before he was truly able to trust her completely.

She crawled up onto the bed and knelt up between his wide-open knees so he could see her without lifting his head. Pulling her nightgown over her head, she cupped her breasts, watched his eyes widen and fasten on the sight of her hard nipples. She pinched them and rolled them between her finger and thumb. His tongue came out to lick his lips as if he was fantasizing that he was the one sucking her. Holding his gaze, she let her fingers drop lower to her sex. She gasped as she touched her swollen bud and then moved lower, finding her own juices and using them to penetrate her cunt.

"I know you want to do this, Mr. Maclean, but you can't. You are just going to have to watch me."

His whole body tightened as if he was going to try and throw off his bounds and then he seemed to remember himself and settle back, his breathing harsh, and his hands still on his thighs.

To reward him, she leaned forward and brought her soaking wet fingers to his mouth. She enjoyed his groan as she smeared her juices on his lips and then allowed him to suck them clean. His cock rested against her stomach, moving against her as he sucked. But he couldn't thrust at all. She stayed where she was, her knees hugging his arms and resumed finger fucking herself.

"This is a lesson in self-control, Mr. Maclean. The more you fight the ropes, the tighter they will become. I want you to relax. I want you quiet and watching me. All I expect to be hard is your cock."

"I can't—"

His stomach muscles flexed as she rubbed her wet fingers over his warm skin. "Take a deep breath and let it out slowly. Lie back and enjoy watching me and do not expect anything for yourself."

"That is . . . hard for me to do."

She smiled as she circled a finger around her clit and shuddered. "I've already told you. The only thing I want hard about you is your cock. Give in to the ropes, Mr. Maclean. Accept that you are bound and at my mercy, and that I can do anything I want with you. Accept the restraints and enjoy them."

She eased back until the very tip of his cock was wedged against her clit and held still. "My will, my choice."

He held her gaze as his breathing slowed and he sank back

down into the bed, the rope marks on his wrists and ankles lessening.

"Very good, Mr. Maclean." She undulated her hips, pressing the crown of his cock hard against her needy clit and allowed herself to come, knowing he'd feel the throb of it through her clit but not as much as he desired.

She experimented a little more, gripping his cock and guiding it around her clit and pussy lips in a slow finger of eight but not allowing him inside. He remained quietly on the bed, only the occasional tremor running through his strong frame as she played with him.

God, she wanted that big cock inside her, but how to ensure he stayed still? She glanced over at her dressing table and moved off the bed.

"Don't move."

Not that he could, but she wanted him to remain in the same calm state. His gaze widened as she returned to him holding her long-handled hairbrush and a thin red ribbon. She placed the bristles of the brush against his balls, leaving the handle parallel to his cock. Using the red ribbon, she bound his shaft to the wooden handle.

He looked . . . Diana sat back and admired the view before rubbing her finger over his shaft and spreading his pre-cum wide. He remained quiet under her hands, which made her want to smile. This was the first time she'd felt he was truly hers; his fighting spirit aligned with pleasing her rather than thwarting her every suggestion. Perhaps he needed to be hit on the head more often . . .

"My lady?"

His voice was hoarse with need, the Scottish burr much in evidence.

"Yes, Mr. Maclean?"

"You look very beautiful tonight."

"Owning you?"

"Aye."

"Then lie very still because I haven't finished yet."

She straddled his hips and carefully positioned herself over his ribbon-clad cock and slowly let him inside her, the smooth wood of the brush handle widening her along with the already considerable girth of his cock.

They both groaned and he sucked in his stomach muscles as she took him deep, imagining the way the bristles of the brush were pressing against his already-primed-to-come balls.

"Ah, God . . ." he breathed. "That's . . ."

"Tell me." She held still, getting used to the throb of his cock and the hardness of the rigid wood inside her.

"I . . . can't move my cock. I can't change the angle even if I could move my hips. If I tried the bristles would press into my balls like a thousand stinging needles."

"So what do you think you should do, Mr. Maclean?"

He opened his eyes wide and looked at her. "Lie still and let you fuck me?"

She squeezed her internal muscles hard. "Well done." And then she began to move carefully up and down his trapped and bound shaft until she climaxed and held still, her arms braced on his shoulders as the waves of pleasure thundered through her.

He moaned when she moved off him, his cock suddenly cold and exposed after the burning heat of her clenching cunt. She undid the rope across his hips and then the one across his chest, followed by the one around his ankles.

"Kneel up, Mr. Maclean."

It was hard for him to manage without the use of his hands, which were still bound to his thighs. It was also difficult to bend his knees after them being so wide apart, but he managed it eventually. She retied his ankles, which were now behind him, to the rope that wound around his arse and trapped his hands on his thighs.

"Look at me."

He raised his head and felt the knot of the rope around his neck tighten and the corresponding pull on his balls where the hairbrush bristles still prickled against his skin.

She touched him. Her hands sliding over his heated skin, shaping his muscles, the curve of his arse and thigh, the flat planes of his stomach. His cock throbbed along with his heart-beat as he remembered to breathe slowly and to simply enjoy the moment of her stroking him as if he were a prized stallion. He felt safe. . . .

The scent of her desire floated up to him from his cock, mixed with his own need, making him even harder. He thought he groaned in protest when she stopped touching him.

His gaze dropped to his cock, where she was carefully untying the red ribbon. He couldn't help thrusting a little into her hand as his shaft was released from the rigid prison of the wood and the scratching torture of the bristles.

"What would you like me to do with this brush, Mr. Maclean? Fuck you or spank you?"

He couldn't speak, his mouth dry with anticipation.

"Or perhaps, this?"

He bit back a growl as she stroked the brush down the rigid length of his cock and then back up and over the straining crown. She did it again and his hips bucked forward, fucking the brush and her moving fingers. And then he forgot how to breathe as she kept going until he was incapable of keeping still or being silent.

Pleasure and plain crowded his senses until he could no longer watch, just experience the need to come, to not come, to soak her hand in his seed, but not disappoint her . . .

"Come for me, Mr. Maclean."

He obeyed without conscious thought, his whole body letting go and just becoming a rutting animal with no purpose other than releasing his come. She reached for him and brought his head down onto her shoulder, offering him support and something to hold on to, to withstand the onslaught.

Even while he struggled to breathe, she was busy untying him until there was nothing holding him in place except her body, her arms lowering him to the bed and surrounding him. He started to shake and she enfolded him in her embrace, drawing his head to her breasts until a wave of exhaustion swept over him and he shuddered through a yawn.

Her fingers tangled in his hair.

"You must remind me not to force your weight onto your injured leg."

"I didn't feel a thing."

"You will tomorrow. I could see the muscles starting to knot and tighten."

"Is that why you stopped?"

"Please don't stiffen up like that, Mr. Maclean. I don't want to hurt you when you are with me. I have a duty to take care of you." Her voice was soft in the darkness. "I achieved exactly what I wanted. Did you?"

He opened his mouth to argue and then closed it again. "I didn't fight against my restraints. I've always enjoyed doing that. It felt . . . strange to lie quietly. The pleasure I gained from doing as you asked me was different but equally satisfying in its own way."

"I'm glad to hear it." She yawned. "Now we should sleep."

"You still wish me to stay?"

She kissed the top of his head. "Yes."

He rolled onto his back and she lay half across him, one knee perilously close to his aching cock. His headache appeared to have gone, but he suspected it would return after the pleasure of his release dimmed. She was the first woman he'd ever chosen to stay and share a bed with since his wife had died. It felt surprisingly right.

"Do you prefer to be restrained, Mr. Maclean?"

Her sleepy question made him open his eyes again. "If I am being honest, yes." He hesitated, the darkness encouraging him to tell her the truth. "I used to dream about being naked and tied up, and being torn between being ashamed that my cock was hard and wet and that everyone could see me like that and . . . wanting them to see me, to touch and fondle me against my will, to make me even harder and wetter."

"There is nothing to be ashamed of, Mr. Maclean." She kissed him. "I like to see you tied up and hard as well."

"If you are there, it would make it even better."

"Why is that?"

"Because I'd be doing it for you as well as myself."

She chuckled. "And you mention this when we are both exhausted."

"I'm sorry my lady, perhaps I shouldn't have—"

She pressed her fingers to his lips. "You must always tell me what you desire. How else can I give it to you? Now go to sleep."

He kissed her fingers and obeyed. Tomorrow would bring the earl closer and the hunt for evidence back to the fore, but for tonight, he would do as his lady told him, and simply sleep sheltered in her arms.

18

"Yes, my lady. I did see Mr. Theale yesterday. Did you wish to speak to him?" Maddon asked.

"No, I just wondered if he had returned from his travels." Diana forced herself to smile at the butler. "I'm sure he'll be in to see me fairly soon."

Maddon bowed and left leaving Diana contemplating the door. Would Nico come and find her? If he didn't, was that an indication of his guilt?

There was a tap on the door, and her questions were answered with a speed that normally never happened as Nico came in, his expression grave, one hand already reaching for his notebook in his pocket.

"Nico."

He took a seat. "Diana. How are you?"

"As well as might be expected when my rat of a stepson steals the evidence I need to find my father."

"I didn't—"

"Don't lie to me. Only four of us knew what that book contained."

"Four?" He frowned. "Who else did you tell?"

"Mr. Maclean."

"Oh dear. Was that wise?"

She glared at him. "Are you suggesting Mr. Maclean stole the page from the book and then came to tell me about it?"

Nico shrugged. "That's what I would've done."

"Even if that was what he *intended* to do, it was too late, wasn't it? Why did you give the information to Charlotte if you didn't want me to have it after all?"

"It's complicated."

"Then you do admit to stealing it back!"

"I thought that knowing the Westbrook family had been involved in paying for your schooling would be enough for you to drop the matter and move on with your life."

"What gave you the right to make such a decision for me?"

"Because I don't want you getting hurt!" He glared right back at her. "There is no point in forcing the Westbrook family to recognize you. You've already told me you don't want money, or anything tangible from them, so why push the issue? You think you know the truth. Why not be satisfied with that?"

Diana studied him for a long moment. "What are you keeping from me?"

"A suspicion. A sense that there is more to this than meets the eye."

"Do you have evidence to support this feeling?"

"That's what I've been trying to do this week. Find concrete proof."

"About what?"

He sighed. "I'm not telling you. It's so far-fetched that even I can't believe I'm thinking it."

"Nico . . . you have to tell me. This is unfair."

He let out a long breath. "It's just this. Perhaps it wasn't the earl who had a child but his wife."

"Faith?"

"Yes. Maybe she was the one trying to conceal her past."

Diana found herself moving. "Then perhaps I should simply go and ask her—"

As she attempted to brush past him, Nico shot to his feet and grabbed her elbow.

"Let go of me."

"*Listen.*" He retained his grip. "Don't rush into this. *Think.*"

She took a deep breath. "About what?"

"Whether you wish to bring this matter up with the earl if it actually concerns his wife. He loves her. He will do anything, destroy *anyone* who threatens her."

She raised her gaze to his dark brown eyes. "Have you found any evidence to support this ridiculous theory of yours?"

"Not yet."

"Then until you do, I intend to follow through with my plan to ask the earl whether he is my father."

He sighed. "Di—"

"I've waited too long and I'm too close to finding out the truth to be dissuaded now. If the earl denies everything, perhaps his countess will speak up instead. I'm sorry, Nico."

A muscle twitched in his jaw. "I think you will be. I don't want you to get hurt."

He let go of her, and she resumed her seat behind the desk and settled her skirts. "We all have to do what's best for ourselves at some point, don't we?"

He put his notebook back in his pocket. "If I find out anything else before the earl arrives, will you at least hear what I have to say?"

"Of course I will."

"Thank you." He hurried toward the door with unusual speed. "Good-bye, Diana. Be well."

It only occurred to her that he hadn't directly answered her question after he'd left. Who might have paid him to extract it in the first place? Diana rubbed at her temples and considered everything Nico had said to her. It was possible he was just trying to distract her from speaking to the earl. Was it likely that the countess had borne a child out of wedlock? She hadn't been that young when she'd met and married the earl. . . .

Diana groaned and decided to focus on straightening out Malinda Keyes's appointments for the next week. At least such a complicated tangle would keep her mind beautifully occupied.

"There's been no sign of Harry, I take it, Mr. Fisher?" Alistair asked, as he placed the first batch of opened mail on his employer's desk.

"Not that I know of." Adam rubbed a hand over his tired face. "I'm assuming you haven't seen him either." He looked as though he hadn't slept for a week.

"No, sir, I haven't."

"I discovered that one of our footmen has been accepting bribes from Sir Ronald Fairbanks, which was how he managed to get in to our little soirée the other night. He's been dismissed."

"Is it possible that he told Sir Ronald about the list of names in your desk?"

"It's highly likely. It might also mean that Harry stole the list to order."

"To get back into Sir Ronald's good graces, or blackmail him instead." Alistair nodded. "Has there been any unusual activity by the men on the missing list?"

"A little. Two of them have removed large sums of money from their bank accounts recently."

"Mayhap my brother is involved in a lot of blackmail these days. That's the only reason I can think of for his return."

"It wouldn't surprise me. I'm waiting to see if either of them arranges to pass the money over to anyone we know."

"The most pressing of Harry's debts appear to be owed to the Demon Club. If he wishes to settle those, he'll need the money by tomorrow night."

"How do you know this?"

"Because the Demon Club collects payment on the last day of the month in person at their headquarters."

"Harry told you this?"

"Indirectly." Alistair hesitated and decided to go with a half truth. "If one wanted to catch Harry, a visit to the Demon Club on settlement day would be well worth contemplating."

Adam Fisher actually shuddered. "I'd rather follow him into a flooded mine shaft. That place is as corrupt and unpleasant as I assume hell will be."

"I could go, sir."

"I don't think you'd like it either, Alistair. The sexual acts that go on there are quite depraved."

"But someone needs to be there."

"And I'll make sure someone is. Don't worry about that. We will contrive."

"As you wish, sir."

Alistair had a strong suspicion that if Harry declined to attend the Demons, they would come for him instead, and he'd have no choice but to inspect the facilities in the most personal way possible. And if Harry disappeared again, Alistair might be taken in his place. But Harry might come through. He'd always tried to pay his debts to men of his own class.

Which somehow made his behavior even worse . . .

Alistair glanced at the clock on the mantelpiece. In eight hours he was expected at the Demon Club, but he wouldn't go willingly. If Harry had enough money, he'd be there instead, and Alistair wouldn't be needed. After Harry paid his debts,

Mr. Fisher's agent would make sure Harry was apprehended and brought to a safe place for questioning.

And he would have the opportunity to face his brother with some questions of his own. . . .

Returning to his own office, he scanned the new pile of correspondence that had just arrived and sorted it into three piles, one for Lord Keyes, one for Mr. Fisher, and the remainder for the ladies.

He pictured Diana at her desk, her expression preoccupied as she wrote one of her interminable lists. She was as unlike his late wife as a woman could possibly be. Gelis had needed him desperately, but Diana? He was the one who needed her. He found himself smiling as he picked up the pile of letters and headed for her office. He'd chosen Gelis because he'd wanted to be the one in control. But it hadn't worked out that way. Her need had almost destroyed him. . . .

Was that what appealed to him about Diana Theale? That she was a survivor, that in a fight, she might be the one to stab him in the back and climb over his dead body to escape her fate. It didn't frighten him. He would probably do the same. He tapped on the door and went in.

"Lady Theale, I—"

She jumped and so did her visitor.

"I do apologize. I thought you were alone." Alistair slid the letters onto her desk. "Please excuse me." He nodded in a general way at Diana's guest and then looked more closely.

"Charlie?"

"Yes, Mr. Maclean. Good day."

He looked back at Diana. "I didn't realize you two knew each other."

She raised her eyebrows. "I was about to say the same thing. How do you know what Charlotte looks like?"

"I hunted her down at the pleasure house. This is the same Charlotte you were at school with?"

"Yes."

He frowned at Charlie. "You might have mentioned your real name."

"Why? I don't like it. I promised Diana I wouldn't tell her what I was up to with regard to your brother."

"Why?"

"Because she is involved with you. She has standards about that kind of thing." Charlotte rolled her eyes. "I suppose I do have something to tell you, though. Harry is still in London. An acquaintance of mine saw him last night."

"Where?"

"In a brothel." Charlotte snorted. "Where else? I doubt he's still there, but I'll check on my way back to the pleasure house."

"May I come with you?"

She fixed him with an amused stare. "No, thank you. It's not the sort of place a gentleman like yourself would be welcome."

"And you would?" He gestured at her blue pelisse and straw bonnet. "You're dressed like a debutante. You'll be set upon in an instant."

"I'm a whore, Mr. Maclean. A well-known one. I won't be in any danger at all." She sighed. "If your brother is there, I promise I'll send you a message immediately."

"I don't like it, but it will have to do." Alistair frowned. "Are you quite certain that—"

She was already moving toward the door. "Good-bye, *nice* Mr. Maclean. Good-bye, Diana, darling."

Alistair turned back to Diana, who was looking pensive.

"Do you think she will be safe?"

"Charlotte? Yes. She is very good at taking care of herself."

There was a distracted note in her voice that made Alistair study her more intently. "Is something wrong?"

"No, I'm just rather busy. Malinda is quite close to giving birth and wants her house to be perfect. She's driving Lord

Keyes mad, and I'm trying to accomplish miracles so that he doesn't have to."

"That's all?"

"What else could there be?"

He took a step toward the desk. "Were you going to tell me that Charlotte had visited you?"

"Not unless she specifically asked me to, why?"

"You don't think I have a right to know what is going on?"

"I believe we've already discussed this. Charlotte doesn't interfere in my business, and I don't interfere in hers."

"But what about the security of the nation?"

"What on earth do you mean?"

"Harry is implicated in a robbery of governmental evidence. Charlotte is very keen to find him. Don't you think Lord Keyes or Mr. Fisher might be interested in speaking to her?"

She made an airy gesture. "They already know all about Charlotte."

"So I'm the only person who isn't given the same courtesy?"

"Why does it matter, Mr. Maclean?"

"Because you deliberately withheld information from me about my own brother!"

"For goodness' sake! You tracked Charlotte down all by yourself and neglected to mention it to me."

"Because—"

She interrupted him. "Because nothing, Mr. Maclean. You didn't trust me enough to share the information."

"I didn't think it had anything to do with you."

She threw up her hands. "I *knew* you would take everything the wrong way and assume that our relationship was based on something nefarious."

"You're suggesting that I'm at fault then?"

"I'm saying that the two things are completely and utterly separate."

"Nothing is ever that clear-cut."

"It is if you make up your mind to it." She glared at him. "How else do you survive?"

He stared at her for a long moment as he fought to control his temper. "You demand a great deal from me, Lady Theale, but seem unwilling to offer much in return."

"You were the one who insisted that your submission to me in the bedroom had nothing to do with the rest of your life. Why can't I have the same courtesy from you?"

"Because these two things are not the same! I don't assume you wish to control every single person you meet at the Sinners in the same way you control me. I *assume* that you are a capable, intelligent woman who can understand the difference between being loyal to her friend and being loyal to her country."

"*That* is the most ridiculous thing you have ever said, Mr. Maclean. This isn't about my loyalty to the country, or to the Sinners. You are hurt because I didn't trust *you*."

"That's—" He stared at her, his breathing harsh in the silence. He bowed. "Good evening, Lady Theale."

She picked up her pen. "I'm sure you are just as busy as I am, Mr. Maclean. Perhaps I will see you at dinner tonight?"

He bowed again. "I'll look forward to it."

All he could think as he walked back to his office was that she still didn't trust him completely and that hurt. How had he allowed himself to become so emotionally vulnerable to her? It was all very well trusting her in bed, but with the rest of his life? That was terrifying when he already knew you couldn't even trust your own family. . . .

His steps slowed. There had been something in her eyes that made him want to gather her in his arms and protect her from whatever was worrying her. She'd hate that. Why was she so unsure? What had Charlotte told her? Had she seen Nicodemus?

A thousand questions and no answers. He flung open the door of his office and went inside. A note sealed with a familiar crest lay on his blotter and he broke the seal to read it.

Alistair, That list I stole has a few names of interest on it, including your father-in-law's. If you value your poor dead wife's reputation, meet me at the Demon Club tonight. Harry.

Alistair shook his head. "That's impossible, I would've—" With a curse, he found the copy he'd made of the list and started to read.

"Devil take it, did he inherit his cousin's title after all?" He found the name he sought and stared down at it uncomprehendingly for far too long. "Why didn't I see it earlier?"

With a groan, he rolled up the list and faced the inevitable. Whatever else happened, he wouldn't be dining with Diana at the Sinners or attempting to make his peace with her. He'd be spending his evening at the Demon Club. . . .

Diana stayed at her desk until she had completed all her work and then lingered staring into space. Maddon had confirmed that the earl would be returning on the following day. From everything she'd learned about him she had to assume he had been informed of her recent employment and had perhaps drawn certain conclusions about who and what she was. It wouldn't pay to underestimate the man. He was the head of a spy ring after all . . .

Despite her promise to Nico to wait and see if he could find any more proof of her parentage, she reckoned she would broach the matter with the earl at the earliest opportunity. It was a shame that she'd then lose the most enjoyable employment opportunity she'd ever had and Mr. Maclean. . . .

She groaned. The job could go hang itself. She'd find another. But Mr. Maclean was irreplaceable, and she was so close in gaining his complete trust. . . .

But in order to do that she'd have to trust him in return. Despite what most people thought of the relationships she formed, not all the power was on her side. If Mr. Maclean didn't choose to submit to her, or allow her to give him the sexual pleasure he craved, she'd have nothing. She needed him just as much as he needed her.

And that was the sticking point. She *needed* him. She'd never felt like this before and it was rather frightening. If she told him, would he change? Would it ruin the delicate balance of their relationship or make it even stronger? For the first time in her life, she wanted to find out. She wanted to be able to tell him when she didn't feel strong, or needed his help, and know that it wouldn't change the way he perceived her in the bedroom.

But didn't he already understand that? Hadn't he insisted that just because he needed to be dominated sexually didn't mean he wasn't a strong, capable man in all the other areas of his life? Perhaps he would understand that the reverse might be true for her. That sometimes, just occasionally, she needed to be held and loved and *cossetted*.

And now she'd upset him by withholding information that he deemed valuable to the nation, but was really about her lack of trust.

She stretched out her cramped fingers. Charlotte had asked her to accompany her to the Demon Club. She insisted it was important, and that only Diana could help her. She'd practically begged, which was most unlike Charlotte. It had something to do with Harry Maclean, which meant that Diana was reluctant to be involved at all. But she couldn't let Charlotte down, and she didn't have to participate in anything at the Demons; watching was quite bad enough.

Dinner with Mr. Maclean would have to wait, as would any attempt to mend her fences with him. She'd make sure Adam Fisher knew where she was going and hope that he would conjure up some kind of plan to entrap Harry if he turned up. She had every confidence in the Sinners' ability to secure Harry before Charlotte or her mysterious client got to him.

And then, tomorrow, once Harry was safe, perhaps she'd be able to have that conversation with *her* Mr. Maclean. Diana started to smile and then froze. She wouldn't be talking to Mr. Maclean on Sunday. The earl was returning, and she would be talking to him instead, meaning her relationship with Alistair would be at an end.

"Oh, damnation!" She marched over to her door, opened it, and slammed it hard behind her. "Why does everything have to get so complicated?"

She stomped up the stairs to get dressed for the Demons. Something black and skimpy should do. God help anyone who got in her way at the club. She was in no mood to play nicely with *anyone.*

19

Alistair made no effort to change into his evening dress for his appointment with Harry. He did remember to leave a message with Maddon for Mr. Fisher as to his whereabouts, although he didn't mention the complications that had brought him to that point. There would be time enough to explain his actions when Harry was under lock and key.

He took a hackney cab to the modest building where the Demon Club had its headquarters. It had once been housed in the far grander surroundings of an aristocratic mansion, but was now on King Street, quite close to the far more famous private club of Almack's. A footman in an old-fashioned white wig and black and red livery answered his knock on the front door. He studied Alistair's invitation through his black mask and then invited him to step into a waiting room to the left of the entranceway. There was no one else present, but Alistair could hear the sounds of revelry already reverberating throughout the house.

After a lengthy wait, the footman returned, followed by another man in immaculate dinner dress whom Alistair immediately recognized.

"Mr. Maclean. How kind of you to join us. I thought you were going to be stubborn about your responsibility for the debt your brother incurred, but I see I misjudged you."

"Lord Blaydon Kenrick." Alistair inclined his head a less-than-civil inch. "I didn't come because you ordered me to do so. I came to find my brother and remove him from this place. Do you know where he is?"

Blaydon Kenrick smiled. "Harry always said you were the worst kind of fool, blinded by your perceived obligations and your sense of honor." He took a step closer. "He wanted you to be punished in his stead. Don't you know that?"

"No one will be punished if Harry repays his debts."

His companion laughed outright. "That will not happen."

"Now who is being naïve? If I am here, perhaps I've brought the money to pay off the debt myself."

"I do hope not." All the amusement was wiped off Kenrick's face. "I'll take you to your brother."

"Thank you."

The footman fell into place behind Alistair as if he feared he might bolt. As they moved toward the back of the house, the noise intensified, punctuated by shrill screams and roars of laughter. A man came toward them carrying a woman over his shoulder. Her skirts were rucked up to her waist covering her upper body and head and the man was fondling her naked bottom.

The crowd intensified as they moved forward into a much larger space. Alistair could barely see anything but the backs of people's heads, and the hands that reached out to grab him as he passed.

"Here you are, Maclean."

Before he quite realized what was happening, the footman behind him shoved him hard in the back, and he was sent sprawling into a golden cage-like structure large enough to hold a dozen. The cage was almost full and none of the occupants looked happy. By the time he stumbled to his feet and turned around, the cage door was locked by a smiling Kenrick.

Alistair strode over to him and grabbed the bars. "Why am I in here? You said you would take me to my brother."

"He'll be here in a moment."

"And then you'll release me?"

"Oh no, Maclean. That will be entirely up to the membership."

"What?"

"The Devils preside over everything. They are seated on their thrones on the platform over there." Kenrick blew him a kiss. "Enjoy your evening, Maclean. I'll be betting on you for sure."

Furious with himself for being so easily entrapped, Alistair swung around to view the other occupants of the cage. Some of them were society ladies of various ages, and others appeared to be gentlemen. But that wasn't all. There were a few lower class individuals from the city proper.

"Mr. Maclean?"

One of the bearded older gentlemen sidled over whispering Alistair's name. He looked like the sort of man one would find in a shipping office or a lowly governmental department rather than a gilded cage.

"Yes?"

"You're not the Mr. Maclean I expected." He glanced down at Alistair. "I'm Dobbs. Mr. Fisher sent me."

"Much good you'll do locked up in here."

"I'll be out soon enough, sir. I was one of the first in."

"How do you get out of this cage?" Alistair asked.

"It depends what you did."

Alistair set his jaw as he tried to see past the crowds hanging around the cage. "Can you be more specific, Mr. Dobbs?"

"Aye, sir. The club members play cards and accumulate points. When someone reaches the level of one of our debts, that person is let out of the cage and has to do what the winner of his debt demands."

"I see. How much do you owe?"

"Five guineas, sir. Mr. Fisher wanted me out of the cage and punished before you, I mean, before Mr. Harry Maclean was released. I'm supposed to report back to him if Mr. Harry is here."

There was a roar and sudden movement around the entrance to their prison. The footman beckoned to Alistair's companion. "You."

"Good luck," Alistair said softly.

Diana forced herself to smile as Matthew Partington, one of the current leaders of the Demon Club, slowly backed her against the wall. He looked relatively harmless, but there was a coldness to his eyes that told a different story—one that Diana had learned to recognize and fear in the occasional client at the pleasure house.

"I don't wish to participate, thank you."

"Then why come to the Demon Club?"

"I was invited." Diana looked around for Charlotte, but there was no sign of her friend. "If something or someone takes my fancy, I'll certainly reconsider my decision. It is kind of you to think about my amusement, Mr. Partington."

"I've heard you make an exceptional mistress, Lady Theale."

She fluttered her eyelashes at him. "Not anymore, sir. I fear I had to give up such things when I married."

His smile was colder this time. "I don't think that's quite true, is it?"

She raised her chin and continued to meet his skeptical gaze. "Whatever do you mean?" She hoped to God he knew nothing about her relationship with Alistair.

"Theale married you so that you could continue to minister to his particular needs in the comfort of his own home."

"That is true, sir." She sighed beguilingly. "But since his death, I haven't had the heart to return to the pleasure house.

That's one of the reasons why my friend insisted I come with her tonight. She hoped to arouse my . . . interests again."

He bowed. "Then I hope we amuse you this evening, my lady."

"I'm *sure* you will."

"I can guarantee it. Please come and find me if I can be of any assistance, Lady Theale."

She curtsied low enough for him to get an excellent view of her bosom. "Thank you, Mr. Partington."

He walked away and she let out her breath. He was as charming as a snake about to strike and not to be trifled with. She wondered why he'd sought her out at all. It wasn't reassuring. She spied Charlotte coming back into the main salon with an all-too-familiar figure close behind her. What was Charlotte doing talking to Sir Ronald Fairbanks and why were they looking so pleased with each other?

Just as Diana moved toward her friend, there was a roar from the gaming tables followed by another shout as a man was released from the golden cage and led toward the unknown nobleman who had won his debt at cards. The bearded man looked somewhat familiar. . . .

She couldn't hear the question he was asked, but the vehement shaking of his head and the howls of laughter from the inebriated crowd around him didn't bode well. One of the footmen shoved the man down onto his knees and the aristocrat moved closer, his hand unbuttoning his trousers to reveal the beginnings of his erection.

Whether he wanted to suck cock or not, the debtor was going to have to do it in front of the crowd while the footman behind him held his head in a stranglehold. Diana briefly closed her eyes as the man's muffled shout was silenced by six inches of cock filling his mouth.

While all eyes were on the pair in the center of the room,

Diana made her way around the edge of the salon and came up behind Charlotte.

"What's going on?" she whispered. "Why are you talking to Sir Ronald?"

"Why do you think?"

Diana spun her friend around to face her. "Don't tell me that you are working for him now?"

"He is one of my clients." Charlotte's gray eyes were clear and steady. "I told you, Di, I'll do whatever it takes to get Harry Maclean, and that includes consorting with scum like Sir Ronald. He wants to find Harry too, so I helped him get Maclean to this place for punishment."

"What did you do?"

"What was necessary." Charlotte shrugged. "Please don't worry. I promised I would do my best to keep you and Alistair Maclean out of it and I have. I just wanted you to see Harry brought to justice tonight."

"Here?"

"I suspect it is the only justice he might understand."

"But, Charlotte, the Sinners want him too."

"Then they can have him after he's paid off that thousand-pound debt in the most excruciatingly embarrassing way Sir Ronald and I can devise." Charlotte touched Diana's cheek. "Don't deny me this. Harry will live to face the Sinners, I promise you that. I just want to see his face when he realizes who I am."

Diana sighed. "Do you really think it will make a difference, love? Mary-Louise will still be dead. Nothing can bring her back to you."

"I know that. But I like to imagine she is looking down on us and will enjoy watching her seducer reduced to servicing others and begging—I hope he begs. I hope he cries too." Charlotte smiled. "As Harry's debt is the highest, I suspect it will take a while for him to emerge from the cage."

"He's in there already?" Diana craned her head to see through the throng of people and caught a glimpse of auburn hair behind the gold bars. "Ah, I see him."

"Sir Ronald has guaranteed the money necessary to claim Harry's debt."

"Why does he hate him so much?"

"Because that is the effect Harry Maclean eventually has on everybody. He bleeds people dry. He takes everything and demands more until his lover either loses themselves entirely or breaks free in the most painful way possible." Charlotte's eyes glittered with unshed tears. "He needs to be stopped, Diana."

Another roar from the crowd announced that the entertainment was over for a while. The bearded man staggered to his feet, his hand rubbing frantically at his mouth, and ran toward the retiring rooms at the back of the house. Much laughter and ribald commentary followed his path, but he had paid off his debt, and as far as Diana understood it, he was free to go.

The gaming started up again and the noise level decreased. Diana found her way through to the supper room and helped herself to a glass of wine and some grapes. She wished she could leave, but loyalty to Charlotte and to Alistair kept her there. Did she have time to slip out and send a message to Adam Fisher confirming Harry Maclean's presence?

Adam had assured her that he had a plan in place to trap Harry if necessary, and she had to have faith in him. If he hadn't succeeded in placing his men in the Demon Club, would Charlotte and Sir Ronald take their vengeance too far? She couldn't allow that. If it came down to it, she would intervene herself and hope that Charlotte would forgive her.

Alistair made his way to the back corner of the cage and sat down, his knees drawn up and his gaze fixed on the locked door. He was so furious his whole body was shaking with it. He hoped no one thought he was afraid. Several occupants of the cage were openly weeping and not all of them were women. After watching Dobbs being forced to suck cock, the wailing had decreased as stark terror took its place.

One had to admire the Demon Club in some ways. Maybe enduring such a horrific way of repaying a gambling debt was an effective method of making sure the debt wasn't repeated. He suspected very few occupants of the cage would wish to return to it. If they did he had to suspect either foul play at the tables, or that the debtor was incurable.

One of the bewigged footmen strolled over and leaned against the corner of the cage, his back to Alistair.

"And how are you this evening, brother mine?"

At the sound of Harry's voice, Alistair stiffened and looked up.

"No, don't turn around. If you do, I'll simply walk away and leave you to your fate."

"*My* fate?" Alistair said evenly. "The debt was yours, Harry."

"And the payment for me returning the list to the Sinners is your being here in my place."

"We have a copy. I don't need yours."

"But I went out of my way to warn you about your father-in-law's presence on the list. You still owe me something."

"I expected better of you."

"That was a mistake." Harry chuckled. "I hate trying to live up to your impossibly high standards, I always have."

"Asking you not to steal, cheat, and lie to your own family is too much to ask?"

"There you go again, making everything my fault." A sulky note entered Harry's voice. "If you'd simply lent me the money I asked for, you wouldn't be in this predicament."

"Harry, I don't have a thousand pounds."

"You could easily get it for me if you wanted to though. You just chose not to."

"I chose to stop saving your neck."

"And abandoned me to my fate."

Alistair stared straight ahead as one of the women was dragged out of the cage screaming. An unusual sense of hopelessness fell over him.

"Did you bring the money?" Harry asked.

Alistair closed his eyes. "No. I don't have it."

"You told Blaydon you did."

"To ensure that I was allowed to see you. I didn't expect to be cast into a cage and offered up as some kind of sexual treat to a room full of drunken gamblers." He rose to his feet and turned toward his brother. "In fact, I think I'll ask to be released right now and suggest you take my place."

Harry's eyes narrowed as he took a piece of paper out of his pocket. "Not if you want this. Do you want Gelis's family to be brought down again?"

"As I said. We already have a copy. It will be easy enough for me to warn the new earl. Gelis is no longer on this earth, and her father is above such things now."

"I doubt that. The Scots are still regarded with deep suspicion here at the Hanoverian court. One word from me, a known supporter of the Crown, and he could easily be cast down again."

"You're willing to make another family destitute to avoid paying your debts?"

"Whatever do you mean?"

"What am I saying?" Alistair laughed. "You brought your own father down. Why would you balk at destroying my dead wife's father?"

Harry's face paled, and his eyes glittered black. "Be careful what you say, Alistair."

"Why, because you can't bear to hear the truth? You lying, traitorous *bastard.*"

"Do you know *why* your father-in-law is on this list?" Harry smiled. "Of course you don't. Shall I tell you? Your dear wife was heavily involved with the Stuart cause. Didn't she ever mention that? *He* is implicated through his association with her."

"You're lying."

"A woman doesn't lie to her lover." He extracted another two pieces of paper from his pocket. "If the original list isn't enough of an incentive for you, perhaps these might be. I have a love letter from your wife and a letter she wrote and entrusted to me with some funds for the Stuart cause."

Alistair went still, the roar of the crowd fading to nothing as he faced his brother. "You—"

"I told her how you betrayed our father. She was horrified and sought comfort from me." Harry shrugged. "How could I not oblige her?" His smile was quite beautiful. "I'm sorry, she preferred me to you, Alistair."

With a snarl, Alistair reached through the bars of the cage and grabbed his brother around the throat, slamming him hard against the bars. Almost immediately other footmen surrounded Harry, and Alistair was shoved back and onto the floor. By the time he righted himself, he could no longer tell which of the retreating servants was his brother.

It couldn't be true, Gelis had . . .

"Oh, God," he whispered as he remembered her sudden distaste for him, her refusal to share his bed, and the miraculous pregnancy he'd been too overjoyed to question that had resulted in her death. . . .

He remained on his knees and buried his face in his hands, fighting for composure, fighting the need to howl his rage to the heavens.

Even if it wasn't true, what had he done to make his brother hate him so much? What in God's name had he *done?* And now, due to his temper, he was still in the cage awaiting his brother's fate and hadn't secured any of the evidence for the Sinners. . . .

Time passed in a blur. The occupants of the cage disappeared one by one, and the audience decreased due to drunkenness and lack of funds to keep gambling. Candlelight played off the sinister masked figures of the Demons' court and the intent card players. Eventually, Alistair was the only person left.

The door to the cage was unlocked, and Blaydon beckoned to him.

"Come on, Maclean, you're wanted. Sir Ronald has won your debt and offered you as a gift to the court."

"You have the wrong man. My brother is here. He's dressed as one of your own bloody footmen."

Lord Blaydon smirked. "Of course he is, Maclean."

Alistair braced himself as two of the footmen came into the cage to get him. He was not going to take his brother's punishment meekly. With a roar, he lunged at the first man, knocking him sideways before he turned to the second. A big meaty fist caught him in the guts, and he stumbled backward to avoid the other blow, hitting his head against the bars of the cage.

After dodging two more blows and landing a few of his own in a white-hot flow of rage, reinforcements were gathered and he was caught and held in a headlock, his arm twisted against his spine, and hauled out of the cage. There were still several onlookers who cheered his arrival at the foot of the raised dais.

"Maclean seems reluctant to pay his debt, Kenrick."

Alistair recognized the voice of Matthew Partington, one of the younger sons of the Earl of Woodford, sitting on one of the gilded chairs.

"It's not my debt. It's my brother's." Alistair stated it again more loudly this time. "He's here disguised as a footman enjoying all this. You need to find him and make him pay for his own sins."

A gasp made him look away from Partington and to his left, where Charlotte stood with Sir Ronald. She was probably the only person who cared that he wasn't his brother at this point. Why hadn't he guessed that she'd partner with the devil himself to entrap Harry? Sir Ronald was probably one of the few men willing to pay out a thousand pounds simply to get his revenge on his old lover. It seemed so obvious now. He tried to catch her eye.

"He's dressed as a footman."

Partington came to the edge of the stage and stared down at him. "Firstly, I don't believe you, and secondly, I don't care. Your name was on that paper. You'll do as well as your brother to provide us with amusement. Actually it might be even more fun playing with you than Harry. By all accounts, you're a straitlaced prude."

He nodded at the three footmen restraining Alistair. "Take him into the smaller salon and strip him naked."

Diana was enjoying her second glass of wine and the relative solitude of the supper room when Charlotte came running through the door, her expression stricken.

"Di, you have to help me. They've got the wrong Mr. Maclean. Alastair's in the cage, and he's insisting Harry's here somewhere disguised as a footman!"

"*What?*" Diana shot to her feet. "Why is Alistair here?"

Charlotte gripped her arm. "Apparently, his name was on the debt. I didn't know that until now. I'm so *sorry,* Di, what can we do to help him?"

"Where is he?"

"They've taken him in to the smaller salon."

"Can anyone go in there?"

"I don't know."

Diana nodded. "Don't worry, we can make this right. You find Harry and keep him in your sight until help arrives from the Sinners."

"And what if it doesn't?"

"Then you have my full permission to stop him if he tries to leave this place—as long as you don't kill him."

Charlotte shivered. "I doubt he'll leave until he's seen his brother punished."

"So do I." She kissed her friend's pale cheek. "Don't worry about Alistair. He's a lot more resilient than the Demons might imagine. I'll make sure to keep him safe."

"Do you really think you can?"

"If he'll let me."

Diana headed for the door, slowing her stride into a more sultry sway as she approached Matthew Partington, who was just descending from the dais.

"Lady Theale."

She touched his sleeve and ran her fingers down it. "I hear that you have a Mr. Maclean needing to be taught a lesson."

"That is correct."

She bit down on her lower lip and then licked it. "I know him. I have to work beside him every day at the Sinners and listen to him prose on." She sighed. "He treats me like a whore."

Matthew sniggered. "Then you should come and watch what we have planned for him."

She opened her eyes wide and gazed into the coldness behind his gaze. "*Watch?* Mayhap I could help. I am very good at making grown men cry."

"So I've heard." He touched her cheek and allowed his finger to trail down to her bodice. "It might be amusing seeing Maclean submit to you."

"I would make it far more than amusing, Matthew darling. I'd make him beg for it."

He pinched her nipple hard and she held his gaze.

"Come then, Lady Theale. This could be very interesting indeed."

20

The footmen were deliberately rough as they stripped him out of his clothes. Their hands grabbing and fondling his arse and balls, their comments as to his eventual fate graphic and obscene. He didn't fight them. How absurd was it that his most secret dark fantasy, of being naked and aroused before a roomful of strangers, was about to become a reality because of his brother's cowardice?

It was truly ironic.

His breath hissed out as one of the men squeezed his balls tight and kept hold of them.

"Look at him, getting all hard. He's a sharp one, ain't he? Knows what's coming."

He couldn't stop his cock responding to the coarse handling. By the time Partington and his friends arrived, he'd probably be fully erect and dripping with pre-cum. He had no idea what they would make of that. If he could just escape this place with his cock and balls intact, he'd be fine. He'd survived far worse.

From what he'd seen so far tonight, the object of the game

was sexual humiliation. His only fear was that someone would realize how much he craved the very thing the others hated, stop his punishment, and replace it with something different.

"Very nice, Maclean." Partington stood in front of him, his gaze taking in every inch of Alistair's body and then settling on his thick cock. "It seems you are as eager to begin as we are."

"Go to the devil, sir. You have no right to do this to me, and you know it."

"Your name is on this debt, Maclean. As an honorable gentleman, you must pay what you owe."

"It's my *brother's* debt!"

Partington nodded to the footmen who held Alistair. "Take him over to the rack and hang him up there."

He tried to fight, but there were more of them than him. His wrists and ankles were manacled and chained. The chains were attached to all four corners of the wooden rack. At a signal from Partington, one of the footmen turned a wheel, which gradually tightened the chains pulling Alistair's arms out and up, and then his ankles until he was spread-eagled like a fly trapped in a web.

"Enough." Partington touched Alistair's quivering skin. ""Are you comfortable, Maclean?"

Alistair didn't say anything as he concentrated on readjusting his muscles to compensate for the stretch of the rack. A sharp slap aimed at his mouth made him jerk to attention.

"I asked you a question."

"I assumed it was a rhetorical one. How could a man be comfortable like this?" Even as he glared at Partington, he answered his own question. His body was more alive and willing to be used than his captors could ever imagine.

Partington snapped his fingers, and Lord Blaydon handed him something. "You can be quiet now while we eat."

He was gagged with a velvet scarf, and another was added to

take away his ability to see. And now he was naked in a room full of men who meant him harm and he was still hard and wet. He concentrated on the loud drunken voices, the scent of the food, and the rare female laugh or satisfied scream.

Occasionally someone came over and touched him, fingered his nipples or the curve of his arse, or rubbed his cock until it ached like a swollen tooth. He was still hard and he'd stay like that for as long as he could. Was Harry still watching, or had his brother worked out that he was the one who was supposed to be trapped on the rack and disappeared? He'd always had the ability to avoid unpleasantness. But he'd probably enjoy seeing Alistair suffer even more.

He eased more of his weight back on his heels and remembered not to fight his chains too much. He might need his strength later. He suspected the Demons would demand far more of him than this tame display of nakedness and a hard cock.

The blindfold was whipped away, and he blinked into the candlelight and went still. Partington was in front of him and nestled in the curve of his arm was Diana. She was smiling and dressed in a thin black crepe gown that slid off her shoulders.

Doubt shook through him. Had she come with Charlotte and Sir Ronald? Had she hoped to see Harry tied to the rack, or was his predicament a far more satisfying sight to her after all? Perhaps he had misjudged her completely, and she'd always been on Charlotte's side and simply used him to draw Harry out.

"What do you think, Lady Theale?" Partington asked.

She considered him with her head to one side. "I think he needs humbling, don't you?"

"He's a Scotsman. They all need to remember their place."

He glared at the laughing pair, his mouth still shuttered behind his gag.

"He treats me appallingly at the Sinners. It will be a pleasure to master him for you, Mr. Partington." She reached forward and fondled his shaft, her nails digging into his heated flesh, making him groan and buck against her hand. "I'm going to enjoy this."

And he knew that regardless of whether she was on his side or Charlotte's, she *would* enjoy bringing him to his knees. It was in her nature just as it was in his to submit.

"Do you like being touched like this, Mr. Maclean?"

He shook his head and she gripped him even harder. "You prefer a man's touch?"

"No!" He shouted it through his gag and she laughed. "How did you intend to proceed if I wasn't here, Mr. Partington?"

Partington shrugged. "We intended to keep him naked and hard until everyone who wanted to use him had done so. And then we thought to give him to the staff to play with too."

"An admirable revenge." Diana paused. "While you gentlemen enjoy your port, I could put a collar and leash on him and lead him around the room so that anyone who wished to use him could simply call him over and take what they wanted." She leaned closer to Partington and whispered, "Unless you wish to take him to bed and fuck him there?"

"No, I want to see him crawling from man to man sucking cock."

Diana turned back to Alistair, her hand still wrapped around his shaft. "Do you think he might be violent if we untie him?"

"Not if we give him a good thrashing first. I doubt even Maclean would turn on a woman." Partington glanced around the room. "If he did resist, we'll just tie him up and use him like that instead."

"Would you hurt a woman, Mr. Maclean?"

He held her gaze for a long moment and then shook his head.

"Do you swear on your honor?"

This time he nodded. Regardless of what happened between them, he knew in his soul that she was the only person whom he could trust to keep him safe. He had to endure this if he stood any chance of getting Harry to give him those incriminating letters.

"Thank you."

Blaydon strolled over and ran a hand over Alistair's muscled buttock, his thumb lingering and dipping to circle Alistair's puckered hole.

"Did Maclean go to school, Partington? I'm not sure I remember him at Harrow or Eton."

"I don't believe he did," Diana said. "He mentioned his family weren't wealthy."

"Then perhaps he's never been buggered before."

Alistair tried to jerk away from Blaydon's finger, which was rimming his arsehole, but there was nowhere to go, and no give in the chains restraining him.

"Then perhaps you need to ease your passage, Blaydon." Partington chuckled. "I wonder if he'll like a big stiff cock being rammed up his arse? I wonder if he'll beg for more and come all over his stomach?"

Alistair closed his eyes as Blaydon's finger burrowed deeper. He had to withstand this. He had to let it happen if it meant he was eventually free to find his brother and strangle him with his bare hands.

"Mr. Maclean?"

Diana's voice.

She cupped his cheek, and he opened his eyes and focused on her. Even if she intended to leave him he could trust her now.

"I'll get you through this, I promise." He nodded once and she stood on tiptoe and kissed him, making all the men cheer as she whispered, "Try and pretend it's just you and me. I know you won't want to disappoint me."

Good Lord, Alistair looked beautiful to her at that moment, chained to the rack, his muscles taut, his limbs stretched, and his cock hard . . . And despite the doubt flickering in his green eyes when he'd first seen her, he still believed she would help him.

"Lord Blaydon, do you wish me to carry out Mr. Partington's instructions, or do you wish to proceed first?"

The Irish aristocrat stood behind Alistair, one hand on his captive's naked hip and the other between Alistair's buttocks.

"I'll wait." He sighed as he moved away. "But make sure you bring him around to me. I want him to suck my cock before I mount him."

Partington handed her a long birch cane. "If he didn't go to school, he's probably not experienced this either. Nothing like a caning from a schoolmaster to heat your arse followed by a good buggering."

Diana took the cane and flicked her wrist, enjoying the sound of the birch whistling through the air and the quivering reaction Alistair couldn't quite conceal. She didn't immediately start beating him. Instead she walked around him, using the tip of the cane to examine his body, rubbing it over his nipples, between his spread thighs and his buttocks.

His breathing shortened as she touched the cane to his gag and shoved it down.

"Kiss this rod, Mr. Maclean, and say thank you for the beating you are about to receive."

He bared his teeth at her, and she smiled before bringing the birch down his sternum and over his flat stomach to rest on his thrusting cock.

"Here then, Mr. Maclean?"

He went still as she rubbed his foreskin until the tip of the cane was as wet as his cock, and then dragged it lower, passing between his balls and the soft smoothness of his taint. The gentlemen had fallen silent, their gazes fixed on Alistair as she taunted him with the end of the cane.

"I could bugger you with this, Mr. Maclean, all three feet of it?" He shuddered. "How much could you take before you were stuffed full? How much more would I make you take anyway?"

She returned the cane to his shaft, rubbing it against the stream of pre-cum until the tip gleamed and he was attempting to arch into every stroke. Removing the cane, she walked around him, smiling at Partington and Lord Blaydon, who were watching avidly, and positioned herself behind Alistair.

His whole body jerked as she snapped the cane and landed her first perfect blow across his right buttock. She followed with five more, three on each buttock, until his pale Celtic skin was marred with six perfect red lines. With a sigh, she watched the colors deepen and spread and the way his body was now tensed against the next anticipated strike.

Instead, she stroked his arse and he moaned.

"Don't fight me, Mr. Maclean."

"Go . . . to . . . hell." He spoke between his teeth.

She wanted to smile at his aggression, but she recognized it for what it was. A desperate attempt to stop their audience from realizing how much he was enjoying what was happening to him. The least she could do was play along.

Still holding the birch rod, she walked around and grabbed his chin in her hand.

"I beg your pardon?"

"You heard me."

She slapped him hard, once on each cheek, making his head snap back. "Perhaps we need to wash out your mouth, Mr. Maclean." She glanced over at one of the silent footmen. "Can you lower the chains so that he is kneeling instead of standing?"

"Yes, my lady."

While he was being repositioned, she beckoned to Blaydon. "Do you wish him to suck you now?"

"While you finish beating him?" His odd silver eyes gleamed. "Damn right, I do."

He strolled closer to the rack, opening his trousers with one hand to reveal his already thick cock.

Alistair growled at him. "If you put that anywhere near my mouth, I'll bite it off."

Blaydon raised an eyebrow and turned to Diana. "Do you think he means it?"

"We can prevent it." She looked at Partington. "Do you have something here in your dungeon that will keep his mouth open, or do I need to improvise?"

"We have something. Many of our guests are strangely reluctant to take a man's cock in any orifice." Partington chuckled and went to one of the tallboys that lined the far wall. "This should work."

Diana examined the brass ring and the two ribbons attached to it. "It is perfect. Hold still, Mr. Maclean." Before he understood her intent, she managed to get the ring in his mouth, ordering the footman to hold it in place while she tied the ribbons together at the back of his head.

The guttural sounds from Alistair's throat sounded threatening, but there was nothing he could do in his present position to close his mouth. Diana smiled at Lord Blaydon.

"Go ahead, my lord. He can't do anything to stop you filling his mouth with your cock and coming."

She took her place again and waited until Lord Blaydon sheathed his cock down a still-protesting Alistair's throat. All sound except the ragged cheer of the watchers and the whistle as the birch cane came down ceased as she concentrated on giving her slave the best experience she could. Her vision narrowed to the slightest movement of his body, the signs that he was going away within himself to a place where the pain became his pleasure and he became completely hers.

She knew he hated being fucked or handled by men, but she also knew, because she had trained him, that he would accept such treatment if she wanted him to. And there was more to come yet. He still needed to survive whatever the Demons came up with next.

The twelfth stroke landed lower, just catching the underside of his balls, making his breath hiss out around the pounding presence of Lord Blaydon's shaft. His own cock was hard and so wet now that he was surprised no one had commented on it.

"Ah, God." Blaydon shoved forward one more time, his hand in Alistair's hair, forcing him to stay put, and pumped his load down Alistair's throat.

Alistair hardly cared, the pain of the beating simply enhancing the humiliation and secret excitement of being used in front of the Demon court. When Blaydon released him, his head fell forward, as he sucked in some much needed air.

Diana's soft hand touched his shoulder as she buckled a thick leather collar around his throat and attached a leash. As she bent to fasten the buckle, she licked his open lips.

"I like you hard, Mr. Maclean. You are so wet and desperate too."

She waited patiently with the end of the leash wrapped around one of her hands as the footmen released him from the manacles. His arse was stinging, but the thought of being led around like a dog and forced to service the Demons brought him some dark perverse satisfaction. He was just something for them to use, a hole for their cock to penetrate without resistance. There was nothing he could do to stop them, so he simply had to endure. He'd stay hard for his lady and damn them all.

As he obeyed the jerk on his leash and crawled toward the dining table, he kept his gaze on the floor. Would Harry give him the letters his wife had purportedly written if Alistair completed this task and wiped out the thousand-pound debt? Did he dare look up and see if his brother was actually there?

The end of the leash snapped against his already tender buttock.

"Mr. Maclean? I believe Mr. Partington wishes you to suck his cock."

Eventually even the Demon court had enough of him. As the first rays of dawn filtered through the black curtains, Alistair was sprawled naked on his stomach on the rug in front of the fire. Someone had decided to leave him tied up so his ankles and wrists were manacled together in the small of his back putting far too much pressure on his cock.

But he didn't care. He'd retreated to the place in his head where he could accept anything and enjoy it—a peaceful haven where he lived for the pain and the pleasure. It was a place most people would never be able to understand. What kind of man thrived on being used or being owned? What kind of man craved being hurt and humiliated?

The soft rustle of petticoats reached him, followed by the lavender scent he associated with Charlotte.

"Mr. Maclean?" Diana whispered.

He groaned as his ankles and wrists were released from the ropes, but the two women were already rubbing his limbs, bringing both warmth and movement back into them. Eventually he was rolled onto his back. His beaten arse protested, but merely added to the high whine of pain that somehow also soothed him.

"Alistair." Diana cupped his chin.

He licked his lips and realized the ring had also been removed from his mouth at some point.

"Where's Harry?" he croaked.

"He's safe. Charlotte has gone to find your clothes, and we have a carriage awaiting us outside."

"Don't need . . . clothes."

"A cloak, then."

He forced himself to meet her gaze. "Need you."

She swallowed hard and he thought he saw a glint of tears in her eyes, which confused him. "I promise I'm not leaving your side until I have you tucked up in your bed at the Sinners."

"Not yet," he whispered.

"What do you need?"

"Finish me."

Her gaze dropped to the swell of his cock.

"I . . . don't want to hurt you."

"Wrap the leash around my balls and make me come hard for you."

Her fingers trembled as she touched his unshaven cheek. "Are you sure?"

"I only want to come for you. Make me."

She wrapped the end of the leash around her hand and looped it under his balls, bringing them up high under his shaft.

"Now make me come."

He moaned as she grasped his cock with her leather-wrapped hand and started to move it up and down his oversensitive shaft.

"God, yes. I don't know if I can come anymore, so sore now, so long since I came . . ." He was whispering, babbling, but he knew she would understand.

"You'll do it for me right now."

Her calm voice reached him, and he brought his hand up over her working fingers and began to move them more crudely.

"Need it like this . . . rough and hard."

"I want to see you spill all over your stomach. Then I want to cover your nakedness in a cloak and take you home." She tightened her grip. "Naked and dripping, Mr. Maclean. I could let anyone see you, touch you, let them fuck you again. I could get you hard again as we travel and make you beg."

He shuddered so powerfully that he couldn't stop, and then his come pumped from his cock in huge jets coating their fingers, his stomach, and the expensive rug he lay on. She leaned in and gathered him in her arms and held him as he continued to come, each violent motion making him shiver and hold on to her like a drowning man.

"Diana?"

Dimly he was aware of Charlotte's voice, and then he was wrapped in a cloak and carried out to a waiting carriage. His head came to rest on Diana's shoulder. She let him stay there as he struggled to keep awake and listen to the quiet conversation going on between the two women. He couldn't think. His mind was still trapped in that place of pleasure and pain and not yet ready to deal with anything other than the basics of existence.

He yawned and couldn't even raise the energy to cover his mouth. When the carriage stopped, he was again carried out and then up the stairs to his bedroom. He noticed it was the bearded man from the cage who held him so carefully.

"Dobbs," he said faintly.

"That's right, sir. Now you bide quiet like, sir, and I'll have you between these sheets in no time at all."

"Thank you."

He wondered what Dobbs thought of having to carry a naked man stinking of sex to bed. Had he watched at the Demons, or was he considered too low to be admitted to the inner sanctums of the club? He'd know if he ever met the man again. Such knowledge would distort a saint's perception of him, and Dobbs was just a man. . . . Although a man who had been forced to suck cock himself might have more sympathy for Alistair than he might have imagined.

"There you go, sir. You rest now."

"Thank you."

Diana appeared behind Dobbs's shoulder, her expression stricken. He tried to smile at her.

"I'm quite all right, my lady. I just need to sleep."

She sat down on the side of the bed and took his hand. "Don't worry about anything. I'll take care of you."

"You always do."

A maid brought a bowl of scented water, and Alistair lay quietly as Diana carefully washed him and then pulled the covers up to cover his nakedness.

"Charlotte brought your clothes. I'll leave them on the chair," Diana said as she unfolded a piece of paper. "The Demon Club left this on top of the pile." She showed him the document, which had "paid in full" scrawled over the original debt amount and four signatures.

"Give it to Harry."

Her expression hardened. "He doesn't deserve such consideration."

Alistair swallowed hard. "Please give it to him. He . . . should give you something in return."

Her grip on his hand tightened. "Is that why you were there? To retrieve the list? Oh, Alistair, why didn't you *tell* anyone?"

"I didn't intend to go."

"I thought, we *all* thought you'd gone to clear your name because Harry had forged your signature on the debt."

"I'm not that much of a fool. I went because Harry intimated that someone I . . . cared about was on that list."

"Who?"

"My wife's father."

"But surely you would've recognized his name immediately, or did you simply not tell Mr. Fisher the truth from the outset?"

"*No!*" He took a weary breath. "The man recently inherited a title from a distant relative. I was unaware that he had succeeded to the earldom until my brother pointed it out. I was concerned about what Harry would do with that information, and agreed to meet him."

"Without telling anyone." She sighed. "You insist I am the one who doesn't trust people, but you are far worse."

A faint thread of annoyance stirred in his gut. "Why were you there?"

"Because Charlotte asked me to accompany her."

"To see my downfall?"

"No, because she believed she had finally found a way to trap your brother and make him pay for his crimes. She had no idea that you were going to turn up in his place."

"You didn't mention that to me."

"When we last spoke, we were at odds with each other."

"Yet you already knew you were going. Charlotte must have come to the Sinners to ask for your help."

"She did."

"But you didn't tell me, so I assume you knew what she planned and thought it best if I remained in ignorance of your plot."

"It was Charlotte and Sir Ronald's plot. Not mine."

He closed his eyes against the flare of indignation in hers. "I did what I thought was right to aid the Sinners."

"No, Mr. Maclean. You did *exactly* what your brother wanted. You damn well walked into his trap and allowed him to escape his punishment. If you'd told Mr. Fisher about the threat to your father-in-law, he would've understood. He would not have expected you to put yourself in danger for a man who gives you nothing but trouble!"

"Why are you so angry with me when you went there yourself?"

She eased her hand away from his. "If you don't know that, Mr. Maclean, you are a fool."

"Because I am your property?"

"Because I—" She sighed. "Because *I* am a fool."

Despite his best efforts to open them and concentrate on the betraying quiver in her voice, his eyes stayed closed. He felt the mattress shift as she stood up.

"Don't . . . go."

"I promised you I would stay and I will do so. We can speak again in the morning."

"Thank you." The effort to say the words almost drained him. "Don't be angry with me."

She sighed. "I'm angry because you put yourself in an intolerable situation for that rat of a brother of yours. I'm angry because you are an honorable, wonderful *idiot* . . . Now go to sleep before I forget that you need your rest and beat you myself."

He was asleep before his mind caught up with the puzzling complexity of her words, and for once he was grateful.

21

"Alistair said that Harry blackmailed him into attending the Demon Club." Diana sat on the chair in front of Adam Fisher, who wasn't looking his usual smiling self.

"How?" Adam leaned forward, his hands folded together on the desk.

"By threatening the family of Mr. Maclean's late wife. Apparently, the father inherited an English title against the odds, and Mr. Maclean wasn't aware of it. The father was on the list."

"Why didn't he *tell* me this?"

"I asked him the same question. He managed to evade answering it by wondering why I was at the club."

Adam shoved a hand through his hair. "You are both as bad as each other. I know you left messages for me with Maddon, but still. What possessed you both to go running headfirst into that den of iniquity?"

Diana shrugged. "Loyalty, I suppose. I went to support Charlotte, and Mr. Maclean to safeguard the reputation of his dead wife's family."

"I'd forgotten Alistair was even married."

"When did his wife die?"

"About six years ago, I think. She died in childbirth."

"He never speaks of her."

Adam cast her a rather too astute glance. "I know nothing about the marriage except those two facts."

"Why would you think I wish to know more?"

"Because by all accounts, you were the one leading Mr. Maclean around on a leash last night at the Demon Club, which suggests to me that you know him rather well."

"I did what was necessary to protect him from those animals."

"Because you already know his limits?"

"Yes."

Adam raised an eyebrow. "I'm not accusing you of anything. I have no issue with you having a relationship with Alistair Maclean."

Diana forced a smile. "I wouldn't worry about that too much, Mr. Fisher. One way or another, we will not be together for much longer."

Adam looked past her to the open door. "Ah, Mr. Maclean. Do come in and please sit down."

Diana waited as Alistair brought another chair over and positioned it next to hers. He looked pale but resolute, and his movements were rather careful. Had he heard her last comment about the approaching end of their relationship? There was no sign that he had, but that meant nothing. He was a master at hiding his emotions. As soon as the matter of Harry Maclean was dealt with, she would seek out the Earl of Westbrook and speak to him about her future. After that . . .

Alistair nodded to Diana and then fixed his attention on Adam, who was displaying more of his steel than she had ever seen before.

"Mr. Fisher, I apologize for not giving you more notice of

my intent to attend the Demon Club last night. By the time my brother sent his message, you had already left the Sinners."

"I still don't understand why you felt it was imperative to go to the Demon Club. We had a copy of the list. All you had to do was ask Maddon for my exact whereabouts and we could've settled things between us quite easily."

"I thought I could deal with the matter without bothering you, sir."

"Obviously."

Alistair visibly gathered himself. "Do you have my brother in your safekeeping?"

"Yes."

"I . . . would like to see him."

"And why is that, Mr. Maclean? Do you hope to set him free?"

"I can understand why you might doubt my loyalty, Mr. Fisher, but there are good reasons why I need to speak to him."

"Which are?"

Alistair set his jaw. "He claimed to have other incriminating documents to use against me personally, sir. If they exist, I would like to have them in my possession."

"What kind of documents?"

"Letters of support for the Stuart cause."

"Written by you?"

"No, sir. By my wife." He raised his head to meet Adam's hard gaze. "I went to the Demon Club to tell Harry that we had a copy of the list, and that nothing he said would make me give him any more money. He told me that my wife was the Stuart sympathizer, and that he had additional evidence to prove it." He let out a breath. "I stayed to cancel out the debt and hoped that Harry would give me the letters she wrote entrusting him with money for the cause. I couldn't allow him to destroy my wife's memory."

"Ah."

Silence fell in the office. Diana had an overwhelming urge to reach over and take Alistair's hand.

Adam stood up and came around to Alistair, who had also risen.

"Let me take you to your brother."

Alistair followed Adam and two of the footmen down to the basement of the Sinners, into the cavernous wine cellars, and the specially fortified cells beyond the wine racks. A single guard sat outside one of the locked doors reading a book by lamplight. He immediately stood up when he saw them coming, his pistol at the ready.

"Mr. Fisher. Mr. Maclean."

"Open the door, please, Reading, let Mr. Maclean in, and lock the door behind him." Adam consulted his watch and then nodded at Alistair. "You have fifteen minutes."

"Thank you."

Alistair stepped into the cell and heard the door shut behind him. Harry was sitting cross-legged on the narrow bed contemplating the thin stream of light coming through the barred upper window. He looked a little tired and his clothing was rumpled, but there were no signs of strain or anguish on his face.

"Alistair! To the rescue, of course."

"I haven't come to save you."

"Don't be silly. Of course you have. You're my big brother. It's practically your duty to get me out of scrapes."

"You call stealing information from the government a scrape?"

Harry shrugged. "I needed money. You wouldn't give me any. I did what was necessary to survive." His lip curled. "No one except you would blame me."

"I paid off your debt at the Demon Club."

"So I saw." Harry's smile was smug, but enough to put Alistair on guard.

"Then I would like you to return my wife's letters." Alistair held out his hand. "Surely it is a fair trade?"

Harry patted his black silk waistcoat. "I'm not sure I have them on me."

"You had them last night."

"And I had plenty of time to dispose of them while you were in the cage."

Alistair turned toward the door. "Then we have nothing more to say to each other."

"Wait!"

He looked back over his shoulder as his brother's most charming smile emerged. "Don't be so hasty, Alistair."

"Either give me the letters or I'll go."

"And leave me here to rot?"

"You've always been so theatrical, Harry. You aren't going to die here. The Sinners is a government-sponsored endeavor. They'll try you quite legally. Now, do you have the letters or not?"

"No, damn you!"

Alistair knocked on the door. "Good-bye, Harry."

"You can't leave me! You're my brother. You owe me your loyalty!"

"Not anymore."

The door opened, and Alistair stepped out and kept moving past the guard and the silent figure of Adam Fisher. He walked up the stairs to the ground floor and then to his office, where he closed the door and sat at his desk, his hands clasped tightly in front of him.

His blotting pad wavered and blurred as he fought to control a wave of anguish. Images of Harry as a child, as a young man as . . . his best friend in the world streamed through his mind and fell as tears with a steady *drip-drip*. He had to rip himself free of this never-ending cycle of hope followed by despair, but it was the hardest thing he'd ever had to do in his life.

"Alistair."

He jumped as a soft hand touched the back of his bowed head and then turned blindly to seek the comfort being offered to him. With a soft sound, Diana wrapped her arms around him and held him to her bosom.

"I . . . failed him."

"No, he failed you." She stroked his hair. "He doesn't deserve your love and your loyalty."

"He said she was in love with him, that she was carrying his child when she died."

"Your wife was?"

"Aye."

"My poor, dear man." She hesitated. "He was probably lying to enrage you, or force you to support him."

"No, he was probably right. He could never bear for me to have anything he didn't. It would've amused him to seduce Gelis and take her from me. And I damn well *knew* something was wrong between us, that her pregnancy was mathematically impossible, but like a blind fool I simply went along with it because to believe anything else would've destroyed my sense of control, of my stupid sense of *worth*."

"I'm so sorry, Alistair."

He forced himself to take a deep breath and pull away from her. "Harry said he didn't have the letters with him. Could you ask Mr. Fisher if he can ascertain if that is true? Otherwise, he hid them at the Demon Club or gave them into someone's keeping."

She perched on the edge of his desk and considered him. "Is it imperative that you retrieve these letters?"

"I would feel better if I knew they had been burned."

"Then I'll make sure your brother doesn't have a scrap of

paper concealed anywhere on his person, and if that fails, I'll ask Charlotte to search the Demon Club."

"Thank you." He forced a smile. "I should get back to work."

"Not quite yet."

He put down his pen and slowly raised his head.

Still sitting on the edge of his desk, she raised her slippered foot and rested it on the front of his trousers. "You are supposed to be always hard for me."

"You can hardly expect me to—"

She pressed down on his cock and balls. "Be quiet, Mr. Maclean."

"I don't want—" His breath hissed out and his cock stiffened beneath her probing toes.

"I want you hard. Unbutton your trousers and make yourself ready." She slid a hand into his hair and shoved his head down to stare at his lap. "Do it."

"The door . . ."

"Is unlocked and will remain so." She removed her foot. "Get on with it, Mr. Maclean. I'm waiting."

He undid the buttons with fingers that shook, aware that his cock was already erect, as if all the emotional turmoil in his soul was pumping down into it.

"Pull down your trousers and underthings to your knees so that I can see you properly and spread your knees."

He obeyed because she was giving him purpose and he needed something . . . needed this more than he needed to breathe.

"Now wrap one of your hands around the base of your shaft and pleasure yourself while I watch."

He drew his cock away from his stomach and did as she said, his fingers soon moving easily through his own wetness.

"That's better, Mr. Maclean." She rested her feet on the very edge of his chair and leaned forward to watch him work his length through his fingers. "Slow down, I don't wish you to come yet."

The normal sounds of the Sinners faded as he concentrated on his cock, on the dangerous rise of his pleasure, and on Diana's keen gaze. After a while she gripped the arms of his chair, bringing her head down close to his now aching shaft.

"Mmm . . ." She blew on him and he shuddered. "Is your arse still sore? I enjoyed whipping you yesterday. Did you enjoy it too?"

He nodded as she glanced up at him, but he kept his mouth shut.

"I placed each stroke very precisely. Did you notice that? Can you feel each individual welt throbbing now in time to your cock stroking? I do hope you can."

He gripped his slippery cock, his hips rolling into the motion as he watched the very tip of her tongue emerge and hover over the slit of his crown. But however he moved she wouldn't close the tiny space between them and lick him. He tried harder, planting his feet on the floor so that he could bring his arse off the seat, which only added to the ache of each welt as he flexed his muscles.

"You're close to coming, aren't you?"

He fought to breathe and could only moan as she sat up and stared into his face.

"Take your hand away, and rearrange your clothing over that big hard cock of yours."

She held his gaze as he silently screamed a denial, releasing his eager flesh and carefully, very carefully, pushing his stiff, unwieldy shaft back against his belly and inside his underthings and trousers.

"That's better." She slid down from her perch. "Now you can get on with your work."

"Yes, my lady."

Blindly, he searched for his pen, his heart pounding along with the pulse in his cock.

"I'll go and speak to Mr. Fisher, and then, depending on what he says, I might need to write a note to Charlotte to search at the Demons."

"Yes, my lady."

"I'll report back to you as soon as I can."

"Thank you."

She walked out, leaving him with the monstrous bulge of his cock tenting his trousers and his mind curiously calm. At least he had something else to think about other than his brother's treachery. And with his emotions harnessed and owned, he was certainly less likely to harm anyone else. When she returned he'd still be hard. He knew she'd check.

He let out a long, shuddering breath. How had she known how to deal with him? Making him obey her had somehow given him back control of his emotions . . .

There was a slight tap on the inner door and Adam came into his office. Alistair shoved his chair closer to his desk to conceal his lap.

"We'll be moving your brother into a more secure holding place today."

Alistair looked up at his employer. "What do you think will happen to him?"

"He admitted he stole the list and the two men he tried to blackmail have confessed to offering him money, so there is clear evidence against him. He'll be tried and sentenced by the judicial system in as private a setting as we can manage. There won't be any publicity about the case, I can assure you of that."

"I don't care for myself, but my mother would be . . . mortified. She has already suffered enough betrayal in her life." Alistair forced himself to continue. "What if he is convicted?"

Adam sighed. "I'm not sure how he will be treated, Alistair. It depends on the judge. What would you prefer to happen?"

"I don't know, sir. I just know that I'd hate to be responsible for sending my own brother to his death."

"I doubt it will come to that. This is a relatively minor

issue." Adam laid something on the desk. "I understand you were looking for these. Reading found them in Harry's coat pocket."

Alistair picked up the two letters, recognizing his wife's handwriting with a sharp pang of guilt. "Yes, thank you. Did you read them, Mr. Fisher?"

"I'm sorry, but I had to scan the contents for security reasons."

"It's all right. I was going to ask you to look through them anyway. My wife is dead. Nothing can hurt her now."

Adam half-turned to go and then turned back. "If I might say something, Alistair, your brother doesn't deserve you."

"Or you, Mr. Fisher. This must be difficult for you as well."

Adam's smile was sweet. "I gave up hope months ago. I'll do my duty to the Crown, as will you."

He went back into his office leaving Alistair in peace to read through the letters. After committing them to memory, he scrunched the paper up into a ball and threw it on the fire, waiting until it burned through and dissolved into black fragments, which he obliterated with the poker. He said a prayer for his wife and her family and then, having nothing else to do, went back to work.

22

Diana went down to the kitchen level and spoke briefly to Maddon, who confirmed that Mr. Fisher had taken all of Harry's clothing and his valuables and had already gone to return something to Mr. Maclean in his office. She could only hope it was the evidence Alistair sought. His revelation about his wife and Harry had shocked even her to the core. How could one brother be so ruthlessly amoral when the other was the soul of integrity? She would never understand human nature. . . .

"Lady Theale?"

"Yes, Mr. Maddon?" She looked back over her shoulder at the butler.

"The countess was looking for you earlier. She wants to introduce you to the earl."

"He is back, then?"

"Indeed, my lady." Maddon smiled. "Cook is preparing a celebratory dinner for you all as we speak."

"Then I will certainly go and find her ladyship and pay my respects."

Diana felt a peculiar sensation in her stomach as she realized she finally had to gather her courage and decide how and when she would face the earl. Should she leave it until after dinner? She suspected Alistair might need her support when Harry was taken away during the afternoon. But was she simply avoiding the issue?

Her steps slowed on the stairs. She had to go and see Mr. Maclean and find out if he'd retrieved his letters. And if he was still hard . . . It wouldn't be fair to leave him in such an aroused state all day.

She was being a coward, but surely the countess deserved a few hours of peace with her husband before Diana ruined everything? Damnation, this was becoming harder to do than she had imagined. Maybe Nico was right and she should simply let it go. . . .

Diana dressed for dinner with great care in her favorite green gown with a black ribbon trim and arranged her hair in a high knot at the top of her head. She had almost no jewelry to bolster her confidence, but she did have her pride. And whatever happened, she would never be poor. If she had to go back to earning her living at the pleasure house, she'd do it. At least it was honest work, unlike her job at the Sinners, which she'd only taken to get closer to the Earl of Westbrook.

She loved working at the Sinners. . . .

With a sigh, Diana blew her reflection a kiss and contemplated her already packed bags. Charlotte knew she might be coming and would be there at the pleasure house to receive her. But there would be no Alistair Maclean in her bed to offer her his own particular brand of comfort. Once she'd ascertained that he'd received his letters back, she'd ordered him to sit in her office chair and made him come with her mouth wrapped around his cock.

He'd been so absurdly grateful.

"Enough," Diana murmured to herself and raised her chin.

She had to put such weak thoughts behind her and go and face her fate as she had faced everything else in her life—alone.

Alistair Maclean was not for her. She would not take his security away from him especially now. But it was difficult. She'd come to love his integrity and his ability to submit to her needs whilst satisfying his own. He was the strongest man she'd ever known and yet many would consider him weak for his sexual choices. She respected him even more for them and suspected she would never find another man who completed her so perfectly.

To her consternation, everyone had gathered for dinner, including Lord and Lady Keyes, and Nico. Even Alistair had appeared, his expression bleak and his silence evocative of his struggle to let his brother face the consequences of his own actions. He took the seat to her left, and briefly smiled at her as he laid her napkin on her lap.

As the dinner progressed, she found herself almost unable to eat a thing or reply with more than the barest of civilities to the conversation going on around her. She was aware of the countess's concerned gaze falling on her occasionally and Alistair's calm presence shielding and protecting her.

Beyond him, at the head of the table was the Earl of Westbrook. Diana couldn't take her eyes off him. He was a tall man with brown eyes and darker skin than one would expect on a peer of the realm. To her dismay, he also appeared to be very nice, taking pains to speak both to her and Alistair at length and to welcome them to the Sinners. His knowledge as to what was going on seemed current as he commiserated with Alistair about Harry and joked with Malinda about her upcoming child.

She was surprised to find that she was enjoying herself, lulled into a false sense of security, that she was among people who cared about her . . . The way the earl looked down the table at his wife made her feel even worse. The love and respect between them was palpable.

And she was about to ruin everything. . . .

Eventually Faith rose and caught the gazes of Diana and Malinda.

"Shall we leave the gentlemen to their port?"

Diana obediently stood, only to be stayed by a gesture from the earl.

"Before you go, my dear, I believe Lady Theale has a matter she wishes to discuss with me." He turned his gaze on her, his brown eyes calm. "Lady Theale?"

She managed to swallow. "It is hardly a matter that needs to be discussed over the dinner table, my lord."

"Why not? There are no secrets here. No one will betray you." He glanced around the table, his gaze lingering on his wife. "In fact, I think it is time the truth came out, don't you?"

"I don't wish to . . . hurt you or the countess, my lord."

"That's very noble of you, but I hardly think your suspicions will change anything."

"Because your wife already knows?" Diana asked, her gaze locked with the earl's.

"Faith knows everything." He shrugged. "But *I* would like to know what I'm accused of."

Alistair took her hand and squeezed it hard. "Tell him. And whatever happens, know that I will be there to support you through it."

Diana held his gaze and nodded before taking a quick breath and turning back to the earl.

"I believe you are my father."

The earl sat back and studied her. "On what grounds?"

"I was born in Cornwall, on the Pelly estate."

"And you believe that while I was courting my countess, I was also dallying with the local women without thought to the consequences of such actions."

"Yes."

"And why would you think that?"

"The woman you paid to care for me after my mother died was something of a gossip. She said you were known for your . . . profligate ways."

A slight crease appeared between the earl's brows. "May I ask how old you are?"

"I'm not quite sure. When I was sent to the charity school, they had my age as seven but I'm not sure that was correct. I thought I was a few years younger."

"But you are more than eighteen?"

"Of course I am."

"Then how can I be your father? The only time I visited the Pelly estate was in 1810, when I met my future wife."

"If that is the case, why do the school records show that you were paying my fees?"

"I have no idea." He held out his hand. "Do you have the records?"

"You know I do not. Nico stole them back for you."

"I swear on my honor that he didn't." The earl looked down the table toward his wife and Nico, his smile dying. "Do either of you have anything you wish to say about this matter?"

Diana tensed as the countess rose to her feet. "I asked Nico to steal back the records, Ian."

"And why was that, my love?" The earl angled his head. "Is Lady Theale your child?"

"No, but I was indirectly paying for her schooling out of the Westbrook estate."

"Why?" Diana asked.

Faith sighed. "Because I had a sister and she . . . was rather wild when she was younger and she became pregnant."

"Are you speaking about Margaret?" the earl asked, his expression as incredulous as Diana's. "But she was only twenty-one when I met her."

"And she was fourteen when she had her child." Faith sighed. "My parents were away in London for most of the year, and we ran wild with our cousins and the local children. The Romany families who visited every summer and camped in our fields fascinated Margaret. She'd often steal away to be with them. I assume the father of the child was one because by the time we realized she was with child, he was long gone."

Diana sank down into her chair and continued to stare at the countess.

"I did the best I could for Margaret. She hardly looked pregnant for the longest time, and when she did, I told everyone that she had become delicate and needed to stay in bed, which kept her out of the public eye. While we waited for the babe to be born, I took our old nurse into my confidence, and she agreed to help find the baby a good home."

Faith dabbed at her eyes with a handkerchief that Nico passed to her. "I thought all was well. You were well cared for by a couple who had desperately wanted a child, and my sister became an acknowledged beauty and married an aging viscount."

"Did she ever ask after me?" Diana asked.

"I'm sorry to say that at first she didn't. I took care of paying your new family to keep you from the Pelly housekeeping money, which I managed for my mother. Your new mother wrote to me once or twice a year so that I knew you were thriving and happy."

"Then how did I end up living in London and being thrown out in the gutter when I was fourteen?"

The countess's eyes filled with tears. "As I said, my sister married well and hoped to provide the viscount with an heir. She suffered through several miscarriages and began to ask me about you, where you were, whether you were thriving. I was . . . concerned about why she wanted to know such things and refused to tell her much, but then I became ill myself."

"You were more than ill, my love," the earl said. "You lost a child and I almost lost you. You took months to recover."

The countess gave her husband a grateful look. "Which meant that I neglected my correspondence and the outside world for far too long. Eventually, I found a letter from Margaret dated several months previously, saying she'd decided to find you and bring you to London. Her plan was to have you educated in one of the charity schools and then to take you into her house as a companion. Unfortunately, she died not long after that, and I didn't know where you were."

She drew a shaky breath. "I tried so hard to find you, Diana, but even with all the resources of the Sinners behind me, I could not discover where she'd placed you, or what had become of you. I am so sorry, I failed you quite *dreadfully*."

The earl cleared his throat. "I wish you'd told *me*, love. I have resources even you cannot guess at."

"I promised Margaret I would tell no one. I *hated* deceiving you." The countess sat down with a *thump* and burst into tears, making the earl curse and leap to his feet. He practically ran down to the bottom of the table and picked his wife up, cradling her against his chest.

"It's all right, Faith."

"No, it is not!" She kept crying against his chest, her voice muffled. "I lost her and her mother, Ian. I failed them both."

"But Diana found us, love, which indicates what a fine and intelligent woman she turned out to be all by herself." He looked over at Diana. "Isn't that true, Lady Theale?"

Diana could only nod as she tried to make sense of the countess's words.

"And now that we have found her, Faith, we will give her whatever she needs from us, and make sure that she is never lost or alone ever again." The earl kissed the top of his wife's head.

"But she must hate me."

Diana shook her head. "No, I . . . really don't. You must forgive me. This is just not what I expected at all. I thought—"

"That I was a conscienceless rake who had abandoned a young pregnant girl to her fate?" The earl held her gaze. "When you get to know me better, Diana, you will understand why I could never be that man."

She nodded, aware that Alistair was still holding her hand and that felt as important to her as the earl forgiving his wife was to her newly discovered aunt.

The countess blew her nose and fixed her gaze on Diana. "I suspected you were my niece when you came for your interview, but it has been extremely hard to discover much about your past. It was only after I persuaded Nico to tell me what he knew that I began to believe you might be who I hoped you were." She sighed. "I was waiting for Ian to come home so that I could tell him about you. I didn't realize you were determined to find out the truth for yourself."

"I'm not sure why you are surprised, my love. She is your niece," the earl said and kissed his wife's head.

"If you don't mind, Diana, the countess and I would like to retire to discuss this matter further so that we can have as many answers available for you tomorrow as possible." The earl stood up and tucked his wife firmly against his side. "But rest assured, we are more than willing to belatedly welcome you into our family, and hope that we can make up for everything we have missed."

Diana managed a nod, and the earl and countess left the dining room. Benedict Keyes whistled and went to get the port and brandy bottles from the sideboard.

"I think we all need to have a drink after that. Adam, will you help me?"

Diana suddenly became aware of everyone else around the table as Alistair scooped her up and placed her on his lap. A large white handkerchief appeared in front of her nose, and she took it gratefully.

"I wasn't going to say anything," she murmured to him. "I couldn't bear to upset the countess."

"Then I'm glad the earl did it for you." He kissed her wet cheek and searched her face, his expression serious. "Are you happy about all this?"

"I'm still rather surprised," she confessed, and blew her nose again.

Alistair gave her a glass of brandy, and they both sipped at their drinks.

"Di?"

She looked down to see Nico sitting in her vacant chair.

"You were right as usual," she said. "There *was* something odd going on. Did you find out the truth?"

"Not quite. It was rather a surprise for me too. I'd begun to believe the countess was your mother."

"Instead of my aunt."

He considered her. "I should have realized it earlier. You have the countess's blue eyes."

"She did say I reminded her of someone when we first met." She reached out and took his hand. "I should have listened to you."

He grinned. "As should everyone." He dropped a kiss on her palm. "I wish you every happiness, Stepmama. I don't think you will ever have to worry about being alone again."

"From what the earl said, I think that's true."

"I wasn't referring to the Westbrooks." He winked. "I'll take my leave of you both. Good night, Mr. Maclean, take very good care of her, won't you?"

When Diana looked up, she noticed that Adam and the Keyes were also leaving her alone with Alistair. She rested her head against his shoulder and simply breathed him in.

"I thought I was going to have to leave the Sinners tonight," she confessed.

"I noticed that you had packed your bags."

“Would you . . . have missed me?”

“Not particularly.”

She raised her head to stare at him and found that he was smiling.

“I knew where you were going, and I knew that if I stripped naked and was in your room at midnight every night, eventually you would come to your senses and master me.” He held her gaze. “Don’t you know that yet? That you own every part of me in bed and out of it?” He shifted her slightly on his lap. “That even now, I’m hard for you because that’s what you demand of me?”

“Oh, Alistair . . .”

[illegible] brought her fingers beneath the neck-
[illegible] ing my collar. I’ll wear it for you for-

[illegible] silver band. “I don’t deserve such de-

[illegible] of returning it.”
[illegible] about that.” His green eyes were
[illegible] ut myself completely in your hands.
[illegible] y for making me scream with plea-
[illegible] allow me to be myself, to hold you
[illegible] d to be held, to support you as I’m
[illegible] ed her nose. “We are devoted to *each*
[illegible] as you give me. We *complement* each

She swallowed hard. “Sometimes I don’t want to be the strong one.”

“I know that. It just makes me want you more. Knowing that I am the only man who brings out the mistress in you *and* the woman who just wants to be loved and protected makes me feel like a complete man and not a sorry excuse for one.” He hesitated. "You never make me feel weak for wanting you to dominate me in bed."

"I *never* think of you as weak."

"Many men do." His smile was wry. "I thought it myself until I met you. You showed me what being mastered really meant and how it freed me to be myself. Even if you don't wish to stay with me, I'll never forget that."

She slid off his lap and put her hands on his shoulders, her voice trembling. "Having gone to all this trouble to tame you, Mr. Maclean, do you really think I will give you up so easily?"

He went down on his knees in front of her and lowered his gaze to the floor.

"No, my lady."

She stared down at his gleaming auburn hair. Her slave, her lover, her everything.

"There is one thing I *would* like to ask you, my lady."

"And what is that?"

"Would you consider marrying this sinner?"

She brought her hand to her heart. "I'll consider it, Mr. Maclean. But you are going to have to work very hard indeed to convince me that it is a good idea."

He bent and kissed the toe of her shoe. "Yes, my lady. It will be my pleasure."